W9-CSG-764

THE RAHTRUM CHRONICLES

BOOK ONE

THE DREAM

R.K. MCLAY

FIFTH
HOUSE

Published in Canada by Fifth House Ltd.,
195 Allstate Parkway, Markham, ON L3R 4T8

Published in the United States by Fifth House Ltd.,
311 Washington Street, Brighton, Massachusetts 02135

10 9 8 7 6 5 4 3 2 1

Fifth House Ltd., acknowledges with thanks the Canada Council for the Arts, and the Ontario Arts Council for their support of our publishing program. We acknowledge the financial support of the Government of Canada for our publishing activities.

Library and Archives Canada Cataloguing in Publication
McLay, R. K., author
The Rahtrum Chronicles : the dream / R.K. McLay.

ISBN 978-1-927083-37-6 (hardcover)

I. Title.
PS8625.L385C47 2016   jC813'.6   C2016-901126-7

Publisher Cataloging-in-Publication Data (U.S.)
Names: McLay, R. K., author.
Title: The Rahtrum Chronicles : the dream / R. K. McLay.

Description: Markham, Ontario : Fifth House Ltd., 2016.
First book in a trilogy Summary: "Set in the Yukon Territory, this fantasy-adventure story follows a young caribou named Bou on a journey to find a rare wildflower" – Provided by publisher.
Identifiers: ISBN 978-1-92708-337-6 (hardcover)
Subjects: LCSH: Yukon — Juvenile fiction. Caribou — Juvenile fiction. Fantasy fiction.
Quests (Expeditions) — Juvenile fiction. BISAC: JUVENILE FICTION / Fantasy & Magic.
Classification: LCC PZ7.M353Chr DDC [Fic] — dc23

Editor: Kathryn Cole
Designer: Tanya St. Amand
Map: Stephen Earthy
Chapter Icons: Marla White
Printed in Canada

Chun tú, mo chara,
mo ghrá

Acknowledgements

I would like to extend my heartfelt thanks to the following people: to my wife, my friend, my love, Siobhan; to whom this book is dedicated, and without whom it surely would not exist – a talented (and my first) editor, a resolute contract negotiator, part-time agent and researcher, and all-round cheerleader; I thank you for your help, for the patience and sacrifice inherent in being the partner of a writer, and most of all, for *believing* when I could not muster the strength. To our dear friend, Lucie Bause, who helped teach me what it meant to be an artist. To Remo and his dog Kenai, and Nathan and Anne, kind-hearted friends who helped fend off madness during the long Yukon winter. To Kirby Meister – a most notable, generous and affable conservation officer of the Yukon Territory – who introduced me to the wonders of the Porcupine Caribou Herd. To my dear friends and draft readers: Sara Bayat (whose books I expect we shall all be reading eventually – no pressure, S) and Rachel Lancaster, an expert reader and natural-born editor. To my YA reader, Brynn Harlow. To my illustrator, Marla White, who was first to imagine my characters visually, and with whom it is a delight to work. To my friend and designer-illustrator Stephen Earthy, whose talent and generosity are evidenced in the beautiful map that graces the opening pages of this book. To François Thisdale for his gorgeous cover art. To Tanya St. Amand, our team designer, who with great care and expertise, put all of the parts together to create the package you see before you. To Oscar — Little Bear, my writing mascot. And finally, my heartfelt thanks to Kathryn Cole, an art director, editorial director, publisher and editor who has contributed untold richness to the landscape of Canadian children's literature over the course of her brilliant career. I feel very privileged to call her my editor, but her counsel to me has been wide-ranging, and most days I simply call her Sensei.

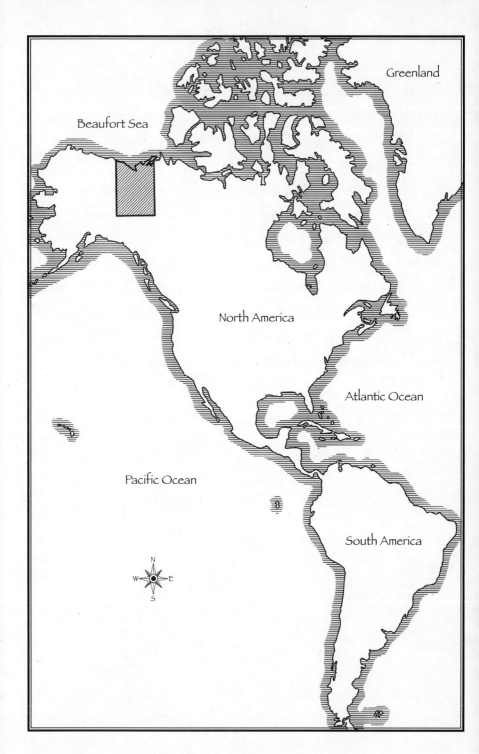

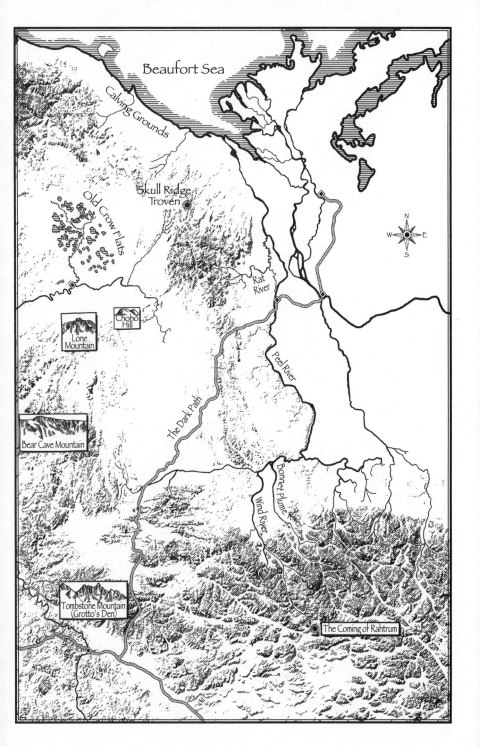

I make war on these pages

do not mistake it,

against your mind

that I may wake it,

against your world

that I may shake it,

against your heart

that I may break it.

Prologue

There is one called Rahtrum, the Binder, who is the wind, the wave, and all the earth and stone they beat upon. His tenderness is everywhere; at rest upon still lakes, cloaked in quiet mist, frozen in the crystal silence of a snowflake. Cold is he, as Antarctica, cruel as the North Atlantic, gentle as Spring rain. He is as mighty as the Himalayas, and his embrace is warm about the equator. His fury is the tornado and the hurricane, and so colossal is his strength that he may shake the earth beneath you. Blue is he, as a sunlit glacier, and black as the Mediterranean Sea bathed in night. He is white as sea salt and golden as the Great Plains in Summer glory. There is one called Rahtrum, the Binder, who binds water to wind, wind to leaf, leaf to tree, tree to earth, and earth to stone. It is he who has bound me to you, and I who am bound to tell this tale.

Rahtrum serves Nature. He is ever watchful. For millennia his vigilance has preserved the fragile harmony that is everywhere and everything. So perfect is his balance, that no plant or animal may count itself more vital than another. He has not shown the Rose more favour than the Thistle. The Blue Whale is titanic, but must follow the tiny Krill to survive. The wild Mustang is majestic, but it is the tunnelling Earthworm that shapes the land where the Horse gallops freely. There is no plant or beast that does not rely upon the whole of Nature for its survival. It has been so for a sea of time, and so it might have remained. Wise was the Binder's counsel to the animals, and each heeded his word. But who can see what lurks in the shadows until it emerges?

In the beginning there were whispered rumours among the animals. It was said that one of the tree-dwelling Apes had left its home in the branches and taken to the plains where it learned to walk upright upon two feet. This was a proud beast, they said, and cruel. Rahtrum spoke to the animals. "Did not the wild Dogs of the south leave their coastal homes and take to the sea? Did they not by degrees learn to swim ever deeper, growing large in the weightlessness of water? Have they not become the great Whales? It is the way of Nature for animals to grow and change." This calmed the animals, and for a time they did not talk of those that walked upright, for they were weak, they said, and fragile.

But the animals that walked upon two feet were prolific and found strength in numbers. As the ages blew over the earth, they grew ever more delicate in stature but in equal measure more cunning. As pack hunters they displayed an intelligence that frightened the other creatures of the World. Whatever Nature had not provided, the upright animals sought out and took for themselves. When cold, they took the life and fur of another creature to be warm. When weaponless, they made weapons. From simple stone came knives, axes, and hammers; from wood they made cudgels and spears. Even the bones of their prey were sharpened and used to hunt others. The two-footed animals bent Nature to their own design and purpose, growing ever more daring in their invention. The other animals called these creatures Cargoth, which means Beasts of Shadow, for they seemed always more clever and proud. Soon their numbers swelled, and it appeared to the creatures of the World that the Cargoth grew as a long shadow with the setting of the sun.

Millennia tumbled past, and as the Cargoth flourished, so too, did their hunger. Rumours spilled out into Nature; stories of dark kingdoms as vast as forests. Many small creatures lived quietly among the Beasts of Shadow, surviving on the waste and spoil that was everywhere among them. It was the tiniest of these animals that first sent forth word of the towering dens and nests built of stone, metal, and glass. Stories of foul air, endless noise, artificial daylight, and stone-smothered earth made their way out to all the creatures of the World, carried by many animals to all the hinterlands and seas. But soon the Cargoth themselves came into the wilderness, and no realm of Nature seemed beyond their reach. They were prodigious builders, tirelessly forging tools to bear them to all the corners of the earth. Upon the land they grew weary of the

Horse, who had been taken into slavery early on and made to carry the Cargoth over great distances. Instead, they built machines that roared and hissed and soon shamed the lordly Cheetah for speed. Upon the water they set giant floating machines that coughed a putrid smoke and travelled as the mighty Whale, who can swim the World over and never weary. Even the wide, blue dominion of the noble Eagle was not spared. With not a feather upon them, the Cargoth took to the air in their most fearsome invention, and with it wrought much harm upon the World, its creatures, and each other. With every tool of travel they fashioned, the Beasts of Shadow inevitably made war upon each other, scorching and scarring the earth as they fought, hungry for possession of the land and its treasures. It became clear to the creatures of the World that the Cargoth, so driven by their hunger, were dangerous even to themselves. A great panic went up among the animals, for they understood that creatures that inflict such harm upon their own care very little for the injury they cause to others.

It was then that a great whispering flowed forth from all creatures of the earth. It passed up into the branches of the tallest trees and became a murmur swept up by the wind. By wind it passed into the clouds, and soon it was heard everywhere: echoing in rolling thunder, hissing in steady rainfall, crying amidst the crash of ocean waves. Rahtrum, with his ear bent to Nature, heard the whispering of the animals, which said to each other, "Where is the Binder of the World? He must see that his precious balance is tipped, for the

Cargoth hunger only for dominion over Nature. Is not Rahtrum's fury the tornado and the hurricane? Will he not come to our aid?"

A great sorrow fell over Rahtrum, for he had toiled endlessly with the Cargoth to repair the balance that must be everywhere if Nature is to survive. Rahtrum came to see the Cargoth's shadow had grown too quickly; that he had spared them too long. They had become so like a plague, that to halt their pestilence would require a fury of such magnitude that the Binder might lay waste to much of what he wished to preserve. A great stillness fell over him and he retreated into Nature's dark places to reflect; to the shade of the Sequoia, the eternal gloom of the deep-sea trenches, into the fissures, caves, and canyons of vast mountain ranges. He sat, still as night, in the twilight of the tropical canopy, and roamed the icy desert of the Arctic Winter. For an age he wandered the dusky places of the earth, visited only by the Tuatha De Danann, the Faeries, who brought news and held council with him. But as the age drew to an end, the Tuatha De Danann came no longer; to see so great a weight upon Rahtrum was too much for them to bear. Instead, the Faeries sent forth a young Gnome into the barren north to seek counsel with the Binder and deliver dark tidings. For the Cargoth had unleashed new and terrible weapons upon each other. Rahtrum heard how the Beasts of Shadow had learned to forage stars from the sky and hurtle them to the earth at will, so that a gale of fire blew across the land, scorching, killing, and destroying all in its path. Now Rahtrum turned his ear and heart again to Nature and recoiled, overwhelmed by the poison and open wounds he felt there. So it was that at the close of the last age, the Binder held council in the north with a brave and wise young Gnome whom he quietly sent forth into the sub-Arctic wilderness. In the darkness of the passing years yet another whispering went up among the animals, and it was said that Rahtrum searched for a way to awaken the Cargoth to Nature and the World. If he could not awaken them, they said, then he would stay his hand and let their hunger run its course. His balance would slip unchecked, the seasons would waiver, and the oceans would rise up against the land. There would come hurricanes, tornadoes, drought, flood, fire, and all manner of pestilence. Many would be lost, they said, Cargoth and animals alike.

In The Shadows

DECEMBER

A creature moved in the shadows, stealthy as night, black as fear. It paused once in the deep snow to scent the crisp air, and then moved deftly down into a silent valley to a ravine on the tree-lined bank of a river. There it slipped into a dark cave to curl into itself and rest. The wide valley around it gasped quietly with the scurrying and flitting of life, as though waking from a nightmare.

In the depths of Winter, the cloudless Yukon sky is a canvas of eternal night, sequined with stars and constellations. When the moon rises full, the snow-covered land glows silver, and her contours are draped with long, blue-grey shadows. When the moon sets low behind the mountains, the Northern Lights whisper across the heavens in ghostly rivers of green and blue and violet. They are the lights of the Aurora Borealis, and on this deep, December night they glimmered and snaked across the sky over Tombstone Mountain.

Three shadows soared high and silent across the wavering light. They spiralled in slow circles and descended lower and lower, until the satin rustling of their black wings could be heard overhead. They were large Crows, and one of them cawed loudly. Another answered with a hollow rattling noise. Their calls echoed across the solitude of the valley. They circled low into a stand of Balsam Poplars near the banks of a wide river. The river stretched out in a still ribbon of ice that curled along the valley below the looming silhouette of Tombstone Mountain. The valley was broad and gentle, buttressed on either side by the high, snow-covered slopes of the Ogilvie Mountains. It tapered and ended at Tombstone Mountain, which thrust, jagged and foreboding, into the sky. Each of the birds alighted on low, barren branches of different trees. The trees bordered a large outcropping of rock on a ravine above the riverbank. There was a wide opening in the stone. This was a cave, and its entrance was obscured by the night. The Crows exchanged glances and moved back and forth nervously on their branches. The middle bird was thinner than the others, and he lowered his head, puffed his neck feathers, and cawed long and loud. The sound bounced down the valley. A deep snarl rose from the shadows of the cave, then rolled out onto the cold air in a cloud of misty breath. The Crows fluttered their long wings and bobbed their heads.

A voice bled warmly and slowly from the darkness of the cave entrance. It was a growl wrapped in a hiss. "Be silent, Crow. Will you announce my den to all the north?"

The middle bird spoke. "I was only calling —"

"Do not call, fool. Crows boast great intelligence, but who can teach them to be quiet? Why are there three of you? Hugin and

Munin, I have summoned you, but who is this that sits between you and shrieks like a hatchling?"

Hugin and Munin glanced uncomfortably at each other.

The middle Crow answered proudly. "I am Turin, of the Fortymile Murder —"

"Be silent, fledgling," the voice rumbled. "Do not make me say it again. Hugin, why have you brought this fool with you?"

Hugin shifted on his talons. "He followed behind us, hidden high against the darkness. We would not have discovered him but for the light rivers that run in the sky even now. Munin spotted his shadow against the green glow. But we were upon your den already when we turned to confront him. He is young of feather, and like all Crows he is curious. It is our strength and weakness." Hugin glowered at the young bird. "We cannot fault him for it. But he swore to secrecy if we brought him with us, and we did not wish to delay. We are sorry."

A deliberate silence hung for a moment in the mouth of the cave. "It is well you are sorry, Hugin, but it is done. Now let him be silent if there is any sense in him."

The two older Crows stared at Turin, who shuffled on his branch sheepishly.

The deep voice continued. "Today marks the heart of Winter, and soon the light will linger as the Spring reaches out her green arms. In the Autumn I bade you fly to my den on this day, and so you have. But why have you come? That is what the fledgling wonders." A hot, white mist wafted from the edge of the shadowed cave and billowed into the starlight. The young Crow perched tensely. "Speak my black-winged friends, tell him why you have come to my valley under the mountain in the pit of Winter. Tell him how I have ranged far over the northlands, hunting. Speak to him of how I have cached and shared my spoils with you, Munin, and you, Hugin. He is eager to hear how I have eased the sting of your hunger, how you have prospered in my service. Even now his little mind flies. *Is this how these two have grown fat and healthy though the seasons have been bleak?* he wonders. *When others of our Murder have starved and struggled?*

Turin was confused and looked nervously back and forth at Hugin and Munin. Munin ruffled her wings. "You have been generous with us. It is as you say."

"Yes, I have been generous with you. I have fed you in your hour of need. Watched over you as if you were helpless kits. Always I have told you this day would come. I have done service to your hunger, but mine has burgeoned, wide as the black sky. I have grown beyond my kind, and I have learned much out upon the land. Now the season has come, and you will serve me."

Turin looked anxiously at the other Crows. He was bewildered and ruffled his feathers as he spoke uneasily. "Crows serve none but their own."

Hugin and Munin stared hard at the young Crow, and Hugin made a low, gurgling noise at him. Turin fell silent.

A deep, breathy snarl rumbled in the shadows of the cave, and a plume of white vapour drifted up into the star glow.

Hugin spoke. "It is as we agreed at the first of the barren

seasons. It is our pledge, and so we will honour it. We are bound, by our pledge and by our fear. Even we Crow cannot fly forever, eventually we must come to land."

"Yes, Hugin, it is well that you fear me," the voice hissed slowly. "You speak wisely, for it is true, even the Crow must come to land."

Munin shifted. "What would you have us do?"

The deep voice paused a moment then continued. "You will fly east to the Wernecke Mountains. Circle high in the air near Rackla Pass, close to Bear River. There you will find Caribou."

Hugin spoke. "Caribou of the Porcupine herd? That is far south and east for Caribou."

"Yes, and yet they are there, wintering. There is a bull yearling among them. Look for him, but be stealthy and wise; you must watch without watching. Others might observe you. This yearling is like other Caribou in appearance, but like me, he is something more than his kin."

Munin cocked her head. "What, then, do we watch for? There will be many bull yearlings. How will we know the one you seek?"

The voice in the shadows huffed and snarled in contemplation. "You will know him, Crow. Three moons past I came upon a Messenger Hare and pinned him on his back. He shook, breathless with fear, sputtering and whispering in my ear to save his skin." The rumbling voice now rose to mock the Hare's pleading. "'Please,' he begged. 'I bear a message to the Tuatha De Danann from the Eye of the North. You are bound and must release me.'" The voice in the cave hissed with laughter. "I ask you, Hugin and Munin, what is an Arctic Hare but a short message bound inside a shorter meal?"

Hugin and Munin looked quickly at each other, but did not answer. Turin seemed shocked. The voice continued.

'Give me your message, Little One, and I will release you,' I said softly to him. He shook like a trembling aspen as I held him. He stuttered like a fool as he tried to speak. But at last he gave me the message as it was meant for the Children of Danu. 'Before Spring is upon us,' he whispered, 'Rahtrum, the Earthshaker, will seek a bull yearling who winters in the Wernecke Mountains, west of the Bonnet Plume Range. He is the one they whisper of. He is the one called Moshee.'" The voice paused a moment as though lost in thought, then resumed. "This is all the Hare would say. He could tell me nothing else. That is the wonder of the Hare; that he bears a message he cannot understand. No matter. This Caribou serves a purpose for Rahtrum, and it is this purpose that will reveal him to you. Go, and seek this Caribou. He will not be like the others. Keep watch for the Binder, and when you discover his coming, you will be sure you have found the yearling. When you have news fly quickly to me. That is all I will tell you now."

"And what became of the Messenger?" Munin asked meekly.

The voice responded in mock tenderness. "What of the Hare asks kind and gentle, Munin? A Messenger in the service of Rahtrum?" And then it grew dark again. "I am not bound as other animals, Crow. I do not fear the Binder. What use was left of this Hare but as a meal? Go now, and bring word when you find the yearling."

Hugin spoke. "And what if you range north, upon the land? How will we find you?"

"You will know without knowing. I know you, Hugin, and you, Munin. I am in your thoughts, and they will lead you to me."

Turin shuffled and mumbled timidly. "I cannot go to the Wernecke Mountains, I must return to Fortymile." Hugin and Munin exchanged quick glances.

A wide, black muzzle, rowed with white teeth and fangs, appeared in the dark mouth of the cave. "You will not go with these two, fledgling." The voice was deep and soft and damp as fog. "You will stay here with me, and I will teach you to be silent."

A long, dark form exploded from the gloom of the cave and moved like lightning up the trunk of the middle tree. Hugin and Munin screeched in fear and leapt into the air from their perches. Their black wings whistled as they cut through the cold and climbed into the sky. Behind and below they heard Turin call out long and panicked. Then there was only silence as the two Crows pumped their satin wings to gain the safety of the sky.

Munin spoke, and her voice was deeply troubled. "What have we done, Hugin?"

"It is done, Munin. Did you not see him lunge from his den? He has grown larger. He is even more now than he was. It is done. What good can come of questions? I do not wish to pass like Turin. Did you not hear him cry out? We cannot fly forever, eventually we must come to land. And there he will wait for us if we hinder him."

Munin was silent as the two Crows ascended into the sky. Two winged, black figures that crossed the green glow of the Aurora Borealis like shadows.

chapter 2

Winter's End

MARCH

The dream was of a Bear. It stood up on its two hind legs and with its forepaws pressed hard against a towering White Spruce. The Bear reared and bore down upon the tree like a windstorm. Its wide, clawed paws crashed forward, its muscles hardened like wood, and its thick, brown coat shivered with the force of the blow. The tree shook beneath the weight. The Bear reared again and fell upon the tree; once more it trembled beneath the awful force that was at work upon it. But now the tall Spruce was left leaning and weakened, unable to endure the awesome power of the Grizzly. Once more the Bear loomed over the tree, and then with a sudden motion, let fall all its weight upon the wounded trunk. A hollow cracking leapt onto the air. The tree collapsed, and the forest floor embraced it in soft, damp arms, all carpeted with Moss and Lichen. The Bear dropped down upon all four of its massive paws, breathed a cloud of vapour, and was still. A calm was upon the animal as it stood over the fallen Spruce with the hushed silence that follows a storm. Then it swung 'round, and its two deep, forest eyes stared at little Bou, who shivered out of his dream and was awake.

The small Caribou shook his head and peered about, frantic for his mother, Taiga. She was not far, only a few steps away, busy digging a crater in the deep snow with the hollows of her front hooves, searching for Sedges hidden beneath. It was mid-March, and other cows foraged nearby with their new calves and yearlings; thirty or so Caribou in all. Bou struggled onto his four sure legs and shook the snow from his reddish-brown coat. He stood only half as tall as his mother. He was not yet a year old, and the Winter had been long and cruel. His rust-coloured fur was divided in two by a dark brown stripe that ran down from the back of his head, along the middle of his back, and all the way to his tail. His belly was all white, as though covered in snow, which it very nearly was. The deep snow reached high up his legs, and he sometimes had to hop just to move about. He did this now, leaping as best he could over a powdery drift of snow to join his mother in her search for food. The two foraged for many hours along the northern ranges of the Wernecke Mountains. Soon a light flurry twirled down about them, and Bou peered up into the sky.

"Does the sky never empty, mother?" asked Bou. "Just when I think there can't be any more, it starts snowing all over again. Won't it ever end?"

"Never," Taiga replied.

"Never? But what about Spring?"

"It will end," she said, bumping her calf playfully so that he stumbled into a snowdrift. "Rahtrum has bound Winter to Spring. Soon the snows will be gone."

This answer did not satisfy Bou, who was puzzled by Rahtrum. He had heard this name spoken many times on the journey south to the Wintering Grounds.

"What is Rahtrum?" he asked, as he kicked the snow from his legs.

"Rahtrum is the Great Binder; the Earthshaker, some call him. He keeps the balance of Nature, of all that surrounds you."

"But I've never seen him."

"Have you seen the wind that moves the trees?

"No."

"Rahtrum is like the wind," Bou's mother said wistfully, as she gazed around the forest.

"He can't be seen?" Bou asked.

"If you look carefully you will see him everywhere, in everything. But you wonder if he can be seen like a tree or rock, or a Caribou? It is said he may take whatever form in Nature he wishes but one, and that some among the Gnomes and Faeries still speak with him directly."

"I would like to see Gnomes and Faeries, too."

Taiga nodded her head slowly. "Perhaps you will see a Faerie one day. They are strange and mischievous creatures. But Gnomes are secretive. It is said they do the work of the Binder. You may live your entire life and never see a Gnome, even had one travelled by your side all the while."

But the young caribou wondered to himself whether he had already seen a Gnome, and he said as much to Taiga. "I think we might have seen a Gnome, Mother, don't you remember? He was a little fellow that followed us from tussock to mountain in the Autumn, when my legs were still new."

Taiga stopped and looked questioningly at her yearling. "I cannot remember seeing a Gnome. I do not remember ever having seen one. If you saw a Gnome, why did you not say something, Bou?"

Bou lowered his head and sniffed at the snow. "Because everyone ignored him, so I tried to ignore him, too. He sat, still as a stone to watch us when we stopped. Even when the Flies came, he sat without moving, and they didn't seem to bother him. I wanted to ask someone how he could do such a thing, but nobody paid him any attention, not even the other yearlings, and I didn't want to seem foolish."

"We paid him no attention because we did not see him, Bou. What else? Tell me all that you remember." Taiga listened intently. *I have seen you distracted, Little One,* she thought to herself. *There has been a difference in you from the beginning, from your very first step.*

"I remember that he was larger than a Porcupine, and smaller than a Wolf. His body was long like an Ermine's, but he had ears and eyes like an Arctic Fox, the muzzle of a Bear, and stout legs and paws. I remember how he stood often on his haunches like a Ground Squirrel, and that he could travel some distance that way, upright, just as the Cargoth are said to walk. His Summer coat was grey, but he had begun to molt to Winter white. He moved along with us, always silent, like a shadow as we travelled. Twice, as we journeyed, Arctic Hare came bounding up to see him; once during the day on the plains, and once at night in the mountains. Each time he spoke a little with them, and he then sent them off at a run. All the while the herd ignored him, so I pretended to ignore him too. But I stole glances and watched him when I could. Then one night at first snow, he was gone, and I haven't seen him again."

"This you remember? All of it?" the old Caribou asked with surprise.

"I can close my eyes and picture it. Was he a Gnome? Why did no one else see him?"

"I'm certain he was a Gnome, and that is why no one else could see him. But you saw him, Little One. You saw him when we could not." *And you remember, you remember such detail as we Caribou cannot.*

"But why could I see him?"

"You have a special gift, Bou. There is something in you that is not in the others." *And I fear this is why the Gnome came to watch you with his keen eyes. For Gnomes do very little unless some purpose drives them,* Taiga thought.

"I feel different, Mother," Bou sighed softly. "Sometimes I feel that I don't belong. The other yearlings don't remember the way the moon shone low between the clouds on the night of the first snowfall. Or how the snow was so fine that the flakes were like stardust in the moonlight. I've asked them, but they can't remember."

Taiga nodded slowly at the small calf. "It is a beautiful memory to have." *But I cannot remember the moon either, Little One; only that the first snows came, and so we turned south.*

A sudden wind swept down from the mountaintops. It seemed to little Bou that the wind was at once warm and cold, and upon its back there rode scents the Caribou did not recognize. As it passed through the forest, the White Spruce trees around them swayed this way and that, and some, with cone-heavy tops, bent over before the blast. Then it was gone. Bou and Taiga continued their foraging side by side, as the other Caribou wandered nearby, weaving through the Spruce trees and digging in the snow for food.

Bou paused and looked inquisitively at his mother. "When Spring comes will we travel north to the sea?"

Taiga raised her head from the snow to answer. "Yes, Bou, it is just as I have told you; we will journey north to the Calving Grounds."

"Why?"

"Because there is much food there. Near the sea the ground is fertile and open, and we can see predators when they come."

"And in late Summer?"

"We will move together with the bulls between the Coastal Plains and the foothills."

"But that's what we did last Summer. Why will we do it again?"

"Because the Flies will come again in that season, thick as fog, and we must move together for protection and search out the wind for relief."

"And when the Autumn shortens the light and the Winter snows come, we'll travel south just as we did last year?"

"Yes, Bou. We will come south to shelter from the storms of

Winter and dig in the snow for food, just as we are doing now. That is our way."

"And that is the way we will travel every year?"

"That is the way we will travel." Taiga said, amused by Bou's questions.

"Why?"

"Because we are Caribou, Little One. And that is what it means to be Caribou." As Taiga spoke a group of cows and calves foraging nearby were drawn to the yearling's questions, for they, too, had sensed a difference in him and were curious.

The yearling stared silently at the snow for a moment. "I want to travel north and return to the sea. To see the dark blue of the water. I remember the way it moved and sparkled in the sun. But I don't understand. If we travel north every Spring, and south every Winter, year in and year out, do we not grow weary of it?"

The old Caribou was confused by this question, and the nearby cows and calves looked at each other with surprise. They stared at Bou's mother to hear her answer. "We are Caribou, Little One. We can travel all the year long and never grow weary." The other cows seemed satisfied with this response and nodded quietly to one another before shifting their eyes to Bou. But Taiga's mind raced. *You ask things I do not understand and cannot answer, Little Yearling.*

Bou spoke with a frustrated tone. "I don't understand our going back and forth. We go north to travel south again. We go south to travel north again. Round and 'round, year after year. Why is this our way?"

Now Taiga sensed the other Caribou watching her and grew frustrated. She answered abruptly. "Because we are Caribou, and that is what it means to be Caribou and to live here in the north. We travel to survive." The eavesdropping animals shifted their expectant gazes back to the yearling.

Bou seemed disappointed and said softly, "I just imagined there was something more. That being Caribou meant more than walking in great circles, again and again."

Bou's mother was confounded, and the other cows and yearlings exchanged puzzled looks, then grunted and mumbled dismissively before wandering back to their foraging.

Taiga stared quietly at her yearling as he resumed digging in the snow. *We do not look for greater meaning than what we are. Your questions are strange to me, Little One. You are Caribou, like us, but something more stirs in you.* She watched her calf a moment longer, then she, too, pressed her nose down into the crater she had dug in the snow.

High overhead two big, black Crows circled the forest. Their rattles and caws pierced the crisp air and tumbled down the valley.

Winter is the time of sleep, and all the northlands slumber. Willow, Birch, Spruce, and Balsam stand, dreamy in the cold. And though all the land lies asleep, the Caribou do not, forever searching out the buried Sedges and Lichens, which sustain them — wandering symbols of life in the midst of a frozen, dormant world. Bou and his mother had spent much of the Winter doing just this, for the previous Autumn, when Bou had still been very young, they had travelled with the other cows, calves, and yearlings down from the Porcupine River, following the way of the Old Crow. They had crossed the dark path of the Cargoth in the night and made their way into the Southern Mountains where they then wintered. But now, much of the Winter had passed, and Bou longed to go to the sea where he had been born. His mother had often told him of the journey, and he was eager to make it, for young Caribou are fearless and bold travellers.

"When will we begin?" Bou had asked his mother repeatedly during the Winter, and always the answer was the same: "When the Winter takes the Spring in its arms and the land is roused from its rest, we will go."

But the Winter seemed always to go on, and the snow always to come again, so that Bou thought perhaps the Spring had grown too distant for the Winter to reach, and he worried that the land would never wake up. But as the Winter's end drew near, there came an extraordinary visitor into the forest, and the little Caribou forgot about the sea for a time.

chapter 3

The Coming of Rahtrum

MARCH

Bou was startled awake from his dreams. The night lay about him in a thick blanket of darkness. He turned to see his mother, who lay nearby. She, too, was roused from her sleep, and her ears stood up, turning this way and that before pointing into the black forest before her. The other Caribou lay soundly sleeping here and there in the snow, amongst the Spruce trees.

"What is it, Mother?" Bou asked in a whisper, frightened now by the alarm in his mother's alert posture.

"Quiet, Little One," replied his mother gently. "There is something in the forest; something that comes this way."

Bou was terrified by this answer and the uncertainty in his mother's voice. He found himself wishing to dash away, but did not want to be alone in the darkness while something unknown lurked in the woods. Instead, he lay where he was with his ears, eyes, and nose all trained in the same direction as his mother's.

For some time the two Caribou lay quietly watching, listening, and sniffing at the air about them. The silence was unnatural, and

Bou began to tremble. Then it was upon him. It came first to his nose, borne somehow upon the still air, a scent that filled him with wonder. Lush Sedges, Mushrooms, Bear Root and Juniper, marsh and salt air all mixed into one. The odour filled Bou's nostrils, then his lungs, and a warmth spread through his young body. With the scent there came a vague understanding of that which was in the forest. Bou could feel its presence now.

"He is coming," the yearling whispered as he stared ahead into the night.

Taiga turned to look at him and asked breathlessly, "Who comes, Little One?" But Bou's senses were lost in the darkness, and he could not hear his mother. He could feel a presence approaching. It was something immeasurable, greater than himself and the forest and all the creatures of the forest. Next, it came to his ears, like a slow drumming in the distance, and he knew this to be the weight of the creature upon the forest floor as it approached. Bou felt the earth quivering against his belly with each of the creature's steps, and as the drumming grew louder, so the shaking of the earth became more severe. Now Taiga felt it too.

Suddenly, there was a distant light, bright and warm, moving in the forest toward the two Caribou. At first Bou worried that it was fire, but it shifted and wove through the trees in a way that fire cannot. The light was like a wide orb of moon-glow, drifting ever nearer, winding around the Spruce trunks, casting long shadows that swung and arced through the forest. As it drew closer, the two Caribou could see the source of the eerie, magical light. For wherever there was light, there were Faeries, the ancient Tuatha De Danann. Twelve of them circled in the air like little stars, casting great, sweeping rays of light this way and that. They looked to Taiga like tiny, slender Cargoth, naked of fur but with wings of glowing dust, which were as thin as frost and beat as quickly as a Hummingbird's. Each of the Faeries sprinkled a gentle mist of Spring Dust through the forest as it flew.

Upon the ground before the Tuatha De Danann, there marched six Root Trolls that walked upon two legs but were short as Foxes. Each one was as thick and gnarled as the roots of a tree, with skin of bark, eyes as green as sunlit leaves, and a beard of fine, wispy Lichen. Behind the Root Trolls there came three Gnomes, lean and graceful, walking upright upon their haunches, their long, furry tails drifting in the light behind them. These three moved in a triangular formation, the lead Gnome wore a thick, tawny-grey coat, and he turned his head slowly back and forth as he moved. He seemed to scan the forest and the other sleeping Caribou with eyes that were like wet, black stones. The Gnomes spoke a strange language in unison, as the Tuatha De Danann scattered Spring Dust along their way. Where the Dust fell, the snows melted and sank into the ground, and tiny plants and flowers blossomed out of the earth: Baneberry, Fireweed, Wintergreen, yellow Sweet Clover, Arnica, and many more.

Amazed as little Bou and his mother were by this strange procession, all of their attention fell upon the last figure that marched through the forest toward them. This final creature was the most wondrous and frightening, and its shape seemed to shift and change as it approached. First it was like a Polar Bear — but much greater in stature — so large that the floor of the forest shook beneath its towering mass. Then, as though it were made of water, the creature's shape wavered and shifted, and when at last it settled, it had changed into an immense, grey Wolf with piercing eyes of yellow. No sooner had it likened itself to the Wolf, than two great wings shot out from its sides. Its grey hairs blurred and fused into feathers as a majestic Golden Eagle took shape, its great wings driving a strong wind through the trees. Bou and Taiga quivered in fear at the size of the Eagle as it drew near, for sometimes on the Calving Grounds, the Golden Eagles would dive from the sky and snatch up newborn calves. But as the creature approached, its two wings folded down into one and stretched to the ground, splitting as they did so into four long legs ending in wide hooves. An enormous body emerged from the legs, and a huge head from the body. Upon the head there wove high into the air a magnificent rack of antlers, and now, where there had just been a giant Eagle, there stood an extraordinary bull Caribou, mightier than Bou or his mother had ever seen. The ground shook beneath the shape-shifter as it moved through the forest toward Bou and Taiga. The Root Trolls stood in a large circle about the two Caribou. The Gnomes stood quietly outside this circle, scanning the forest with their dark eyes and alert ears. Little Bou looked on in amazement.

As the Gnomes all found their places, the Faeries filled the air above the two Caribou, flying every which way and driving back the night with their light. Last came the great shape-shifter. It came near and stood before Bou and his mother in their image, though many times larger. The two Caribou peered up at the immense creature and wondered what would become of them.

Now the shape-changer spoke, and to the Caribou it was like many voices speaking together. One was gentle as a warm Summer shower. Another was broad and murmuring, like the running of a vast river. Yet another was deep, like the distant rumbling of an avalanche. All of the voices spoke as one to the Caribou saying, "Shed your fear, Little Ones, as you shed your Winter coats, for you will have no need of it. I am Rahtrum, called the Binder by some and Earthshaker by others, and on this night I have come, humbly, seeking your help. Will you hear me?"

Rahtrum looked tenderly down at the two Caribou who were still too afraid to answer. "You are Taiga of the Porcupine herd, and this is your yearling, Moshee, whom you call Bou. I bear tidings of despair and of hope. The Cargoth grow ever bolder, their shadow ever longer, and though there are many more here in the north than the eldest of your kind can remember, it is as nothing compared to the south, where the Beasts of Shadow swarm and swell and overwhelm the land and water and sky and all that once lived upon it. But here in the north you have felt their new power rising, have you not, Taiga? Have you not smelled it in the seasons? A shortening of Winter and a cracking of sea ice? An early breaking of frozen rivers, and a lateness of Fall? Mild Autumn winds that bring rain out of season? Have you not seen birds overhead that you do not know? It is the long shadow of the Cargoth that reaches into the north like venom. They swell like a black tide in the south and girdle the earth with their hunger. The ways of the first Cargoth are forgotten. They have tipped our precious balance, and we must call them from their sleep. It is time." And then Rahtrum lifted his head into the air so that his huge rack of antlers stood up in the Faerie light and cast intricate, pointed shadows through the trees. A darkness entered the Binder's voice, and it boomed out like thunder.

"Awake, Cargoth, and step into the light! How proud and forgetful you have become! You think yourselves above the other creatures of the world, but it is your brothers and sisters in Nature that hold you up so high. Awake, Cargoth, shake your dreamy heads. Rahtrum walks the earth this night!"

All of the forest shook beneath the Binder's wrath. Bou and his mother pressed their heads into the ground, for they had never heard or felt such fury. Many miles away, in the small northern strongholds of the Cargoth, the ground seemed to tremble and a fierce noise tore through the night air. The Beasts of Shadow came to the entrances of their dens to peer out, for they were uneasy, and something deep inside them stirred, but they could not draw it to memory, and they withdrew inside their dens to shut out the cold.

Rahtrum stood quietly, peering up into the sky, his anger now passed. Bou and his mother slowly lifted their heads up from the forest floor, anxious to know what would happen next. The Great Binder sighed deep and long, and a damp ice fog fell about the forest. Now the Faeries truly looked like tiny moons suspended in the misty night air.

Rahtrum looked down at the two small Caribou and said softly, "Tomorrow the Winter will take the Spring gently in its arms and begin to rouse the land. Your long journey north will begin once again, and I would set a great task before you. Spring will pass into Summer, and the Summer will grow old. There is a forgotten wildflower that grows in the north, where I bid it, once every fifth Autumn. A single plant, with roots that cling to stone, and four white flowers that bloom at the first bite of Winter. It is called the Breschuvine — ancient and rare among flowering plants — and none may scent or see it, except those bound by me."

Now Rahtrum looked straight down at little Bou. "This wildflower you will seek, Moshee. When the cold winds come, turn south from the Beaufort Sea and be true. Counsel will come to you in Summer, and you will learn where upon the land you must seek the flower. You will find this plant, and you alone must consume it. I will send you keen eyes upon the ground and high up in the sky to aid and watch over you."

The Earthshaker's eyes grew wider, his long face closer. "This I ask because you are Caribou, and you may travel all of the year and never grow weary. This I ask because Moshee is your true name, and you are more than Caribou. This I ask because we must wake the Beasts of Shadow, or much will be lost. You will wake them."

Bou's eyes were wide with wonder and confusion.

"You have many questions, but you are yet young, and time is short. Answers must wait for their season."

Now Rahtrum took two great steps away from Bou and his mother and spoke quietly to the ancient Tuatha De Danann in a forgotten tongue. The tiny Faeries flew brightly above the two Caribou, singing softly and sprinkling shiny Dust down upon them. The Dust swirled about them and blew into their eyes. It was a sleeping spell, soft and ancient, and the Caribou drifted off into warm, restful dreams so that they would be ready for their long journey.

Rahtrum and his strange procession slipped away to the north and travelled for a time in that direction, up a steep slope to a high peak where the Tuatha De Danann dimmed their lights. Rahtrum whispered quietly to the assembled creatures and then took the form of a giant Gyr Falcon that flew swiftly into the south. The Root Trolls turned and burrowed into the scree to travel beneath the earth and stone. The Faeries departed to return to their Trovens, three in each direction; north, south, east, and west. The three Gnomes stayed together on the high peak for a short while and spoke softly in their old language before one departed to the east, and another to the west. The last Gnome, with his tawny-grey fur and obsidian eyes, turned south again toward the sleeping Caribou. As that Gnome began to climb deftly down the mountainside, there was already a whistling of wings in the valley below.

Two dark shadows alighted, high in the Spruce boughs above Bou and Taiga, and muttered quietly to each other.

"He has seen us, Hugin!" Munin hissed. The Crow shifted her weight back and forth nervously. "That was surely the Earthshaker, even the Gyr Falcons do not grow so mighty. We cannot have escaped his eyes. He has seen us."

"Calm yourself, Munin. What of it? There are Crows everywhere in the north, from mountain to sea. The Rackla Murder is just south, the Bonnet Plume Murder is there, just to the west." He pointed with his beak. "Why should the Great Binder take note of us when everywhere there are crows?"

"But he is Rahtrum, Hugin. Who can say what he sees?"

"You let your fear run over the banks of your reason and flood your mind, Munin. If you must, fear him that we serve. He will be hungry for news of the yearling called Moshee and of the coming of Rahtrum and of the Breschuvine. And he will grow angry for every wasted minute. Fear his anger, Munin – and his hunger. We must fly to him, we must fly without food or rest to find him, or it is he who will find us."

Munin stared quietly at the sleeping yearling as Hugin spoke, and then the two Crows spread their dark wings, rose up into the sky, and flew west. Behind them the sun stirred beneath the eastern horizon. Then slowly it rose to cast a glow of deepest blue up into the sky.

Bou and Taiga lay in the snow between the Spruce trees, asleep in the twilight along with the other Caribou that were scattered through the valley – piles of brown fur in the snow. The slim antlers of the cows poked up here and there, like Willow saplings. During the night, Spring had crept into the forest, Winter had taken it into its arms, and the land had slowly begun to awaken.

chapter 4

The Land Awakens

APRIL

Little Bou lifted his head from a deep sleep and shook it gently until the last grains of Spring Dust fell from his eyes. These twinkled once or twice in the bright sunlight that streamed over the mountain peaks before disappearing altogether. The forest around Bou seemed almost to move, as though it were stretching its vast, cramped body after a long hibernation. The very air about Bou felt alive, filled with the waking breath of so many sleepy trees. A slight breeze carried the sunlight about on its back, clear and golden. Upon this breeze Bou noticed a happy sound that was very faint, drifting all around him. The sound was like no other he had ever heard, and he decided that if the twinkling of Faerie Dust had made a noise, it would sound very much like this one. It was, of course, the sound that snow and ice make as Winter embraces Spring, for even water must sleep in the Arctic cold until the sunlight stirs it from its crystal silence into a sparkling song of melting, dripping, and splashing.

But Bou heard another melody between the melting and the trickling. He cocked his head and little antlers to one side and squeezed his eyes shut, listening intently to the strange harmony. For several minutes the little Caribou sat, still as a mountain, listening. He listened first to the melting snow so that he recognized it, then to the tiny trickling streams so that he could pick these out as well. Then he concentrated on the music in between...until suddenly he exclaimed out loud, "It's a song! Someone is singing!" To Bou's surprise, there came a warm voice from just in front of him.

"Would you not make a melody if you had been frozen, stiff as a tree, all the while the Winter was about, Moshee?"

Bou's eyes sprang open as he backed away from the mysterious visitor and into his mother, whose eyes were still full of Faerie Dust and lost in sleep. The young Caribou's rear legs stumbled against his mother's body and he sat down abruptly in the snow on his rump. Standing before him was the tawny-grey Gnome with big, black eyes, like wet stones; the one who had led the other Gnomes when Rahtrum had come in the night. The Gnome stood, upright upon his sturdy haunches, as high as the yearling's shoulder. His long, furry tail curled and undulated behind him like a creature all its own, and his forepaws hung from his bent arms, poised and ready. His pointed, black-tipped ears turned independently to listen to the surrounding forest as his sharp eyes looked deeply into the young Caribou's. Bou was too surprised to speak and stared, wide-eyed, at the Gnome, who continued.

"The young Faeries are terribly fond of pollen, which is sweet to them, and some are unduly adoring. When they have had too much, their little heads get woozy and they sleep like Bears, though

Bears are meant to sleep for such a long time as Winter. But if the Tuatha De Danann nod off in Autumn with heads made heavy by pollen, they are sure to be covered with silver dew. And if the Autumn should take the Winter into its arms while they are yet sleepy and wet, then they have lingered too long. The dew about them freezes, and they are caught like little icicles in the Winter's cold embrace — until the Winter takes the Spring into its arms, which sets the land to waking."

Little Bou stared at the Gnome, who cocked his head to one side, blinked his black eyes and said, "Are you listening, Moshee? It is the young Faeries you hear, The Children of Light, all turned to singing now that their icy tombs have melted. A very foolish crowd they can be, if you want my opinion. Having escaped the cold, they will all be so delighted with their freedom that they will keep singing and fall to their pollen and become just like little icicles again when the Winter returns from the north."

At that moment a high-pitched whistle echoed through the forest. It was so piercing that all of the Faeries quickly fell silent. Bou's ears stood up straight as he searched for the source of the new sound. But as quickly as it had begun, the whistling slowed and stopped. Silence hung everywhere in the forest. Bou looked to the Gnome, but he stood with his head bowed down and his eyes tightly closed, as though he was still listening to a sound that he alone could hear.

A great grey cloud obscured the sun, and a breeze leapt up off the ground and came howling from the north. It blew dead twigs and needles across the snow-laden floor of the forest. Bou pressed in against his mother for shelter, but the wind was cold and seemed to whisper low and long, "No time."

The little Gnome slowly lifted his head. He muttered to himself at first, "On with it, Blinn." But then he looked deep into Bou's eyes with his, and said, "The Binder sends me, for you are Moshee, a Caribou, chosen of Rahtrum. I know your ways and can help you along them."

Now Bou gathered himself and blinked at the Gnome. "My name is Bou, of the Porcupine herd, not Moshee. Who are you?"

The Gnome replied with a very small and formal nod of his head. "My apologies, Bou, calf of Taiga and yearling of the Porcupine Caribou herd. I am called Blinn by my kin, and by some, the Eye of the North. I am a friend of the Earthshaker. We are bound, he and I, and it is he who gives you the name Moshee."

"Why? Why does he call me Moshee?"

"I cannot say why. Only that as he calls you Moshee, and so then do I. You are different from other Caribou, do you not feel it?"

"Yes, I do. I see things others do not. I have seen you before," Bou replied.

"You are still groggy with Faerie Dust. It was I who walked with the other Gnomes when Rahtrum came to you in the night," Blinn told him.

"But I have seen you before last night. I've seen your eyes shine black under the midnight sun when you moved in the tussocks beside our herd. You kept on with us and were like a silent, tawny-grey cloud that molted white and followed us into the mountains. None of the other Caribou saw you, but I did. And I watched you until you left us at first snow."

The Gnome stood in silent contemplation of the yearling for a moment, then spoke slowly. "Your eyes are keen already, young Caribou, as is your memory. It is now two seasons past that I tracked your herd, and we Gnomes are not easily detected. We may walk cloaked in a dark gloom of forgetfulness when we wish it. We stride in the shadows of Grizzlies for days on end and are never scented. We even travel the bright, Summer hummocks of open tundra beneath far-sighted Falcons without being seen. But you, Moshee, you see what others cannot, and you remember. This, too, is why you have been chosen among Caribou for the task the Binder sets before you."

The yearling dropped his head and replied in a confused tone. "But what has he chosen me for?"

"Rahtrum has chosen you to help him wake the Cargoth, Moshee."

"I do not understand. Why should we wake them? Maybe it's better they sleep. What harm can they do while they dream?" Bou asked.

Now a seriousness crept across the Gnome's face, and his voice grew low and gentle. "They do not sleep quietly like the Bear, Moshee, or harmlessly, as a Winter Faerie trapped in frozen dew." The Gnome turned his head for a moment and peered silently into the south. "They are industrious, these Cargoth. Always their minds are at work. But there is something deep inside them that sleeps, an older, better part of them that is forgotten. And now there is a place in their memories and their hearts that has grown hollow. It cries out to them to be filled. They stand astride the earth, lost in the dream of a hunger that will not abate. If we cannot wake them from this dream, they will consume all they can to fill their emptiness. They will swallow all the world into their shadow, as they once swallowed the Musk Ox from the north and the Buffalo from the wide, golden plains."

Bou was confused and shook his head slowly. "But it is said the Cargoth take what they will from Nature. If they take all they want, how can they still be hungry?"

"It is the emptiness within them, Moshee. They cannot fill the hole that is left by what they have forgotten. Take what they will, still they hunger for more. Their shadow does not wax and wane with the bounty of the seasons, but grows ever larger. There is nothing in Nature — plant or beast, water or stone — they cannot consume."

Bou fell silent for a moment. He tilted his head to one side and asked thoughtfully, "How will a tiny flower fill so great a hunger? How will the Breschuvine awaken the Cargoth?"

The Gnome's black eyes narrowed as he pondered the Caribou's question. "The Breschuvine cannot fill their emptiness, Moshee. Nor will it wake them from their slumber. Still, you must find it. The Binder sends you to do what he cannot. There is but one path to waking the Cargoth from their sleep, and the Breschuvine lies upon it."

There was a hint of frustration in Bou's voice. "That is more riddle than answer. What must I do with the Breschuvine when I find it?"

The Gnome's voice grew impatient, and he spoke quickly. "Answers will come in their season, Moshee. Though you plant a question in Spring, it may not grow into an answer until Summer. You must be patient. If it is not enough that the Binder himself sets this task before you, then you must say so now." Blinn hung his head to sigh, and his voice grew somber. "You are one path Rahtrum has chosen." As he said this, he lifted his head and his black eyes widened and stared deeply into Bou's. "If you are not bound, if you will not go in search of the Breschuvine, then he will wake the Cargoth by another route."

As Bou began to answer a great peel of thunder rumbled across the sky.

Blinn peered up quickly at the clouds and interrupted. "The seasons are not mine to waste, Moshee. Know that I am near, and be comforted. Remember, young Caribou, not every animal is to be trusted, nor every animal to be feared. Now, begin!"

As the Gnome spoke, Bou felt his mother stir in her sleep and turned his head to look at her. She huffed softly into the snow around her muzzle and slowly shook her head. He gave his answer as he swung his head back to face Blinn. "I am bound. I will go, Blinn. I will do as Rahtrum asks and seek the Breschuvine." But the Gnome was no longer there and Bou could find no trace of him, not even a track through the deep snow.

As the yearling looked about frantically for Blinn, he felt his mother stir and climb onto her four, sure hooves.

She peered up into the sky and sniffed at the wind. "It is time, Little One," she said. "We must go."

Bou said nothing to his mother about Blinn, the singing Faeries, the sudden whistling, or the whispering of the wind. He only rose up onto his hooves and quietly followed his mother as they began the first leg of their journey toward Bear River and beyond to the Peel River.

chapter 5

The Peel River

APRIL

The two Caribou walked rhythmically through the snow on their broad hooves. They travelled over the foothills of the high valley that flanked Bear River, climbing and descending through days that widened with Spring sun. When they reached the big valley of Wind River the Caribou wandered along the eastern slopes of the vale. They wove through White Spruce and thickets of Willow, pausing here and there to dig for Lichen before moving on again. The valley grew steeper, and at last they climbed the high edge of a mountain to look out over Spruce-filled lowlands that gently rolled out of the Wernecke Mountains. Here the Caribou turned away from Wind River to skirt four high peaks and graze in the wide dale, where they foraged in the long hours of daylight. They stopped sometimes to lie next to each other in the snow and rest their sturdy legs.

Bou struggled to keep pace with his mother. They had travelled for six days, and though the young Caribou was excited to journey north toward the sea, it was difficult to move as quickly as his mother through the deep snow. He still felt uncertain and a little anxious about the visit from Rahtrum and Blinn at the Wintering Grounds. He pondered their coming as he and his mother lay beneath the Spruce shade in the lowlands.

There are so many Caribou, why does he send a yearling? Why not a mature bull, who will turn south from the Beaufort with high antlers, stripped of their velvet and ready for the Fall rut? Why doesn't he send an animal that is seasoned and knows the northlands? What if I cannot find the Breschuvine? What if I fail? The young Caribou closed his eyes and rested his wide muzzle in the soft, grey hair of Taiga's haunch. He thought again of Rahtrum and the Tuatha De Danann, and of the Gnomes and Root Trolls. He wondered to himself what other marvels he might see as he journeyed in search of the Breschuvine, and then he drifted into a restful sleep.

"Must we travel so quickly?" Bou asked his mother as they walked.

"We must, Little One," Bou's mother apologized. "The seasons have no patience. The Great Binder has roused us and sends us with haste to find what he seeks. The Spring comes early, she is strained and stretches out over the land while the days are still growing. It is the Cargoth that call her forth before she is ready. We are before the other cows that will come north first with their young, farther behind will follow the bulls, who come last toward the sea. But look there. Wind River lies over those hills. We will reach her eastern banks before the sun lies down again. The river will be frozen, and we will graze both shores as we follow it to the Peel River where we must cross. I hope to find the Peel River still frozen, so that we may walk across its back and not disturb its wintry slumber." Now Bou's mother lowered her head and seemed troubled. "But the Cargoth have roused the seasons early, and if the river is awake, and the ice has broken, then there is much peril in crossing."

At twilight the two Caribou crested a gentle hill that was smooth with untouched snow that lay in drifts of blue and purple in the low light. Taiga was encouraged to find Wind River still frozen, but it was much smaller than the Peel River and meandered around many gravel bars. The Peel was swift and deep, and it took the lives of many Caribou each Spring when it awoke. Taiga said nothing of this to Bou. *He is young now, but the seasons will make him strong. He must remain fearless for what lies ahead.*

The Caribou wandered along Wind River, stopping here and there to sleep, or to search for Sedges and roots to maintain their strength. Bou's legs were sore, but he was becoming accustomed to the constant motion and thought that he was well suited to it. Days passed and the Caribou followed the river as it wound ever lower into the Peel River basin.

Late one night, when the sun laid down in the west to sleep in the Bering Sea, Bou began hearing a new sound, like the rushing of wind in the distance. When he asked his mother about the new noise, the old Caribou stopped and listened attentively.

In a somber voice she replied, "It is the river. It stirs and is awake. It has taken its first breath of Spring, and now it shakes the icy scales from its back. I cannot remember it waking so early. It is the shadow of the Cargoth at work in the north. It is the voice of the river you hear, daring all to cross. It is a half moon's walk upriver to a safer crossing, but we cannot waste the early season. We must answer its challenge."

Bou stared into the distance and listened to the river. He thought of Rahtrum and Blinn. "I don't want to challenge the river, Mother. I only want to cross it."

The cow sighed, and a loving look came into her eyes as she said, "Then let us go and cross, my brave, young Caribou."

Mother and son continued along the bank of Wind River. The rushing sound of the Peel River grew, and it seemed to Bou that the river was whispering to him. He shivered and continued on his way.

The Peel River appeared suddenly in front of the two Caribou. Like a Lynx stepping from a shadow, the river slid out from the night. The darkness of Spring nights was upon them now; the deepest pitch of black washed with moonlight. Neither Caribou had seen the river until they had very nearly stood at its edge.

Now Bou was certain the river spoke to him, hissing, "Come, enter, rest, sleep," as he peered out at its wide, inky body. Upon the river's back there was much ice, newly broken by the great strength of the water. The moonlight clung to the floating ice, giving it a dull glow. As he watched, it seemed like ghostly Caribou were drifting by, silent and still, as they stared back at him and his mother before being swept along in the river's icy embrace.

Taiga did not hesitate, but walked to the water's edge and plunged into the cold river. She was quickly swept downstream. Bou looked on in horror as he watched his mother float quickly away.

He stared after her, seeing clearly now that the old Caribou was moving across the river, swimming strongly and carefully across the current, avoiding the ice floes as she went, but she was quickly lost in the darkness. Bou did not want to be left behind. He walked to the place where his mother had entered the river and stared at the dark, rushing water as it called to him again, "Come, sleep, rest."

Peering back at a stand of Poplar trees behind him, Bou hoped to catch a glimpse of Blinn. This seemed a good time for the Eye of the North to come and comfort him, but Bou could see nothing in the quiet forest. He breathed deeply and leapt out into the icy river. As he broke its dark surface the frigid water seeped into his thick, Winter coat and stung his skin. The icy-cold wrapped itself tightly about him, squeezing the air from his lungs. Bou swam with all his strength across the current as he had seen his mother do, but the river stole his breath away. The journey had sapped some of the young Caribou's energy, and now the river seemed poised to swallow what remained. Bou felt himself growing heavy in the water. The river tormented him, whispering, "Rest, Little One. Sleep and be warm." Bou could feel himself sinking deeper into the water's frozen grip. With great effort he kept his head up so that his muzzle broke the surface and he could breathe. Cold and fatigue crept into his legs and he began to wonder if he might not rest a while as the river suggested. His eyes grew heavy. What remained of his strength was gone. *I am only one little Caribou,* he thought to himself sleepily, and he began to slip deeper into the water.

The crossing had been difficult even for Bou's mother, who had been buffeted by ice in the water. She had just struggled up the slick riverbank into darkness. The old Caribou found her footing and turned to peer up the river, looking for signs of her yearling. *He is strong; many do not cross in their first Spring, but Rahtrum has chosen him. He will cross. He must.* The old Caribou stood still, straining through the moonlight to see Bou. She watched carefully, but only ice drifted by, strangely lit by the moon-glow. The river raced on, but no little figure could be seen struggling up out of its dark water. Still she kept her watch.

When at last too much time had passed, she sighed deeply and turned east to follow the riverbank, for she believed she must have missed Bou in the darkness and would find him farther downstream, safe and wet. But as she walked, she felt the darkness close around her, for the cruel river had touched her with its icy fingers and made a little place in her heart where she could find no hope.

Bou was surrounded by the whispering of the river. "Sleep, yes, sleep," it hissed from every direction. The river had him in its cold spell and he slipped beneath the surface of the water, beyond the reach of air. *I must sleep. I must rest a little while.* But just as he gave up paddling altogether and began to sink into the weightless embrace of the river, something hard and jagged knocked into his side and started him awake. He tried to gasp, but there was no air. Panic gripped Bou, and he struggled to the surface to take a large breath. Now the hard object floating in the water struck him again. This time it threatened to push him back down into the freezing depths. He summoned what strength he could and swam bravely around the object, so that he could study it without being battered by its weight.

Bou discovered that he had been struck by a large, flat piece of newly broken ice. *I'll escape the river and ride upon one of its own discarded scales.* It was torturous to try and climb up onto the ice floe with so little strength, but Bou would not give up. When at last he caught hold of the ice and dragged his shivering body up, the dark water gave a splash of rage and whispered to him no more. Bou could resist resting no longer. He collapsed on the ice and was asleep.

Bou's mother continued walking along the bank of the Peel River. She could not help but watch the dark water as it rushed past, wishing with all her heart to see her yearling struggling across the current amid the ice floes. The old Caribou grew more concerned with every step, for if Bou continued east, he would pass the place where the Bonnet Plume River emptied into the Peel. *If he has taken refuge on ice then he may sleep. He will not recognize his danger. The river is swift and when he has passed the Bonnet Plume and Snake Rivers, he will be carried north as the Peel, swollen with Spring water, rushes for the sea. Even if he escapes the river in time, where will I search for him?* Taiga stared downstream, wondering if he was already ahead of her, racing toward the sea. As the old Caribou glanced forward, she noticed the shadow of a small figure standing at the river's edge. For the tiniest moment hope leapt up in her heart, but it was clearly too small a shadow to belong to Bou. As the old Caribou watched, she imagined that this figure was staring at her. She stopped to look more carefully. Now the tiny shadow turned away and leapt with surprising agility out onto a passing ice floe. Then without pause, the strange figure jumped again to an ice floe farther downstream, and then to another, as it quickly disappeared, leaping downstream faster than the powerful river could run.

Rahtrum sends us aid. Taiga ignored her aches and pains and increased her pace.

Gentle darkness cradled Bou as he lay on the ice floe, sleeping. He dreamed again of the Grizzly Bear. It toppled the tall, straight Pine tree as it had before, and then, standing on all fours, it turned its horrible gaze toward Bou, but this time the Bear spoke to him. "Wake, Little One, time is short. You must rouse yourself or the Bonnet Plume will soon be passed, and the river will grow wide and more dangerous."

The great Bear wavered, like the heat of the sun, and the dream faded. Bou was awakened by a soft tugging on his leg and a firm voice in his ears. He opened his eyes to find Blinn's black eyes staring back.

"Here is a proud and brave Caribou to take an ice floe for his bed," said the Gnome. "If you are finished with your slumber, may I suggest we remove ourselves to the shore? Rise, Moshee, you do not know your peril!" Blinn's voice was sharp, and Bou stood up quickly to survey his surroundings. The river had gathered speed; of this the little Caribou was sure. The voice of the river had also returned, but it whispered and hissed no longer, now it was mad with laughter.

Blinn looked hard into Bou's eyes, and spoke in an ominous tone, saying, "If we pass the Bonnet Plume and Snake Rivers, the banks of the Peel will grow wide as it rages stronger, having swallowed up the last of its brethren on its journey toward the sea. Can you hear the river's laughter? It is in celebration of its first Caribou. The river believes you will be the first of many this Spring."

Now Bou understood the river's laughter, and he shook as Blinn continued.

"Escape is a simple matter. You must follow me as I leap from one ice floe to the next and guide us safely to shore."

Bou looked around at the surface of the river. The moon was gone now behind a stretch of cloud, and the water looked like a dark, writhing mass. He could not see the ice floes and was afraid he might leap again into the icy torrent and be lost. He turned to Blinn. "You are the Eye of the North, and a very keen eye you must have, but I can see nothing upon the dark water. I am only one small Caribou, and you are smaller still. How will I follow you if I cannot see you?"

The little Gnome moved to stand in front of Bou. He drew the yearling's face down close to his with his broad paws and studied his eyes. "Now you may be small, and I smaller still, but watch, young Caribou, and see if I do not lead you from this river. Do you think the Great Binder sends one who is not resourceful?" And with that, the tiny Gnome stepped back, peered up into the sky, and let out a whistle so piercing and loud that Bou lay down on the ice and pressed his head against its cold surface.

When the ear-splitting sound at last subsided, all was quiet, and even the river's laughter fell momentarily silent. The little Caribou peered up at Blinn, but the Gnome still stared up at the sky, as though waiting for a reply. Bou joined the Gnome in watching the high, black clouds, edged silver with moonlight. Several moments passed, and Bou thought to himself, *Surely we will drown if we remain here like this*. But no sooner had the thought entered his mind than a strange shadow crossed a crack of moon-glow in the sky. Bou found it very hard to follow the gloomy figure in the darkness, but Blinn watched carefully as the shadow grew larger and said, "She comes." Soon the shadow drew near enough, and Bou saw that a massive bird descended out of the darkness at extraordinary speed.

He turned quickly to Blinn and cried, "It's an Eagle! Now if we're not swallowed by the river, we will be caught in this great Eagle's talons!" Bou cowered against the ice, but Blinn stood up straight and let out another piercing cry. The Eagle halted its descent, flapping its enormous wings fiercely to slow its speed. Then, in mid-flight, it called out with its own shrill cry and raced off into the west, disappearing into the night.

Blinn watched the western sky long after Bou had lost sight of the great bird. When at last he drew his gaze from the heavens, he turned to Bou, saying, "Windshim she is called by her brethren. She is mightiest of all Golden Eagles, and in the north her eyes alone surpass my own. I have called her away from her hunting in the south much earlier than was expected. She does not come willingly, but she is bound, and she will serve you well. I have sent her to summon the Tuatha De Danann, and soon you will see how the tiniest of creatures may save you when you cannot help yourself."

Bou's mother toiled along the bank of the Peel River. She was near exhaustion and would soon need to rest and find food.

Surely Bou cannot be far, I have seen the shadow of the strange little one who leaps among the ice floes. The Great Binder must have sent such a creature as this, agile and cunning. A Gnome, perhaps, who has chosen to reveal himself to me.

As the old Caribou struggled on, wondering to herself what manner of beast Rahtrum had sent forth as aid, her thoughts were interrupted by a distant cry out of the east. She froze where she stood and listened carefully. Again, there came a shrill cry, and then a third piercing call. Taiga remained motionless for several moments afterward, but nothing was to be heard. She resumed her trek along the Peel River, and after only a little time had passed, another cry split the shadowy sky above her.

Taiga froze where she stood and peered up. Overhead a wide shadow flew up the river, and much wind was disturbed beneath its wings. As quickly as it had appeared, the winged shadow was gone, swallowed by the night.

Bou's mother was confused. *First the nimble river-walker and now a mighty Eagle? Can both be in the service of Rahtrum? My little yearling, you cannot know what eyes watch over you, and here am I, Taiga, your mother, helpless. Still, I will take no sleep until you are resting at my side.* And with that thought, she bent her head forward and continued on her way.

The murky river had resumed its mad laughter. Bou clung close to the ice, afraid that at any moment a rock or rapid might break their frozen raft into pieces.

Blinn stood by and gave the young Caribou what reassurance he could. "Do not be afraid, Moshee. Windshim has outraced a tempest, and the Tuatha De Danann are swifter still."

Bou was surprised at the thought of one of the Faeries moving with greater speed than the Golden Eagle. He asked Blinn what sort of creatures the Tuatha De Danann were, to possess such swiftness.

The Gnome cocked his head to one side for a moment. "There is little time for so long a tale."

But Bou persisted, insisting he would be glad for the distraction. Blinn's eyes softened, and in an effort to divert the yearling's attention from the river, he spoke softly.

"The Tuatha De Danann are wise creatures, possessed of long life. Their only real folly is the late Autumn pollen, as I think I've told you. But it's no harm done – a frozen Faerie, that is – no harm to any other creature but themselves. It is the way of the Tuatha De Danann to do no harm. It is their covenant to each other. No creature in Nature treads more softly upon the earth. Some call them The Children of Light." Here the Gnome paused and stared away into the west for a moment.

Bou looked after him but could make out nothing in the darkness.

Blinn turned to the little Caribou and continued. "You will see in a moment why they are called this. Make ready, Moshee, the Children of Danu come swiftly and quietly."

Bou's mother struggled east along the river, watching carefully for some sign of Bou. The old Caribou grew ever more weary, and hope faded in her heart, for she began to wonder if the Golden Eagle was only hunting along the river and knew nothing of her yearling's plight. Perhaps she had only imagined the ice-walker.

After all, you can live your entire life and never see a Gnome, even had one walked at your side all the while.

Still, she plodded on because she could not think what else to do. As the blackness of the night began to settle down upon her heart, a voice came out of the crisp air, clear and bright, like the glint of sunlight off an icicle.

"Lift up your head, Taiga of the Porcupine herd. I am called Ainafare, First Light, by the Tuatha De Danann. It is we Faeries that hasten now to the little one's aid, and none may go more swiftly."

Bou's mother stopped in her tracks and searched in the direction of the mysterious voice. As Taiga stared on, the tiny Faerie that had spoken to her gave out a pulse of clear, white light, then streaked off eastward over the river and into the night.

But this Faerie was followed by a multitude, and the other Tuatha De Danann answered Ainafare's pulse of light with their own, as they darted past the Caribou at dizzying speeds. Taiga watched with wonder as a constellation of tiny shooting stars streaked overhead, leaving traces of light in the air. Not until Rahtrum had come into the forest had she seen anything so wondrous. When they had all gone, Taiga stood staring after them. Then, as though waking from a dream, she shook her head and crashed forward through the brush after the Tuatha De Danann. Bramble and dead wood splintered and fell before her.

Blinn moved closer to Bou and said calmly, "You must keep your eyes upon me. Fix them to me and do not be distracted. The Bonnet Plume grows closer, and we must make the shore before the Peel begins its mad rush to the sea. Stay near, Moshee, it is time."

The Gnome moved carefully to the edge of the ice floe, and Bou followed close behind. He was confused, for he could still see nothing of the river in the darkness. But the tiny Gnome stood straight and still at the edge of the floe, staring out toward the shadowy bank. Without any warning Blinn raised his arms into the air and shouted into the night, "Slowly my friends, or you will blind him with your brilliance."

Hovering in the air above the river, a tiny Faerie began to glow, and then another, and another. They shed their light slowly at first, one at a time, so they would not injure Bou's eyes. But when enough were lit up to cast a dull glow across the entire river, they began to light more rapidly, until the river was awash in the splendor of the Tuatha De Danann, Children of Light. The little Caribou was so dazzled by the illumination of the Faeries that for several seconds he stood fastened to his spot.

Blinn turned and barked at him, "Watch only me, Moshee, only me!"

Bou remembered his danger and locked his eyes onto the Gnome. Blinn did not pause to see if the Caribou was watching but leapt immediately to a nearby ice floe, turning only then to see if Bou followed. Bou leapt after him, losing his balance slightly and then regaining it, never taking his eyes off Blinn. The Gnome was away again to the next ice floe, and Bou struggled after him. Blinn moved from floe to floe at a masterful pace, and Bou followed without hesitation, sometimes falling on his side, sometimes landing perfectly only to spring away again after the agile Gnome. In this way, Blinn led the yearling to shore under the bright watchfulness of the Tuatha De Danann.

When Bou finally made the safety of the riverside, he was so frantic and excited that he hopped twice more up the bank, lost his footing, toppled back down to the water's edge, and then recovered his balance. He stood and shook the water from his coat. Then he looked up again only to find that the Faeries had put out their lights, or were gone. All was dark once more. He peered about for Blinn, who was nowhere to be found.

chapter 6

A Shadow Lurks

APRIL

Bou guessed that Taiga would be walking along the bank of the Peel in search of him. He was exhausted and in need of rest, and the darkness made him feel even more alone, so he gathered his strength and began to walk in search of his mother.

The nights of April were growing shorter, crowded by the daylight. The sun still lay down in the west to rest, but she slept lightly there and crept north a little more each day. In the coming weeks she would grow restless with the green tide of Spring and sleep no more, eventually skirting the horizon altogether, ending the night and ruling all the hours of the Arctic sky with her burning, yellow glory. As Bou walked slowly along the banks of the Peel River in search of Taiga, the waking sun bruised the eastern sky cobalt blue behind him, and the stars nearest the horizon began to fade.

Why is Blinn so secretive? One moment he is here, and the next he's gone, Bou thought as he walked. *I wonder if Mother will believe me when I tell her about the Children of Light?* Ahead of the yearling the river's edge jutted out sharply, and a stand of Poplar and White

Spruce stood, most of their length in the deep blue shadows of the waning night. But the sun now scraped the tips of the eastern hills and licked the tops of the trees with its orange light. As Bou looked at the glowing treetops there was a noise ahead of him that echoed sharply through the grove. It was the sound of dry timber cracking and squeaking in the cold air as some slow-moving weight pushed through it. The young Caribou stared in the direction of the noise, and at last, Taiga, walking slowly and wearily, stepped from the trees, looked up, and paused to blink at Bou, who grunted and raced to her side.

The old Caribou nuzzled her yearling with her nose as he stood near to her and pressed against her warm flank.

At last Taiga nodded her head at Bou and spoke. "I wondered where I would find you, Little One. I began to believe that in your haste to reach the Beaufort Sea, you had chosen to swim there."

The yearling could not contain himself. He pranced in tight circles around his mother as he spoke. "The river whispered to me. I was so tired and afraid. But there was ice, and I climbed onto it and fell asleep, and a Gnome came to wake me! The very same Gnome that came with Rahtrum into the forest, and that I saw following us through the Autumn tussocks. His name is Blinn, but some call him the Eye of the North. And there was a Golden Eagle, called Windshim, and she went in search of the Tuatha De Danann, whom Blinn calls the Children of Light. They came and lit up the night like the sun! Do you believe me, Mother? Do you?"

"I believe you, Bou. The Gnome made certain that I saw him out upon the river, and the Eagle passed overhead."

"And did you see the Faeries? Did you?"

"Yes, those I saw too. For one stopped on her way to you to ease my fear with her light. Ainafare, she said her name was, First Light of the Tuatha De Danann. Then all the rest passed me by like shooting stars."

"What does it mean, Mother? What does it mean to see such wonderful things?"

"I do not think that any Caribou has seen what you have seen, Bou. But I cannot say what it means, only that Rahtrum watches over you in his way." But Taiga's thoughts were troubled. *The Binder does not send aid lightly. He does not bend what should not be bent. But you slept upon the river, and you are a yearling. Most would not have survived. Yet Rahtrum reached out for you, and bent his careful balance to keep you safe.* The old Caribou wondered what else might lie ahead for her yearling as Bou carried on excitedly about the events on the river.

Together the pair wandered up the north bank of the Peel River and into the shade of the Balsam and White Spruce. The sun was rising quickly, the morning sky was clear and blue, and the air fresh with the first taste of Spring. Taiga was exhausted from her search, and Bou, having told her all he could about his adventure, grew silent as he was overcome by fatigue. The Caribou lay down in the snow next to one another. There, in the lee of the Spruce trees, dappled with green and blue shadows, they closed their eyes and slept deeply as the sun arced across the sky and was lost behind dark grey clouds that billowed out of the northwest, bringing Spring snow in the late afternoon.

When Bou and Taiga awoke, they lay comfortable and warm under a new coat of snow. Taiga nudged her yearling with her muzzle and he lifted his head to shake the snow from his fur-covered nose. Together they stretched their legs and rose.

"We must continue," said Taiga, and she turned and began to walk as Bou followed. They wound through the last of the Poplars that grew in the low, dark soil near the river. The Poplars soon made way for White Spruce. As they wandered farther away from the river and through low valleys, the White Spruce were fewer, and Black Spruce took their place.

The Caribou rose out of the lowlands of the Peel River as Taiga followed the contours of Mountain Creek into the southern climbs of the Eastern Mountains. These mountains stretched far to the north and piled high on the shoulder of the great river delta where the Peel and Mackenzie Rivers emptied into the Beaufort Sea. As the Caribou rose higher into the old range, only Shrub Willows poked up through the Winter snow here and there on the south slopes. The northern inclines were windswept and barren of shrubs. The long hills and steep slopes were a difficult climb for Bou, but he kept pace with his mother as they followed age-old paths. Taiga traversed the eastern flanks of the Richardson Mountains with an easy strength and grace.

By this time, Bou had begun to cock his head regularly to peer over his shoulder as they walked. He did so discreetly, as he did not want to be noticed. Something was bothering him. He said nothing to worry his mother, who walked ahead of him, but he turned it over again and again in his mind as they plodded through the long hours of waxing daylight. *A shadow lurks behind us,* he thought. *It is twice now that I have seen it waver to our rear and then melt away. I cannot make it out, but I do not think it is a Gnome. It is too large. And it is strange, for although I'm sure I've seen some part of its shape, my eyes cannot recall it. It's like a darkness that cannot be held in memory. It could be some beast the Binder sends to watch our path, but I do not trust this shadow. There is something unnatural about it.*

The light of day stretched ever longer as the Caribou walked the edge of the mountains, leaving deep trails through the snow and exposing dark rock where the Winter lay thinly on the mountainside. They foraged in valleys, at the headwaters of creeks and streams, and slept out of the wind whenever they grew tired. They travelled late into the month of April, and when Taiga saw that they had passed the wide Eagle Plains, she turned and began to cross the worn, stone shoulders of the Richardson Mountains toward Rock River.

It was late one night in the last breath of April that the low sun filtered through a blanket of cloud and cast a soft yellow pall over the land. Long, purple shadows crept beneath the crags and peaks as Bou and Taiga readied themselves to bed down in the crook of an old mountain that stood in the middle of the range. Then, as the sun lay down behind the hills for a short rest, the amber light leached from the clouds and the purple gloom deepened. At the top of a small, rock outcropping the Caribou lowered their tired bodies into the snow and fell asleep near to one another.

As Bou slept he dreamed again of the bear. In his dream it was nighttime, and a round moon shone in the clear sky. A tall Spruce tree stood before him at the top of a high barren hill. The land all around fell away into a valley that circled the hilltop. The air in the dream held the last warm scents of Summer: Blueberry, Cinquefoil, and Labrador Tea. But the Autumn skulked in a breeze that blew across the mount and ruffled the fawn-coloured hair of the Grizzly that stood beside the Spruce. Bou trembled at the site of the big Bear. But the Grizzly ignored the yearling and the tree and raised its muzzle in the cool wind to scent the air. Suddenly the Bear spooked, wheeled to the east, and bolted over the edge of the hillside. Its thick coat shook along its flanks and loose rock scattered as it ran wildly. Bou watched in amazement as the bear galloped out of view. Then he looked again to the tree and saw why. Where the Grizzly had stood near the Spruce, there now lurked a shadow. And while most shadows lie flat across the surface on which they are cast, this shadow hung in the air and seemed to shift like black fog in the moonlight. It was long and low, smaller than the bulk of the Grizzly and closer to the ground. Bou could not fix its shape from the darkness because he could not make out all of its edges. When he concentrated on one part of the shadow, the rest blurred and wavered. The Caribou was terrified and shook as he lay against the hard ground of his dream. The shadow moved slowly nearer and emitted a low snarl that quivered the night air. A plume of hot, moonlit mist rose out of the creeping darkness. As the cloud cleared, Bou could make out the shadow's eyes for the first time. They were the only part of the dark creature that was easy to discern, and they peered sharply at the yearling. They were small and set near to each other, and they glowed, frost-white as Faeries' wings in the light of the moon. The eyes drew nearer and nearer, until they seemed to hover, directly over the Caribou. Bou was near panic, and he closed his eyes tightly in his dream and wished to be awake. It was no use, he could hear the shadow breathing; it huffed and sniffed long inhalations around the yearling's head. The breathing filled Bou's ears and his hair stood up on his back and neck. Then the dark visitor let out another deep, rolling growl that sounded to Bou like a distant peel of thunder. Another cloud of hot breath crowded around Bou's muzzle, reeking of meat, long dead and rotten. The yearling tried not to breathe. Then the shadow spoke, as though to itself, in low, whispered tones.

"So, this is the bull yearling called Moshee. Now I know you, Caribou, and I have your scent. I seek what you seek."

There was a new sound in the dream, a shrill call that seemed to rain down from the sky. The sound seemed very real to the yearling; it was high and clear and somehow familiar.

The shadow stopped speaking, and Bou could hear it sniff up at the sky. The piercing call came again and then once more. As Bou listened, the shadow huffed and snarled and turned away. The call came once again, and seemed closer. Bou opened his eyes slowly, still frightened, and realized that he was no longer asleep. As his heavy eyes came into focus he saw a long, dark shadow slip over the edge of the rocky outcrop and disappear. Again, the sharp cry came from above, and Bou looked up quickly to see a great Eagle spiralling against the first red streaks of dawn. Twice she circled before she flapped her broad wings, angled her tail, and raced away, chased by the rising sun. "Windshim," Bou whispered to himself, but she was gone.

Bou was alert now and scrambled quickly to his feet to check on his mother. Taiga still slept, with her muzzle on her hind legs and her antlers resting in the snow. Her breath rose, pink, into the cool air, lit by the first light of the red sun. Bou surveyed his surroundings and found wide, new prints in the snow around him. The tracks pooled with violet shade in the growing light of dawn. They led to where he had made his bed in the snow, then away to the edge of the outcropping, where Bou had seen the dark shadow disappear. The young Caribou stepped slowly, with legs that still quivered, and followed in these tracks to the edge of the blunt cliff. A short drop below, the trail continued in the snow. The lumbering gait of the prints widened quickly to a gallop as they faded into the valley below. The high sides of the vale wore Dwarf Birch scrub but in its crook there was a long forest of Black Spruce. The shadow that had lurked in the darkness had vanished into the Spruce trees and Bou could see no sign of it. This brought little comfort to the yearling, who was still shaken by the encounter. He peered up into the sky again for Windshim, but she was already leagues away to the west, soaring ever closer to Lone Mountain. *Where are you, Blinn?* Bou wondered to himself. *This shadow lurks, and you are nowhere to be found. The creature says he seeks what I seek. Can he mean the Breschuvine? But why? What does he want with it? What can it mean? Blinn, where are you?* There was a noise behind Bou that startled him. He jumped as he turned, half expecting to see the Gnome standing in the snow. But it was Taiga, rising out of her bed and shaking the snow from her antlers.

She looked surprised to see her yearling up before her and spoke gently to him. "Are you rested, Little One? Usually it is I who wakes you from your sleep."

Bou did not want to frighten his mother and decided to say nothing of the shadow. "I woke with the sun. I'm rested and ready to journey to the sea."

Bou's mother nodded her head at him and replied, "Well, it is still some way to the sea, but every step draws us nearer." Taiga turned, and Bou was relieved she did not notice the strange tracks in the snow.

As the Caribou continued on their way, Bou made certain to watch the landscape carefully, stealing glances to see if the shadow followed them. But there was no sign of the dark one, and soon the young Caribou began to relax. They climbed together into the morning sun as it stained the high slopes as blood red as bull's antlers, newly freed from their velvet.

chapter 7

Dark Path of the Cargoth

MAY

April slipped away in the Richardson Mountains, and as the Caribou journeyed into May, Bou stopped looking behind him altogether. He could find no evidence that the shadow still tracked them, and in the brief darkness of the last Spring nights there were no more visits from frost-white eyes or stinking breath. The air had warmed slightly, and the high southern slopes had begun to lose their pelts of snow to the sun. Just as the Caribou began to molt their grey Winter coats in exchange for the brown of Summer, so the mountains began their long molt from Winter white to the rust and black and green of Spring thaw. In some spots Shrub Willow and Birch could be seen tasting the season with buds of green. But cold air still ran in rivers through the valleys, where the Spruce and Poplars stood to their knees in the damp snow, waiting for the new warmth that would come with Summer.

The Caribou descended a steep ravine out of the mountains as the sun stood high in the east. They crested a round embankment. There, Rock River lay in the distance, beyond hills mottled red with willow tips emerging from the snow. From this vantage point they could see a great distance. At the edge of their vision they saw the long, dark path of the Cargoth as it snaked down from the Eagle Plains, rose out of a valley bottom, and disappeared into another, only to crawl up into view again and wind in a long arc over a hilltop plateau before fading beyond the horizon.

"Why is it called the dark path?" Bou asked Taiga.

She stared into the distance at the long trail that cut through the land before she answered. "Here the Cargoth make a path of shale and gravel, piled high above the frozen ground. But far in the south it is said their paths run wide as rivers across the earth, and are made from stone, blackened with earth-blood they draw from the ground. It is partly because of their appearance that they are called dark paths. But remember, Little One, it is the Beasts of Shadow that travel these wide trails, carried along by giant, growling creatures that breathe foul air. It is by these trails the Cargoth's shadow moves over the land. These are the tendril roots of their darkness, and it is for this reason that we call them the dark paths of the Cargoth."

Taiga looked at her son, who turned his head to survey the length of the path, and continued. "It stretches to the north, almost to the sea. There is no way around. We must cross here."

The Caribou followed their shadows through the morning until white clouds billowed overhead and obscured the afternoon sun. As they drew near to the path, the Caribou descended a steep embankment to Rock River and followed its deep valley.

Soon Taiga stopped and turned to Bou. "It is near, Little One.

I will walk ahead to scent it, just as I did when we came south in the Autumn. It is my hope that it will be quiet. Always there are Cargoth upon it, but in this season the Peel River runs with ice to the north, and they cannot cross. Still, there are some that travel this way and we must be wary of them."

Bou looked nervously through the woodland brush that bordered the river before he replied. "Will I wait here alone while you go ahead?"

"I will not be long." She hesitated. "What troubles you? Have you seen something?"

The yearling thought of the dark creature with frost-white eyes, but answered quickly. "No, I haven't seen anything. I will wait here for you, beside this Poplar."

"I will be quick, but I must make sure there are no Cargoth upon the path, waiting with their thunder." Taiga turned and walked through the brush toward the dark path of the Cargoth.

Taiga walked quickly through the Spruce and Alder and the snow that still lay deeply in the valley near the river. Soon she saw a steep incline, and the dark path rose like a ridge in front of her. It was piled high above the permafrost with crushed stone, to a plateau where nothing grew. Bou's mother stood and wondered at it. No matter how many times she saw or crossed the path, it always filled her with awe and fear. *What creatures can build such a thing? I have heard stories*

of Wolf dens, dug deep into the hills. And I have seen Eagles' nests that sit high in trees or upon stone cliffs, as big as a bull Caribou. But this path is more than any of them, more than all the Beavers of the north could accomplish in a hundred seasons. What creature can divide the wilderness from north to south? As she pondered, she pushed through the brush to the edge of the gravel slope. It rose in front of her at a steep angle beyond the height of her antlers. Taiga huffed and sniffed the air before stepping onto the embankment and starting up the side. But just as she climbed high enough to see over the flat surface of the path, she heard a rustling in the forest behind her. She looked around, concerned that Bou had followed her too soon, but he was nowhere to be seen. Instead, a Snowshoe Hare, already molting its Winter white, came bounding between the tree trunks. Taiga stood perfectly still at the side of the path and watched him approach. He paused as he neared her tracks in the snow and sniffed at the air with his little black nose. His long ears busily turned every which way. He shuffled forward until he found the old Caribou's prints in the snow and stopped suddenly out of her view behind some Alder scrub. His nose twitched almost frantically, and then he began to whisper in a very nervous voice as he lumbered toward Taiga. His front paws bore his tiny weight as he lifted his furry little rump and drew his large, rear paws forward. His ears stood guard all the while.

Quietly he whispered, "Moshee of the Porcupine herd? I bear a message, are you there?" The Hare spoke so softly as he sniffed at the Caribou tracks that the cow could only just understand him. "Moshee, I bear a message from Blinn, Eye of the North. Are you there?" The rabbit's ears strained in every direction.

As the Hare crawled through the brush and into full view, the old Caribou could see that the new brown fur on his back stood up a little where the Winter white was falling out, and that he seemed to shiver. She spoke. "I am Taiga of the Porcupine herd."

At the first sound of Taiga's voice, the Hare leapt straight up into the air, fell back into the snow and raced back into the forest in three lightning bounds before hitting a Spruce tree and sitting back on his big rear paws, stunned.

Taiga strode to the bottom of the dark path and called to the Hare, whose rump pointed out at her from the tree he had struck. "Moshee is my yearling. I am Taiga, his mother."

The Hare's ears circled back, like two thin Weasels, toward the Caribou's voice. Then the rabbit regained his balance and turned to stare at Taiga with his round, black eyes. "Moshee is here?" he squeaked nervously.

"He is nearby, but hidden. What is your message? I am Taiga, his mother."

The Hare blinked and sniffed the air as he spoke quietly to himself. "Taiga? Yes, yes, Taiga. The mother, Taiga. She can have the message." Then he addressed her again with his high, nervous voice. "Will you be bound? Will you receive the message of Blinn, Eye of the North, Taiga, Mother of Moshee?"

"I have asked you for it already," the Caribou replied sternly.

The Hare sniffed the air again and peered this way and that as once more he spoke softly to himself. "Why does she not give the answer? Ask her again." The Hare addressed the Caribou in a shrill, distressed voice. "Will you receive the message of Blinn, Eye of the North, Taiga, mother of Moshee?"

Now Bou's mother seemed agitated as she replied, "I have said as much. Yes, Hare. I am bound. Give me the message."

This answer relieved the Hare of some of his distress, but still he remained nervous as he approached Taiga in short, careful hops. "Yes, yes, yes. That is the answer we need," he muttered to himself. Then he addressed the Caribou anew. "Here is the message I bear, Taiga, mother of Moshee. The Eye of the North bids you to cross the dark path and travel north. Let Rock River set you a course and stay upon it."

"Why, Hare? Why does he send us this way? We can travel by another way to skirt the Porcupine River and reach the Calving Grounds just as easily."

The rabbit seemed agitated by this response and murmured again to himself. "What does she say? Did she not hear? Perhaps. Yes, yes, perhaps she did not. Give her the message again." And once more the Hare addressed the Caribou, though this time he spoke more slowly. "Here is the message I bear, Taiga, mother of Moshee. The Eye of the North bids you to cross the dark path and travel north. Let Rock River set you a course and stay upon it." Now both his ears bent forward in anticipation of Taiga's response.

The old Caribou huffed and shook her head, then she studied the nervous little rabbit. "It is well, Hare. I have your message." But even as she spoke a low growling reverberated through the air from a small distance away on the dark path of the Cargoth.

As Bou watched, Taiga turned and strode toward the path. He thought again of the black creature that had stalked them in the Eastern Mountains. How it had crept near to stand over him while he slept. *The days have grown bright, and I have not been watchful. What if he has tracked us here? He stood over me as I lay helpless, yet no harm came to me. He seeks what I seek. That is what he said.* At that moment, in the branches of a tall White Spruce there was a sudden caw, followed by a sharp rattle. The yearling was startled from his thoughts. These sounds were answered by a throaty chortling in another nearby tree. The yearling looked up to find the source of the noises and saw two large Crows turning their heads from side to side and staring back down at him.

"Hello." The Caribou said hesitantly to the Crows. "I am Bou, of the Porcupine herd."

The Crows looked at one another then back at the Caribou, before the smaller of the two spoke. "Greetings, Bou, of the Porcupine herd. I am called Hugin and this is my companion, Munin. It is rare to find yearlings travelling alone. You are not lost I hope?"

"I am not alone. My mother, Taiga, has gone ahead to see that the dark path is safe for crossing. She will return for me soon."

Hugin made noises at Munin, *"Kek, kek, kek."*

Munin answered, then turned her head sideways at the Caribou and spoke. "It is early to be this far north. You cross the dark path already? Where are the other cows of your herd?"

"We are before the other cows. They will not be far behind," Bou replied.

They ruffled their feathers. Hugin clicked and rattled. "That is passing strange, Bou of the Porcupine herd. Why do you travel before the other cows?"

Now Bou tilted his head to look more closely at the Crows. As he did this he remembered Blinn's words. *Remember, Moshee, not every animal is to be trusted.* The Crows were polite and seemed harmless. He wanted to tell them how Rahtrum had come into the forest, but he decided to be cautious. Turning his head to look into the distance, the yearling tried to sound at once both disinterested and mysterious. "I cannot tell you why we are here before the other cows."

Munin squawked.

"He does not know why he is here," Hugin rattled.

"I do know why we are here!" Bou protested.

"Then why can you not tell us?" Munin demanded.

"Because I cannot trust you," the yearling declared.

"You cannot trust us? *Ark, wok!* Nonsense! You cannot tell us because you do not know!" Hugin retorted.

The yearling burst, "We are before the other cows because Rahtrum himself has set us to a task!"

"Rahtrum?" The Crows said in unison. "What does the Binder want with Caribou?" Hugin bobbed his head slightly and warbled. Bou felt the Crows were laughing at him. Munin warbled in return and shuffled from side to side on her branch.

The yearling felt mocked and annoyed by the Crows. "Rahtrum sends us to find the Breschuvine!"

The Crows stopped their warbling and Munin spoke softly. "You seek the Breschuvine, yearling?"

"You know of it?" Bou said, surprised by the Crows' familiarity.

Hugin interrupted quickly, "We are Crow, Caribou, there is much we know that others have forgotten. *Click, click.* Why do you seek the Breschuvine?"

"We were chosen of the Caribou to seek it, by the Earthshaker," Bou said proudly, feeling he now had the Crows' attention. He paced a little way from where he stood so that his back was to them.

Hugin ruffled his feathers and glanced at Munin. "*Wok.* But where will you seek the Breschuvine, young Bou? Is it not lost from memory in the north — known only to Rahtrum?"

Bou was not expecting this question, which he had no answer for, and not wanting to appear less important to the Crows, he replied carefully. "I cannot say where we will seek the Breschuvine."

"*Caw, kek, wok!*" Hugin raised his head, stretched out his wings, and tucked them in again. "You cannot say? You do not know! We are Crow, Caribou, keepers of secrets. Why will you not tell us?" he said sharply.

Munin cooed at Hugin, who gurgled impatiently, then spoke softly to the yearling. "We can aid you in your task, Bou of the Porcupine herd. Tell us where you seek the flower, and we will go and make certain it is there for you."

This seemed a kind offer, and Bou felt embarrassed that he had been trusted with so great a task, but had not been told where to seek the Breschuvine. He paused in thought and then said confidently, "It is very good of you to offer, but I cannot tell you where we seek the Breschuvine."

Hugin shrieked. *"Caw! Kek, kek!"* He spread his wings and bobbed his head fiercely. "Speak now, Moshee! Foolish Caribou! Tell us where it blooms, and we will aid you as Munin says!"

Bou turned his head quickly to stare at the Crows. "How is it you know this name? How do you know the name, Moshee? It is only two moons since it was given to me by Rahtrum."

But just as the Caribou demanded this of the Crows, a terrible, long howl came rolling from the direction of the dark path and shattered the forest quiet. The Crows cawed loudly, leapt from their perches into the air, and rose quickly above the trees to circle in the sky on their dark wings.

Bou froze as he peered in the direction of the noise. It seemed to move as it sounded again and again. The call was foreign and awful, and for a moment he thought of the dark creature with frosted eyes. Then the howling was suddenly gone, and a silence came into the wood. The yearling charged forward, following his mother's hoofprints toward the path.

As Taiga raised her head to listen to the growling noise, the Hare sensed it too, and was momentarily filled with panic. He darted to his right but changed his mind, bounding to his left. The low growl grew closer and louder. The Hare stopped again and shook with fear before racing past Bou's mother and up the steep side of the dark path.

Taiga turned after him up the incline, calling to him as she did so. "It is not safe, Hare! There are Cargoth upon the path!" She was high enough up the side of the slope to see the big creature approaching. It was as red as fireweed, tall as a Moose, and wide as three Bears standing beside each other. It growled and stared at her with big, wide eyes that glowed as bright as the moon. It charged along the path on round, black hooves.

The little Hare mounted the top of the incline and stretched long to hop with all the speed he could muster across the path. The beast called out suddenly with a long, sharp howl that pierced the air, and Taiga saw briefly the Cargoth that sat inside, behind a skin of clear ice, as it hurtled ever nearer with horrible speed. It called out again, and again, and as the beast galloped up the path, it lifted a cloud of fine snow and dust in its wake that hung in the Spring air. The Hare panicked, and with his long ears pressed back and his black eyes wide with fright he zigzagged across the path to try and save himself. But the beast came upon him like a wind and he fell beneath the terrible, black hooves that galloped without moving. He tumbled beneath the long creature as it charged over him, then lay still in a twisted heap, as the snow and gravel beneath him turned deeply red, and the dust settled, quiet as death.

As Bou charged through the Spruce and Alder, the long ridge of the dark path rose before him. He came to its base and stopped to looked up to where Taiga's tracks mounted the top. The old Caribou was nowhere to be seen, and awful thoughts drifted into the yearling's mind as he climbed the embankment to search for her. As he neared the top, he called out hesitantly for her. "Mother? Are you there?" She stood in the centre of the trail and cantered quickly to him when she heard his voice.

"You were to wait in the forest for me to return, Bou," she said quickly.

Bou spotted something lying upon the path behind Taiga as he answered. "I did wait, and spoke with two Crows that sat in the Spruce trees above me." As he said this he pointed his muzzle toward two, black shadows circling in the sky. "Hugin and Munin they are called. But when we heard the howling they took to wing, and I fled here to find you."

Taiga looked softly at her yearling. "It is well you came, we must cross, there is much danger, Little One." She turned and began to trot across the path.

Bou did not follow and instead stared at the spot where the Hare lay dead. "What is this upon the path, and what was the terrible call we heard?"

Taiga circled quickly to look at her yearling. "That was a Messenger Hare, sent by the Gnome Blinn and struck down by a beast of the Cargoth. It was this very beast you heard howling at us as it passed. There is much danger, Bou. We must cross and leave this place. Come."

The young Caribou stared at the Hare's broken body on the road as he walked slowly toward his mother. A low growl came from north along the path, and Bou jumped and cantered quickly across the trail. Mother and yearling galloped down the west bank of the dark path and plunged into a stand of White Spruce.

Another great beast of the Cargoth galloped south, down the wide path, in a cloud of dust and snow. This one was green, and its round, black hooves ran carelessly over the little Hare and rolled its broken carcass to the edge of the path. When the beast was gone, the newly disturbed snow spiralled slowly through the cool air to the ground. So, too, did the winged shadows that had circled above. Down, down they came until, with the beating of black wings and loud cawing they alighted on the Hare. They grasped the hide with their talons and pressed their long, sharp beaks to the flesh. They grasped and tore, then paused, turned their heads and listened. They gurgled and clicked, and long red strips of meat hung from their beaks and wriggled in the yellow sun.

chapter 8

Shadows in the Twilight

MAY

As Bou and Taiga strode along the eastern flank of Rock River, the old Caribou relayed the message from Blinn, carried by the fallen Hare, to her yearling. She spoke of the Hare's nervousness, and how he seemed afraid of his own shadow, and that this fear had driven him to panic and run foolishly to his death. "Always understand your danger before you run blindly from it, Little One. That is the lesson of the Hare."

The young Caribou spoke of the Crows, Hugin and Munin, and he and Taiga both observed that it was strange the birds should know that Bou was called Moshee by Rahtrum. They puzzled over this as they walked the long sloping pediments that rolled gently down from the Eastern Mountains. They breathed the Spring air, slowly warmed by the watchful sun, and smelled the waking scents of Shrub Birch, Arctic Bearberry, and Locoweed. Clear springs ran here and there with melted snow, trickling down into the valleys to feed the rivers. Coaxed by the sun, more and more of the land was struggling to emerge from the deep, white dream of Winter.

The Caribou followed Rock River slowly for two days, covering less ground than usual as they foraged in Lichen-lush valleys and Spring flood plains. The days grew swollen with sunshine, but still the night came and cast a brief, starry darkness over the land. When day and night reached out their arms for one another, the light and dark embraced, and a long twilight came between them.

On the second night of the Caribou's journey along the river, they made ready to bed down in a stand of Balsam Poplar and Tamarack. As they lay down in the wet snow, twilight hung deep and blue in the sky, speckled with dim stars. Taiga drifted to sleep immediately. Her old legs were tired, and she dreamed of the Coastal Plains, covered in rich Cottongrass tussocks, Sedges, and Lichen.

But Bou was restless, and still he wondered how the Crows had come to know the name Rahtrum had given him. As his mother slept, the young Caribou peered out into the half-light that lay around the trees. A sudden motion seized his attention. A shadow, then another moved in the twilight. The hair stood on Bou's back. His ears stiffened and rotated, searching for sounds of approach. He could hear nothing. He saw another movement out of the corner of his eye. The yearling swung his head to catch what lurked in the growing dusk, but he could make out no plain shapes. Another movement danced past at the very edge of his senses. He scrambled to his feet, shaking a little as he swung his head to and fro, hunting for the shadows that drifted in the deepening blue of twilight. *Always understand your danger before you run from it.* He repeated his mother's words in his mind. *What if it is the dark creature from the mountains? But that was only one beast, and I have seen more than one. They circle us, I'm sure of it. Where are you, Blinn?* The yearling stood in one place, turned his head with his ears pricked, and strained to see into the gathering darkness. As the last shade of blue faded from the sky, Bou's legs shook and his ankles grew sore from standing motionless in the shallow snow. He did not see the shadows again, although he felt certain they still wandered the edges of the night. His eyes grew heavy and his front legs twitched. *Surely, if they were a threat they would have attacked us by now.* As the Caribou pondered the shapes that roamed in the twilight, he hardly noticed that he had lain down again near his mother. He strained his senses as the night circled and thickened. Eventually he rested his muzzle on the ground and only his eyes scanned lazily back and forth through the gloom. But soon even his eyes would stay open no longer, and he slipped into a deep sleep and dreamed again of the Grizzly.

When the light of dawn eventually woke Bou, his eyes sprang wide, and he scrambled to his feet. Taiga, already digging in the wet snow for Lichen, raised her head at his sudden motion.

"Are you well, Little One?"

Bou peered about quickly before responding. "I was startled from a dream, that is all."

On their fourth night, when dusk crept purple and long-shadowed down the hills, the Caribou curled up near the banks of Rock River, in a dell filled with Poplar and Spruce. The twilight sank into night, and as the moon rose high and full, Taiga slept, while her yearling remained vigilant.

The shadows still follow us, I'm sure of it. They are watching. What does it mean? Bou considered his surroundings carefully, as long, thin clouds drifted across the moon, washing the forest alternately in silver light and darkness. The young Caribou peered carefully into the forest when the moonlight fell between the branches. It was not long before he spied them. *They are here.* A shape in the distance backed behind a tree, while another circled quickly to Bou's right, behind a thicket of Alder. *They are hiding from us. Hiding and watching.* The yearling's mind raced as a cloud slipped across the moon and darkness flooded into the dale. *There is no wind, or I might scent them. But they are stalking us, these... shadows. Perhaps they do not know that I can see them, just as I watched Blinn in the Autumn, prowling between the tussocks.*

The moon drifted out from behind the clouds, and suddenly, the yearling had a very un-Caribou-like idea. *They must hide at a distance in the day! Afraid we will see them, lit by the sun against the snow. But they sneak boldly near in the last gloaming of Winter and think themselves safe in the darkness. I see them though. I see what others cannot. I will stalk them. I will take one by surprise and demand to know why they follow us.*

Bou was nervous as he rose onto his four sure legs, but he felt a new determination mingle with his fear. It made his back tingle, and he huffed brazenly into the night as he stood quietly and waited in the moonlight, watching for another movement. He did not wait long.

Directly in front of the Caribou, a grey shape lingered in an open space between the Spruce trees. The Caribou sprang away with hardly a thought and galloped straight toward the dark form, which stopped suddenly and stood its ground. As he charged forward, the tingling in Bou's back spread all over his body, and he felt taller, as though a new strength coursed in his legs. He was surprised by the deep, thudding of his own hooves, and how quickly and easily he covered the distance to the shadow — so swiftly, in fact, that he was suddenly upon it. The figure was also surprised by the Caribou's speed. It pressed low to the ground and backed away as Bou halted his charge. In the moonlight, the yearling saw that his night stalker was a large Wolf, that now lay flat against the ground with its front paws apart, prepared for sudden movement. The Wolf growled menacingly. Fear turned in the Caribou's belly; the tingling he had felt in his hide faded, and he felt suddenly small and vulnerable. Bou froze as the Wolf's eyes, which smoldered deeply gold in the half-light, fixed his own. It rose from its crouched position onto long, grey haunches, with its ears slightly back, its teeth bared, and its head held just lower than its shoulders. The growl grew lower and more threatening. Bou suddenly felt foolish for charging forward and wanted to move; wished desperately to run, but could not, held as he was by the Wolf-gaze. The Wolf stepped very slowly closer and snapped at the Caribou. Bou's eyes stretched wide and his hind legs shook. The night could not hide him, his legs would not answer him, and his voice caught in his throat, so that he could not call for his mother. As the Wolf drew nearer, its growl became more intense. But then a voice, calm and commanding, vibrated behind Bou.

"Be still, Mist, he is but a yearling."

The grey Wolf let his growl fade and fall silent, and then lifted his head without taking his eyes from Bou's.

"A yearling?" he sniffed. "He charges through the night like a grown bull. He is strange, this Caribou, who can spot a stalking Wolf and pursue him. It is unnatural."

The voice answered. "He is not like the others, that is why we watch over him."

Mist continued to stare into Bou's eyes, raising his muzzle to drink in his scent. "Still, he is Caribou. I do not understand why we protect this meal."

"Am I not First Star? Look to your nature. You safe-keep him because I wish it."

"You are First Star, Polaris, but it is the Eye of the North that wishes this Caribou safe."

The voice behind Bou grew deep and snarled its answer impatiently. "Then look to our nature, Mist. I safe-keep him because Blinn, who holds council with Rahtrum, thinks it wise. Now go, circle the others, mark the dale, and make the ground safe. Send Aurora in and take Tundra to the hunt. There are animals here in the north that we do not protect, and I am not deaf to my belly."

The grey Wolf sneered as he turned away, "Rahtrum has let the Cargoth break balance, and the Gnome meddles in our affairs. He does not even come himself to call upon our First Star, but sends an Eagle to Lone Mountain. Still, you heed his counsel before the pack's." Then, without waiting for Polaris' answer, the Wolf called Mist turned and slipped away into the darkness.

Bou remained frozen where he stood and struggled to understand what was happening around him. The voice behind him crept nearer and spoke flatly. "It is not customary for Caribou to charge Wolves, Moshee, of the Porcupine Caribou. Mist is young and impatient, but he is strong of instinct. He is right. There is something strange in you." The yearling heard a sniffing near his haunch. "Even now you expose your heels to Polaris, First Star of the Lone Mountain Pack, and this too, is unwise — even insolent — behaviour."

The young Caribou turned his head first, and from the corner of his eye he saw a large, black shape, wreathed in moonlight, that made him shiver and think of the dark, shadowy creature from the mountains. His rear legs trembled a little as he circled to face the Wolf. Polaris was only a little taller than Mist, his fur was sable black, and he stood easily high enough to stare with his copper eyes directly into Bou's. His ears rose above his fur-widened face, and his muzzle was long and silvered with frozen breath.

Polaris looked the yearling up and down and then spoke. "You are right to fear us, Caribou. Mist speaks truly when he calls you a meal, for that is what you are to us, though Blinn and Windshim, both, would have us believe that you are much more." The big Wolf sniffed at the air and continued. "You reek of fear, yearling, and yet I am here to keep you safe. If there was danger from us, it would have visited you and the old cow three nights ago, for we have tracked you all that time." Polaris' eyes narrowed, and he stepped nearer. "But it is not me you fear. You know what I say is true. Some darkness lurks in your memory. You have seen something upon the land, something that I remind you of. Speak, Moshee, what have you seen?" Bou was mesmerized by the Wolf's copper eyes, and quiet with fright. Polaris growled deeply, "Speak!"

The yearling's head twitched and his eyes widened. "A darkness came in the Eastern Mountains, a black shadow that seemed at first to enter my dreams, with frost-white eyes and stinking breath. I could not make out its form, but it was no nightmare. I awoke when Windshim called from the sky, and I saw the creature slip over an outcrop. I saw its wide tracks pooled with shadows in the dawn."

Polaris dropped his head a little and walked in a slow, thoughtful circle until he faced the Caribou again. "Then it is as Windshim has said, and a new darkness moves in the north."

Bou appealed to the big Wolf. "What is this thing? It haunts my thoughts, and it whispered to me in the mountains. Before it fled it said —" But then the yearling thought better of telling Polaris too much. Perhaps the Wolf did not know that the Caribou had been sent by Rahtrum in search of the Breschuvine. "It whispered something."

The big predator sensed that Bou was withholding part of his story. "You have caution, yearling. That is good. But let us speak no longer of this darkness. You are guarded by four Wolves of the Lone Mountain Pack. There are none in the north that may assail you now." Polaris turned his big head to look in the direction of Bou's mother. "The old one will panic to see us, Moshee, you must calm her when she wakes. Tell her that we are bent by Rahtrum against our own nature; that I, Polaris, have given my word to escort you safely to the edge of your Calving Grounds on the Coastal Plains. She must put aside her fear, for Mist and I will accompany you to Babbage River before we turn south again to our range. She must accept this."

"She is my mother. She is called Taiga," Bou said softly, as he peered through the growing twilight to where the old Caribou still lay sleeping. "Together we've seen many strange things already this Spring. It is possible she will not be as surprised as you expect."

The black Wolf stared a moment at the young Caribou. "That is well. Wake her then, the dawn rises up in the east, and Aurora draws near from her watch to the west."

"Who is Aurora?" The yearling asked.

"I am," came a voice from behind the yearling. Bou spun to see a large, female Wolf standing in the twilight. She was grey, like Mist, with streaks of coal black fur that ran through her coat. Her eyes glowed bright yellow, and a big Hare lay at her paws. "Go and wake your mother, Moshee. Soon she will know all of us."

Aurora's voice was calm and soft, and Bou's fear passed away. He was filled with new wonder at the Wolves and thought to himself that they possessed a grace and nobility he had not expected in such a feared predator. He stared a moment at Aurora, then blinked and turned quietly to look into Polaris' copper eyes. Bou felt the warmth of trust growing in his belly. *It is good*, he thought, *to be watched over by such animals.* And for the first time since he and Taiga had left the shelter of the Wernecke Mountains, he felt they were not alone in their task.

He walked carefully to where his mother lay sleeping, in the blue shadows of dawn, and nudged her lightly with his muzzle. The old Caribou lifted her head and nodded at her yearling. Her eyes widened and her ears pricked up as she scented the Wolves. She clambered up onto her hooves in a panic. Polaris and Aurora stood back in the shadows, and Bou did what he could to calm his mother. Taiga stood beside her yearling, stamped her hooves, and grunted uncomfortably. It took some time to convince her that it was safe, but eventually the yearling motioned the Wolves slowly forward and introduced them to his mother.

"This is Polaris, First Star of Lone Mountain," Bou explained as the Wolves, dappled with moonlight, moved forward. The black Wolf nodded his head once. "And this is Aurora."

Taiga shuffled on her hooves. Still nervous and unsure, she replied, "You I know, Polaris, by your size and colour, and by your eyes. In seasons past many Caribou have fallen to you after crossing the Porcupine River, hauled down from their sure hooves by your great weight and unforgiving teeth. I remember little of old seasons, but fear settles in the memory like a stone in a brook. And now you ask that I trust the Wolf most feared by us in the north for sixteen Winters? Why? Why should we believe you?"

Polaris considered the cow carefully before responding in a stern tone. "It is seventeen Winters that I am First Star of Lone

Mountain, old Caribou. And many more of your kind will fall to me in the Autumn. I am what I am. But I have held council with Blinn, friend of the Earthshaker, and when this moon was still new, he sent an Eagle to Lone Mountain."

As the big Wolf spoke, Mist padded slowly out of the trees and into view carrying a Ground Squirrel in his jaws. At his side strode a female Wolf that Bou had not yet met. She was sleek and black with long haunches and wisps of charcoal grey that marbled her coat. Her pale green eyes stared softly at the yearling as she approached. She carried a lean Snowshoe Hare in her lengthy muzzle and tossed it to the ground beside Mist's squirrel. The two Wolves lay down in the snow next to each other behind Polaris and Aurora, panting quietly.

Polaris paid no attention to the returning Wolves and continued to speak as the rising sun broke over the hills. "The Eagle bore news of you and the yearling called Moshee. Make no mistake, Caribou, I am not compelled by Raptors, nor any other bird. But this was Windshim that flew to us, First Star among the Golden Eagles. She came bearing counsel from the Eye of the North."

Now the big Wolf looked at Bou. "We know of your task, Moshee. That you will seek the Breschuvine, lost from memory in the north for seasons upon end."

Taiga looked surprised and stole a glance at her yearling as Polaris continued. "We know that you are chosen of Rahtrum and that he has set you on a long path. We know that he means to wake the Beasts of Shadow from their dream of hunger." Now he looked to Bou's mother. "Windshim has given me a token to win your faith, Taiga. She bids me tell you that it was Ainafare, First Light of the Tuatha De Danann, who came to you by the Peel River to ease your heart with her light; that only a friend of Rahtrum could know this."

The old Caribou tilted her head, blinked at the black Wolf, and nodded slowly. Polaris paused a moment and looked tenderly at Aurora. "In seasons long past, we Wolves suffered greatly at the whim of the Cargoth's ceaseless hunger. We do not forget how we were hunted mercilessly, and without balance, across all the wide lands that stretch between the great seas. We were driven by them, into the northern wilds, where once their reach was weakened by the long Winter. But now, even the seasons bend under their weight. The bones of Winter grow brittle. The river ice breaks early, and we hear rumours from our cousin the Arctic Fox that the northern seas run blue and open when they should sleep beneath ice. It is said even the great White Bear struggles, where once he reigned supreme. The long shadow of the Cargoth stretches north, and we know well its danger."

The Wolf seemed lost in his own thoughts for a moment. "All that is asked of Lone Mountain is that we escort a cow and her yearling safely to Babbage River, near the edge of the Coastal Plain. So we have come, Taiga of the Porcupine herd. And though Mist would prefer to eat you, we will not." The grey Wolf, who was listening where he lay on the ground, huffed and licked his lips. "This year the Hare and Lemming will wax into the fullness of their breeding bloom. There is much food for good hunters, and you are not the only Caribou in the north. Come Autumn, as every Fall, we will track your herd as it crosses the Porcupine River, and many will fall to us. Such is the binding and the balance of Rahtrum. We are what we are."

Taiga looked to each of the four Wolves and then to Bou. "It seems we have little choice. Never could I have imagined that we would travel in the company of Wolves. We must trust in Rahtrum and in Blinn, who see farther than Caribou. But why does the Eye of the North not come himself to watch over my yearling, as he has come before?"

Aurora stepped forward and spoke softly. "The Eye of the North is out upon the land seeking answers. He will come when he has learned what he wishes to learn. He sends us in his stead. You are not used to the company of Wolves. But it is good company, Taiga of the Porcupine herd, and it is safe."

Polaris spoke next. "Aurora speaks truly. We are mate and First Star together, and we rule with one voice. But these two behind us you have not met, old Caribou. The grey-mane is called Mist, Second Star of Lone Mountain. Pay him no mind. He has little patience for the well-laid plans of Gnomes, but he knows his place. The other, black of hair and green of eye, is his mate, Tundra. Of the two, the patience and kindness is in her. If he is Autumn, she is Spring." Polaris cast his gaze back at Tundra and Mist. The female Wolf lowered her head and faintly wagged her tail. Now the First Star addressed the two younger Wolves. "These Caribou we will defend as our own. This is Taiga of the Porcupine herd, and her yearling, Moshee."

Mist sneezed and looked away, disinterested. He reached his

muzzle back and groomed his hind leg. But Tundra rose and came forward with her dark ears flopped slightly to either side and her tail hanging.

"Hello, Taiga of the Porcupine herd, and Moshee, chosen of Rahtrum." She looked at each of the Caribou with her gentle green eyes as she addressed them.

Polaris spoke firmly. "Go then, Tundra and Mist. Eat and make ready." He turned to the Caribou. "The sun rises. When my shadow is as long as I am tall, we will leave and continue toward the Calving Grounds. Forage now, if you will."

When the sun had yellowed and risen a little higher into the cloud-marked sky, Polaris ran scout and broke trail with Aurora. The two Wolves widened their strides and moved out ahead of the Caribou. Soon they were lost to sight over the rising and falling of the land, but Mist and Tundra stayed back with Bou and Taiga, who steadily and easily followed the First Star's trail.

As the day grew long with sun and blue with sky, the Caribou continued plodding along on their sure legs, flanked by the Second Stars of the Lone Mountain Pack. Mist and Tundra sometimes padded quietly beside the Caribou, and sometimes trotted in wide circles, pausing to scent the air and stare upwind, into the distance. Several times, filled with curiosity, Bou tried to speak to the large, grey Wolf.

"Why is your tail so long? Have you ever seen a Faerie? I have. Why are you called Second Star? How come you want to eat us?" But always Mist groaned impatiently, huffed, and loped away to look over the horizon and taste the wind. And each time Bou tried, Tundra looked tenderly at the yearling with her Lichen-green eyes, then ran to her mate and jostled him mischievously. Always the two Wolves walked near to each other, grey and black tails held high, gently bumping into each other's flanks or nuzzling with their muzzles.

Occasionally Tundra would run playfully at Mist, whimpering and growling, and jump up to scruff-bite him. A gentleness came into Mist when she did this, and he would break from his guard to chase her. Wagging his tale, he ran after her and softly nipped her scruff, but in the end he always rolled onto his long back and let her bite his scruff and lick his face.

Bou watched the Wolves play in this way for much of the day. "Why do they do this?" he finally asked his mother.

She looked over to where Mist and Tundra walked side by side. "That is the way of Wolf mates, Little One. Rahtrum has made them to need each other. With us Caribou it is the herd first, and then our calves. But with them, it is their mate first, and then the pack. I do not understand it."

When the day was old and the amber shadows of evening began to lengthen, Tundra suddenly left Mist's side and came to walk beside

Bou. The grey Wolf paused to watch his mate saunter over to the yearling, then turned, circled wide, and began a sweeping patrol around the Caribou.

Bou, always curious, was happy for the company. "Hello, Tundra."

"Hello, Moshee. Are you well? Do you grow tired?" The dark Wolf asked the yearling. Taiga looked suspiciously at Tundra.

"I am not tired. I am a Caribou and I can travel all the north and never grow weary!" Bou proclaimed.

"That is well." The Wolf seemed amused by the yearling's boast. "I think you will have far to go before you find what you seek."

"Do you know the Breschuvine, Tundra?"

"I know only a very little, Moshee. Polaris first spoke of it after the Eagle came. But he would not tell us its purpose. It was then that he gathered the pack and bid Mist and me travel east with him and Aurora, far from our own territory, to find you. We ran long days with the First Star out in the lead. Never have I panted so hard or felt such weariness. Some among the Wolves call him Land Crow, and now I know why, for I have seen his long black strides swallow the wide country like the wings of a Raven."

Bou listened to Tundra with a look of wonder. "Why does Polaris help us?" he asked.

The sleek, black Wolf gazed up at rolling clouds, each one lit different shades of gold, blue, and purple by the low sun. She scented the Spring breeze that blew from the west. "The Spring comes early by our reckoning, Moshee, and yet it is early each year. Now, if it came when it should, we would call it late. Polaris says the Cargoth are changing the weather. He fears them, and he fears nothing else."

She looked at the Caribou with her green eyes, and her brow softened. "When Polaris was but a pup, he was denned at Lone Mountain with his brother. His parents were called Nightmane and Dawn. They were First Stars and mates, and everywhere they went together they bumped and nudged and walked closely. When Polaris and his brother were still short of tooth and clumsy of paw, Dawn bade them stay close to the den, and she and Nightmane went out to hunt under the big moon. When the sun crept up in the morning, only Dawn returned from the hunt. She howled long for Nightmane, but he would not come. She told her pups how their father's leg had been caught in a trap he had not seen in the moonlight. How he lay and panted, and though his pain was great, he would not yelp or whimper. She lay with him, while the moon set, and licked the wound where the cruel teeth of the trap grasped him tightly. But with the first glow of morning came the sounds of Cargoth, and she told her pups how Nightmane bade her leave him, and how she heard him growl and snarl until a crack of thunder came through the still air, and all was silent. Every night she left her pups in the den and returned to where the Cargoth had taken him. For a full cycle of the moon she returned without fail, to the spot where she could still scent him on the ground where he had lain. There she howled for his return. And when the moon rose full once more, she went again. That morning Polaris and his brother woke to the distant crack of thunder and waited long hours by the den for Dawn, but their mother never came."

Bou stared at Tundra with wide brown eyes. "Why did the Cargoth take them?"

"Whatever great hunger may be in them, they are still animals, Moshee. As Wolves hunt Caribou, so too, do Cargoth. But they hunt Wolves also, and we must take care as well."

"How did Polaris and his brother survive without Nightmane and Dawn?"

"You have seen our First Star, he has the strength and cunning of three Wolves. He and his brother foraged and scavenged and learned to hunt together. They grew large in their second year and attracted mates from other territories. Soon Lone Mountain was again home to a pack. But always with Wolves, there must be a First Star. In time Polaris dominated his brother, and a shadow grew between them. In the Spring of their third year it was clear Polaris would be First Star, and his brother crept off in the twilight with his mate. But he, too, was a Wolf to be reckoned with, and soon he was First Star of another den. Still, neither has ever forgotten how the Cargoth took both of their parents in the space of a single moon. Polaris will say that he does not begrudge the Cargoth their hunting. And why should he? He is himself a feared hunter. He will say it is the long shadow they cast into Nature that he loathes; the breaking of the seasons and the poisoning of air and land and sea. He has heard the whispers that come into the hinterlands, and he has held council with Blinn, Eye of the North. But I say there is a mark upon his heart. That he was wounded deeply when Nightmane was lost, and deeper still when the moon came full again, and Dawn never returned. He is fearless, and yet he fears the Cargoth and their hunger. It is like them, he would say, to take not one parent, but two. To take not a small part of Nature, but all of it that can be taken. This is why he helps you, and this is why you must trust in him. He chooses to believe that one day you will help wake the Cargoth from their slumber."

Taiga looked quietly over her shoulder at Tundra and Bou as the dark Wolf finished speaking, and a new trust came into her eyes.

The young Caribou and gentle Wolf sauntered under the midday sun as Bou told Tundra how Blinn and the Tuatha de Danann had rescued him on the Peel River. Even Taiga, who walked just ahead, quietly added the parts of her story she could remember clearly. But as they spoke of their adventures, Mist came bounding up through the Spring-heavy snow and stopped a little way in front of them.

"Polaris wishes to speak with us, Tundra. He is just ahead." The grey Wolf looked at the Caribou with his golden eyes. "Aurora has moved west to watch your flank and will circle behind you while we go forward."

"What is it you guard us against?" Taiga demanded impatiently. "We have travelled safely for three moons without the company of Wolves."

Mist eyed the old Caribou silently, then turned and strode a little way ahead. He paused to wait for Tundra to follow.

"Remember the river crossing, Taiga," Tundra offered gently, "you were not alone at the Peel." She bumped Bou playfully, ran ahead and nipped Mist as she passed him. He gave chase, and they disappeared over a rise. The Caribou watched the Wolves for a moment, and then followed their trails over the land.

chapter 9

Coney and Rock
MAY

Two bright, blue days slipped past without any sign of the Wolves. In the daylight the Caribou followed the trail of Polaris, whose long strides led always north, skirting the eastern bank of Rock River, toward the distant Calving Grounds. They followed his tracks across several small rivers, until eventually they descended into the Bell River Valley, carpeted with Spruce, Tamarack, and Willow. Here Polaris' route wove beneath the trees and disappeared into the water. The two Caribou forded the cold river, swollen with meltwater and crossed to the opposite edge, where they picked up the Wolf's trail once again. As Taiga and Bou continued along, they sometimes came across the tracks of Aurora, Mist, or Tundra, approaching from the west or east to run for a time by Polaris' side before breaking off and veering out again into the distance.

The prints spoke to the Caribou from the snow. On one hillside Aurora's slender tracks told how she came to the First Star with an easy stride and lingered at his side, bumping against his long, black flank before circling away. And in an open valley, they saw where

Mist's prints joined and paused with Polaris' for a time. A trampled, wet circle in the snow was evidence that they had held council there, and that when they were done, Mist had raced again into the distance.

Mother and yearling followed these tracks and their stories, and though they knew in this way that the Wolves were always somewhere nearby, they also sensed anxiety in the coming and going of the prints, and it had begun to make them nervous. During twilight hours Bou and Taiga stopped to graze then lay down to rest as the short night gathered. But even in the night, the Wolves themselves did not come to the Caribou, and this puzzled the yearling.

"Why do they not come and speak to us? What keeps them? What does it mean?" Bou asked.

Taiga looked up ahead to where Polaris' tracks faded from view in the distance. "Who can say, Little One? They are Wolves. We Caribou travel north and then south again as we have for ages. But Wolves are less predictable. Unlike us, they roam and wander, unhindered by the seasons." *Still,* she thought to herself, *these wolves are formidable. They circle wide to protect us, as though they fear we are hunted. It is strange. What makes them so uneasy?*

It was in the afternoon of the third day that Mist and Tundra appeared over a rock embankment and trotted, side by side, down a long slope to where the Caribou stood looking on. As they drew near, Tundra broke away from Mist and ran ahead to Bou and Taiga.

"Are you well Moshee? And you Taiga?" The Wolf's green eyes shone brightly as she spoke. Mist drifted up behind her, big, grey, and somber. The male Wolf stood a little way apart from the Caribou.

"We're fine, Tundra. But where have you been?" Bou asked. "We have seen only tracks for days."

Mist snarled. "Do not question us, yearling. We are Wolves. Is it not enough that we watch over you?"

Tundra glanced back at her mate, and the grey Wolf fell silent. She turned again to the Caribou. "We have been watching the hills and valleys to the east and west, while Aurora circles far to the rear. She has seen two Crows that hide in the glare of the sun and in the low clouds, following well behind you. Polaris fears they track your movements, that they are but eyes, high up in the sky, that serve another who follows on the ground. So he sends us to scent the land and search for tracks. We are only being cautious, Moshee. All is well."

Taiga turned to her calf. "Can these be the Crows you spoke of at Rock River?"

Tundra looked at the yearling. "You know these birds, Moshee?"

Bou answered slowly. "If they are the same two, they are called Hugin and Munin. I spoke with them near the dark path. They were curious and asked me why we travelled north before the other cows."

Tundra glanced at Mist, and then she addressed the young Caribou again, softly. "And what did you tell them, Moshee? What did you say to these Crows?"

The yearling bowed his head as he replied. "I told them I was chosen of Rahtrum, sent to seek out the Breschuvine."

Mist huffed impatiently and turned in a circle. Tundra glowered at him.

Bou continued. "They mocked me. I said at first that I could not tell them, but they said it was because I did not know," he tried to explain. "In my frustration I spoke of Rahtrum and the task he had set before us. Then they asked where we would go to seek the Breschuvine. They even offered to help, to fly ahead and see whether it was where I was going to seek it. But this I did not know. I still do not know where we will seek the Breschuvine, and I could not tell them, though they pressed me."

Tundra stared into the distance as Bou spoke. Mist lay down gruffly in the snow. Then the female Wolf spoke sternly. "You must trust us, Moshee. Remember. What else did these Crows say to you? What else did you tell them?"

"I said nothing else. It was then that the Cargoth came up the dark path, howling terribly. I ran to find my mother, fearing she was in danger, and the Crows took wing." The Caribou paused, then continued. "But there was something strange. Before they left, the Crow Hugin called me Moshee, though I had not told them of the name given me by Rahtrum." Bou dropped his head and stared at the snow, ashamed that he had been so foolish.

Mist rose onto his long legs and came to stand beside Tundra. His golden eyes flashed in the sun. "If these two black birds know you are called Moshee by Rahtrum, then they will have known already that you seek the Breschuvine. They were likely watching and listening even as Rahtrum came to you in the mountains. You have been a fool, but it is no matter, yearling. They have learned nothing they did not already know. But we know now that they have some design, that some purpose drives them." He looked at Tundra. "I do not trust these Crows, they are scavengers. I will lay out a kill to draw them, in a stand of Black Spruce. I will lie in wait for them and be done with their meddling."

Tundra replied slowly to her mate. "We have a bond with the Crows, Mist. How often have they led us with their black wings to fallen prey frozen under the snow? How often have we shared a carcass with them in gratitude? What would be said among the northern Murders if Wolves from Lone Mountain hunted Crow?"

Mist huffed. "Nothing will be said. Who will miss two prying Crows that disappear in the wide north? Who will give any thought to a smudge of black feathers in the melting snow?"

Tundra was silent a moment. "We must hold council with Polaris. The Eagle, Windshim, told him many things. He will know what to do."

Taiga, who grew more and more apprehensive as the Wolves spoke, now voiced her concern. "Why do Crows follow us? Why should they track us? What is it to them that we seek the Breschuvine? You guard us, but you will not say against what."

Tundra replied carefully. "We cannot say, old one. Polaris has told us little. He awaits word from Blinn, Eye of the North, who seeks answers to these questions."

Bou's mother stamped her hooves in frustration. "Bou is but a yearling, if we are sent into peril, then we should be told what danger awaits us."

Tundra's voice softened. "You speak wisely, but we do not know. We cannot say what our First Star will not tell us." The black Wolf looked up at the sky. "The days grow long, and there is much light left, we must continue, or we will fall behind. Polaris moves like the wind."

Taiga snorted shortly. "We are Caribou, Wolf, perhaps we are not like the wind, but we may travel all of the north and never grow weary. Let us move on then, Crow or no Crow."

And so, as the sun slumped against the western sky and lit a bank of clouds aflame with orange light, the Caribou marched on in Polaris' tracks, the two Wolves at their side.

As the daylight began at last to falter, the four animals turned westward, following the First Star's trail as it veered toward the long, curving arm of the Porcupine River. Together they descended an ancient river gully, now dry, and walked in its long folds. As they neared the end of the culvert, Mist stopped suddenly. The Caribou paused and looked at him. Tundra scented the air.

Bou whispered. "What is it?"

The big, grey Wolf's ears strained forward. "It is Pika. They are cousin to the Hare. There, on the talus slope above the gully bank, arguing like fools." Mist lowered his lithe body to the ground and stalked up to the edge of the culvert where he hid behind a Willow thicket. Above the culvert a long, rocky slope rose into the cradle of a high hill. The others followed him silently and peered through the Willow, over the edge of the gully. The Caribou tried hard to be as stealthy as the Wolves.

Bou whispered again. "What is a Pika?"

The big, black Wolf ignored the yearling.

"They are also called Rock Rabbits." Tundra breathed quietly. "They are like fat, furry mice, only larger. They are wary little creatures. You must be silent, Moshee."

The incline above the dry riverbed was rough. It was an old rockslide, laden with damp snow that hung heavily over the stones and left dark spaces in between. Midway up the slope, two Collared Pikas stood a short way apart, each on a separate rock. They faced each other on their haunches and their chirping filled the air. They looked nearly identical, except one was slightly larger than the other. Both had small round ears that moved independently. Their coats were tawny and brown along their backs but cream-coloured on their bellies. Their small front paws were also lightly coloured, and their rear paws were long, like miniature rabbits' feet. Their brown noses and long, thin whiskers twitched constantly, and each had tiny dark eyes that glistened like wet Blueberries as they spoke. The Wolves and Caribou listened quietly.

"It is too close, Rock," said the larger Pika. "There must be a space between."

"There is a space between, Coney," the smaller Pika retorted. "You are sitting in it."

"If your territory continues to grow, then soon it will infringe on my share of the talus," Coney countered, clearly annoyed.

"I've worked very hard for my share of territory, Coney." Rock spoke with great conviction while Coney stared, twitched, and tapped his rear foot. "Last year, in the first three seasons, I worked long days building my haystack. My twig and stem gathering was extremely successful, and my haystack grew more quickly than in previous years. So in the fourth season, I took some of the hay from my first stack, spun it off to the side in a bundle, and carried it to the edge of my territory to begin a second stack. Now, in the first season of this year, my haystack growth has been even faster. So I simply must expand my territory and take a greater share of the talus," Rock finished with a confident tone.

"I'll chase you," Coney said simply.

"You'll what?"

"I'll chase you off the talus if you expand any closer to my territory."

"You won't," Rock responded indignantly.

"I will. I'll chase you away."

"You're jealous, Coney Pika!" Rock proclaimed.

"And you're greedy, Rock Pika!" Coney replied.

"You're jealous because I have two haystacks and I've earned the right to take more territory than you," the smaller Pika complained. "Soon I will have three haystacks. What do you think of that, Lazy Paws?"

"I think I'll chase you away. I may even bite you."

"You wouldn't!"

"I would. And now I've decided I will bite you. Twice. Once for each haystack, and then I will chase you away. If you build another haystack, I'll bite you three times."

"You won't dare!"

"Won't I?" Coney asked menacingly, and then leapt from his snow-covered boulder after Rock. The smaller Pika chirped loudly and dove into a crevice between two stones. Coney followed him into the tunnels that wound beneath the talus slope.

As the Wolves and Caribou looked on, the two Collared Pika chased each other among the rocks, chirping and arguing over territory as they went. They became so occupied with their dispute that they did not scent or hear the approach of a lithe, agile Ermine that stalked them over the rough slope. The Ermine's body was long with short front legs. She had small, protruding ears and long whiskers, and she still wore her white Winter coat. Her black eyes were bright, and they matched the swatch of dark fur that tipped the end of her tail. Her sleek body moved quietly among the boulders as the Pika scrambled here and there, chirping at each other, oblivious to her presence.

Rock eventually popped up onto a snow-covered stone and began to peer about.

Coney jumped up onto another boulder a short distance away.

Rock chirped a boast at him over the talus slope. "You can chase me, Coney," the smaller Pika mocked, "but obviously you'll never catch me. And you certainly won't ever manage to bite —"

The Ermine struck quickly as the Pika was speaking. Rock chirped and flailed, and then succumbed to the hunter's sharp teeth and fell still in her grasp.

Coney dove down into the boulders to cower in silence and wait for the predator to leave. The Ermine slunk away with her prey.

Taiga looked away as the Ermine snatched up the tiny Pika in her teeth, and Mist saw that the old Caribou turned her head. He spoke with contempt. "You are squeamish, Taiga. That is weakness."

"We hunt only Grass and Lichen, Wolf. Like the Pika, we eat plants." Bou's mother looked Mist in the eye. "Watching the Ermine hunt the Pika is to me like watching the Wolf hunt Caribou. I do not relish it. But this you will not understand, because you are predator, and we are prey."

Mist considered the Caribou a moment, then replied thoughtfully. "It is true, Old One, but I do not understand. Why should it trouble you? It is in the Ermine's nature to hunt the Pika. And these Rock Rabbits squabble like fools. They busy themselves arguing over territory. They quarrel over Nature as though it belonged to them. It is well the Ermine stalks them when they bicker like halfwits. Do you not see, Caribou? She has solved their dispute. Peace is restored." The grey Wolf's eyes glimmered wryly.

Bou looked quietly up at the talus slope as Mist spoke. The Ermine was gone. As the yearling watched, Coney pushed his tiny nose up to scent the air, hopped up onto a boulder, listened intently for a moment, then scurried across the snow-laden stones and disappeared below to nestle in his haystack.

chapter 10

Encounter with Darkness

MAY

The howling was distant, disconnected from Bou's dream. But his instincts could not ignore the baying of a Wolf, and something deep inside stirred him toward wakefulness. His eyes fluttered open and he lifted his muzzle from his forelegs. He was confused at first, his head felt heavy with sleep. Spruce trunks stood all around the valley in the blue twilight, like dark sentinels. The yearling shook his head and blinked his eyes to clear them. The howl came again, rising wide and urgent into the half-light. *Polaris.*

Bou struggled up onto his hooves, shook his pelt, and peered about. He saw that Taiga had lifted her head toward the sound and now stared fearfully in that direction. An empty crater lay in the soft snow where Tundra had slept, curled up near the young Caribou. She was gone. Her tracks led off through the wood toward the howling, now fallen silent. Then the forest was punctuated by new noises. Sounds of panting and cracking twigs disturbed the still air. Bou panicked and whirled to his right to see where these came from. There, in the dimness of the trees, Mist raced past the two

Caribou, like a grey shadow. He had been circling when the cry went up. Now Bou and Taiga watched as he charged through the shadows, unflinching, driven to answer the call of his First Star.

Many hours earlier, Bou and Taiga had walked leisurely through the long day with Tundra at their side. Polaris still ran lead, while Aurora and Mist padded in wide, protective circuits around the Caribou. Polaris had been visibly agitated when the Wolves told him of Bou's encounter with the Crows, and he bid Tundra stay near the yearling and his mother, which she was happy to do, for she had grown fond of Bou and his inquisitive nature.

The young Caribou was playful also, and sometimes Tundra nipped in jest at his heels and Bou would pretend he, too, was a Wolf and chase her in circles around his mother. Taiga ignored this behaviour, for it seemed very strange to her to see a Caribou cavorting with a Wolf. But Tundra put the old Caribou at ease with her gentle posture and attentiveness to the yearling.

As the day wore on, the black-and-grey Wolf walked close to Bou, and they spoke at length.

"I have enjoyed our time together, Moshee," Tundra offered sincerely.

"I have also, Tundra. I've seen wondrous things this Spring, but I never thought I would befriend a Wolf."

"And I never imagined that I would meet a Caribou I did not eat!" Tundra said playfully, then nipped at the yearling's front leg.

Bou leapt to the side. "I am much too fast for you to catch and eat." He bounded in a circle and charged the Wolf with his new, stubby antlers.

Tundra rolled on her back, her tail wagging, and exposed her dark belly. "Please do not eat me, Moshee!"

"Since you have asked so nicely, I will not," Bou said with mock importance. "But let this be a lesson to you."

Taiga turned her head to watch her yearling romping with the Wolf and huffed impatiently. Tundra squirmed onto her side, and then rose up on her wide paws. She bumped against the young Caribou, who had grown taller since he and his mother had begun their journey.

"I am glad you will accompany us to the Calving Grounds, Tundra. I fear Mist does not like us. Even Polaris is very stern, and Aurora is too quiet," Bou said.

The gentle Wolf hung her head.

"What's wrong?" Bou asked.

Tundra looked thoughtfully at him. "I will not come with you to the Calving Grounds, Moshee."

"Why?" The yearling was confused. "Polaris has given his word that he will watch over us until we reach Babbage River, near to the coast."

The Wolf stopped in the snow and looked carefully at the Caribou. "And the First Star will keep his word. But we are with pups, Moshee, Aurora and I." Tundra spoke gently. "It is as Polaris has said, this year the Hare and Lemming will wax into the fullness of their breeding bloom, and there is much food for good hunters.

Because this is so, the First Stars allow Mist and me to have a litter of our own. Soon there will be many pups at Lone Mountain, and our pack will have grown." Now she looked at the ground. "But because I am with litter, Moshee, I must return with Aurora to our den at Lone Mountain. I cannot accompany you to Babbage River. Polaris and Mist will see you safely there."

Bou hung his head low and was silent for a moment. "Then you are leaving us?"

Tundra pressed her dark brow affectionately against the Caribou's flank. "Aurora and I will travel with you tomorrow. We will stay while you rest in the Driftwood River Valley, by the wide bend of the Porcupine River. Then we must part ways and travel beside the Porcupine. There is a place near Lord Creek where we will swim across the big river into our own territory. Then we will make for the den at Lone Mountain. I am sorry, Moshee. I am sorry I did not tell you sooner."

Taiga paused just ahead of Bou and the Wolf. She looked tenderly over her shoulder, at her yearling and the she-Wolf.

"Can we not come with you? To Lone Mountain?" Bou suggested. "You are more than Caribou, Moshee, but still you are Caribou, as is your mother." The black-and-grey Wolf looked up at Taiga with her green eyes as she spoke. "You must make for the Calving Grounds and seek protection there. You will graze in the Summer heat with the other cows, and though Taiga has said nothing, I do not think she will lose her antlers this season. I see by the shape of her belly that she, too, is with calf."

Bou stared at his mother. "Is it true?"

The old Caribou nodded her head slowly at her yearling. "It is true, Little One."

"I am going to have a brother!" Bou cried as he ran in a circle around his mother.

"Or sister!" Taiga interjected.

"Or sister!" Bou echoed.

Tundra barked and ran in circles after the yearling. After two quick circuits around Taiga, the young Caribou wheeled and began chasing the Wolf, who growled playfully and ran off over the tussocks with Bou in close pursuit.

Though the yearling was saddened by the news of Tundra's impending departure, the two new friends romped and talked through the long afternoon, aware now, that their time together was growing short. Twice Mist trotted in from his patrol to walk near his mate and feel her soft, warm length pressed against his flank. When this happened Bou wandered to his mother, apart from the Wolves. He sensed that Mist did not have the patience or interest in Caribou that Tundra had. The big, gold-eyed Wolf was simply fulfilling his duty as Second Star. He did not speak to the Caribou, and only rarely did he even bother to steal a glance at them. Neither did Mist tarry long when he came, and eventually the two Wolves would touch noses briefly or exchange playful scruff bites before he padded away again to keep watch over the hills to the east. At length the trail of Polaris led over several high rises, and it was upon the third rise that Bou saw a broad river winding through a treed valley. Tundra drew near to his side.

"That is the Porcupine, Moshee. It is the northern boundary of our territory. Aurora and I will cross it to return home."

Bou gazed at the big waterway. "It is as wide as the Peel, Tundra, and fast. I did not know Wolves could swim such rivers."

"You know little of Wolves. We swim well. We have even tracked and chased wounded Caribou into the water..."

Bou turned and looked carefully at the Wolf as she spoke.

"...when they sought refuge from us in the river," Tundra finished softly. She looked away from the yearling, out at the thick band of water.

"Why do you hunt us, Tundra?"

Taiga looked on silently from a short distance away. The Wolf stared out over the river in quiet contemplation. She spoke without looking at Bou. "Why does the river run north and west? We are what we are, Moshee."

"But you do not hunt me or Taiga. You protect us," the yearling pressed.

Now Tundra turned to him and spoke affectionately. "It is said that Rahtrum, though mighty, is himself bound to the balance he ministers. That he cannot command even a sleeping squirrel to move against its own nature. But they say he may compel the wind to bend and shake the branches where a squirrel sleeps and send it scampering. It is not in our nature to protect you," the Wolf said, "but we have seen the Cargoth's shadow, and we have felt the Binder's wind. We are what we are, Moshee. And you are what you are; a breeze now, that will become a wind, that one day will gust like a howling gale into their shadow. That is what I believe. It is why I protect you. I believe in you." Tundra turned slowly and walked away along Polaris' wide trail.

Bou stared at his mother, who returned his gaze, and then he turned to follow the Wolf.

For a time they travelled in silence. But soon Bou could stand it no longer and bumped the dark Wolf mischievously. At first she only wagged her tail a little, but the yearling would not relent, and finally he butted her rump soundly with his velvety antlers. Seeing that she was preparing to chase him, he ran a wide half circle around his mother and made for the long slope that rose ahead of them.

"She will catch you, Little One. Here she comes," called Taiga as he passed.

The young Caribou sprinted up the foot of the slope, his wide, hollowed hooves firm and sure through the thin snow. He heard Tundra's rollicking yelps in swift pursuit. His heart beat like thunder in his chest, and though they were only playing, he felt his instincts at work within him, felt them driving his primal flight. He was exhilarated, but he knew also that the Wolf was as fleet as a Summer wind. A tingling spread down his back and spilled like cold water down his flank and legs. Even his head began to prickle. *It is like the night we first encountered the Wolves. This is how I felt when I charged Mist through the darkness.* He rose up the slope at a furious pace, surprised at how easily he drove upward through the snow, toward the crest. Even Tundra's playful yapping seemed to fall behind him until he could no longer hear her.

The yearling felt as though he could run forever over great distances. He swung his head to his shoulder as he neared the crest at a gallop, to look backward, to see if Tundra followed. But he could not see her. As he strained for some sign of his pursuer he mounted the top of the slope in full stride, and as he did so, a deep growl shook the air a little way in front of him. He turned his head. It was Polaris.

The giant, black Wolf stood with his front legs apart and his big head sunk low beneath his shoulder blades. His fangs were bared, and they glared white in the late light. Saliva ran over his teeth and lips. It frothed a little and dripped from his muzzle, stretching out for the ground. His menacing snarl was punctuated with quick breaths of air that hissed in through his nose. His copper eyes floated and wavered in the wide, black sea of his face. The yearling skidded. Polaris' eyes seemed to seize upon his heart. Fear flooded down Bou's body and pushed out the tingling. He lost his balance, and his forelegs spread awkwardly in front of him. He collapsed to the ground in front of the Wolf, staring up at the enormous predator.

Polaris's snarl faded, he sniffed at the Caribou, and his head tilted slightly to the side. His eyes softened with a look of confusion. Tundra padded up beside Bou, panting quietly, and looked at the First Star.

Polaris spoke to her without taking his eyes from the yearling. "You have seen it, Tundra? You saw him as he mounted the crest of the slope?"

"Yes, I saw him." Tundra looked down at the young Caribou. "Though I scarce believe what I saw."

Bou was upset. "What did you see? Why did you growl at me? I thought you were going to attack me. You said you would protect me as your own."

The First Star looked quietly at the yearling. All his viciousness was gone, gathered again like a dark storm within. "I am sorry, Moshee. You came upon me suddenly, I was surprised and I did not know at first that it was you. But let us speak of this later." He looked over his shoulder. "See there to the west? It is the Driftwood River Valley. We will find a place in among the trees for you and Taiga to graze and rest."

Then his copper eyes turned to Tundra. "Aurora has seen the Crows. They are still following. It does not rest well with me. You will stay with the yearling and his mother, through the twilight hours, until it is time for you to depart." As the big Wolf finished speaking, Taiga lumbered up behind them, mounted the hilltop, and nudged Bou with her snout.

The four animals strode down the long decline into the Driftwood Valley. Polaris left Tundra and the Caribou in a Spruce grove to go in search of Aurora and Mist. The Spring light lingered as the Caribou grazed under Tundra's watchful eye. The black-and-grey Wolf wove through the trees around them, keeping watch. But the sun soon slipped behind the horizon and cast a half-light over the north that stretched into the valley. Taiga and her yearling found comfortable spots in the wet snow and lay down to sleep beneath the deep shade of the fragrant Spruce. Tundra surveyed the forest carefully. She circled the resting Caribou slowly and paused to scent the air. When she was satisfied all was quiet, she crept near to Bou and curled up beside him. No animal could draw near to the yearling without her first detecting it, and the others were watching all the other approaches. As she laid her muzzle across her legs, she heard the yearling whisper dreamily, "What did you see, Tundra? Why did Polaris frighten me on the hillcrest?"

The Wolf stretched her head out toward Bou and licked his nose softly. "I think it was you who frightened him," she said with an amused tone. "But sleep now, Moshee. There will be time for such things tomorrow." The yearling sighed heavily and was asleep.

It was the howling of Polaris that woke Bou and Taiga. They stirred and peered about only to find that Tundra was gone already. Then they watched as Mist raced through the long Spruce shadows in the direction the call had come from. The yearling stood staring after Mist, and watched as the Wolf's grey form dissolved into the gloom of the valley. Taiga rocked her weight back and forth, rose up onto her legs and stood beside her calf.

"What will we do?" Bou asked urgently.

"I do not know, Little One."

"Should we follow?"

"I do not know. I do not think so," Taiga responded, indecisively.

A sudden clicking and knocking sound came from behind them,

followed by a familiar voice. "Hello, Bou of the Porcupine herd. Strange that we should cross each other's paths again. Are you following us? *Kek, kek.*"

Both Caribou spun and looked up into the Spruce trees to the source of the voice. There, in the barren branches of a dead tree, perched two large Crows, preening and cooing in the dim light.

"It is you who follow us, Hugin and Munin." The yearling was instantly distrustful. He spoke brazenly to the birds. "What do you want? What is happening to our friends?"

"Friends? *Ark, wok!* Do you hear him Munin? He calls these Wolves friends!"

Munin answered. "Poor Caribou, these Wolves are not your friends, even now they draw you into a trap," she fawned.

"Do not listen to them, Bou," Taiga interjected.

The yearling looked back and forth from his mother to the Crows. In the distance he heard the Wolves growling, barking, and yelping.

"We can help you, Bou," Munin continued. "We can save you and your mother from Polaris and his bloodthirsty brethren. Tell us where you will seek the Breschuvine."

"I — I cannot," Bou stuttered, looking away, toward the sound of the Wolves. "What is happening?"

Hugin lost patience. "They will eat you, fool! Tell us where the Breschuvine will bloom, and we will lead you to safety!"

"No! We must go to our friends! Mother, come!" The yearling turned purposefully in the direction of the Wolves and began to stride away. Taiga followed.

"*CAW! Ark, wok, wok!*" The Crows squawked, leapt into the air, and swooped over the heads of the retreating Caribou with their talons. Their wings hissed and fluttered through the still air, and they cried out frantically as they assailed the yearling and cow. "It is a trap, foolish Caribou! Tell us where you will seek the Breschuvine! Tell us! Tell us!"

Taiga shook her antlers, and Bou lowered his head as the Crows flapped frantically above. The two Caribou quickened their pace through the trees to escape the birds when suddenly there was a light before them. It was as white as new-fallen snow and brilliant as the Summer sun. Shadows fled.

The Crows' feathers glistened as they beat their broad, black wings and struggled to shield their eyes. A voice came from the centre of the illumination, and like the light itself, it was at once soft, yet penetrating. "Be gone, Crow," it said simply.

Hugin and Munin pumped their wings hysterically and rose above the trees, into the waning twilight. Now the blaze of light dimmed until it was but a gentle glow. It lowered through the air, hovered before the Caribou, and approached. Bou's eyes adjusted slowly until finally he saw a figure, suspended at its centre. A Faerie, no taller than an Arctic Wintergreen flower, was suspended in the air. She came closer and closer to the young Caribou until she floated before his nose. Her skin was naked and white, and she had two willowy legs, like a Cargoth's, that hung straight down together. Her little feet pointed neatly to the ground and her arms were crossed in front of her chest. Her face was slender and long, and her eyes, wide and piercing, were as frost-white as her skin. Her wings moved so quickly that they looked like a cloud of moonlit mist. Her light moved about her, spectral and shifting. But as Bou stared, mesmerized by the overwhelming beauty of the Tuatha De Danann, he noticed the tiniest flash of red, flickering at the centre of her pure light. She held the young Caribou with her eyes, and spoke again. Her voice was ice-edged in bitterness and seemed to push through the yearling — through his pelt and skin, through his very bone and muscle — to pierce his heart. "Much will be sacrificed for you, Moshee, chosen of Rahtrum. Do not waver." And then her light went out, and the Caribou stood blinking and shaking their heads in the failing darkness.

Tundra was up on her long, black legs even before she was fully awake. *It is Polaris,* she thought. She recognized his howl immediately as it hung in the cool air. She wobbled slightly as she shook the dreams from her head and snow from her coat. She scented the air and peered about. Bou was still sleeping, but Taiga had raised her groggy head and was looking at the Wolf. "Watch over him, Taiga," Tundra said simply, and then she sprang away west, through the trees.

Moshee will be safe with his mother. I should not leave him, but I must go. When Polaris calls we must answer. As the Wolf ran, she felt nervous. She had never heard Polaris howl like this.

Often he would call them from the top of Lone Mountain, but never with such urgency. She thought of the pups she now carried inside her, and of her mate, Mist. *He is well. He is circling to the south. I will arrive before him. He is safe.* The Wolf ran beneath the trees, dodging scrub and leaping over fallen trunks. When she broke out from the tree line onto the banks of Driftwood River, she saw Polaris. He stood menacingly by the water, growling and barking viciously at a pile of large boulders that towered as high as a bull Moose. The big, granite stones had dark, hollow spaces between them, like cave entrances, and were tangled here and there with driftwood. Aurora stood nearby in the shallow water, her coat still wet from fording the river. She had left her watch to answer the call of her mate. She too, stood with bared teeth and hackles raised, snarling at the rocks. Tundra approached carefully, padding lightly on her big paws. She followed the First Star's gaze and scanned the boulders, but she could not see what made the others so leery. Shadows wavered among the rocks, cast there by the brief twilight of Spring. A slight breeze came up the river, wafting air from the pile of stone and driftwood. She scented the wind for some sign of what might lurk there. And then it came to her, an odour, as pungent as death, laced with a cold, hateful hunger, carried high on the air from out of the rock pile. Her green eyes narrowed as she stalked closer.

You are in there somewhere. You are difficult to see, but Polaris has found you. She peered intently at the deep cavernous shadows in the spaces between the boulders. Creeping low to the ground she approached the rocks from the treeline. She drew nearer and nearer, scanning the black spaces, until she stood closer to the pile than Polaris, who snapped at her. "Keep back, Tundra. It is not safe." But she was sure she saw something, there in the darkness, in the cave-like hollows between the rocks. A thick shadow within the shadows. A figure, absent of light, hiding in the gloom of the boulders.

There is motion. Something is there, it is difficult to see, but it is beginning to move. Tundra froze, her tail pressed down, her scruff hair stood over her shoulder blades. Her head tilted just slightly to one side, and her ears strained forward as she scented the air again. To reassure herself she spoke, addressing the boulders in a firm and impatient tone.

"We know you are in there. Your stink is on the wind. We are Wolves of Lone Mountain. Here are Polaris and Aurora, our First Stars. This is my counsel to you, who cower in the shadows: Come forward and tell us your business. You will not want to be pursued by Wolves such as we. You will be sorry for your error when you are hunted by Polaris, Land Crow."

The gloom between the rocks seemed to shift. Tundra lowered her head and squinted. Then she saw them in the shadows, opening slowly, lazily, in the darkness. Eyes, white as bleached bones, frigid as ice. Eyes without pupils or colour; two waxen orbs staring from the murk between the stones; a frozen gaze that Tundra felt seeping into the pale green tenderness of her own eyes. The Wolf recoiled.

He sees me. He sees my pups. He sees into me and through me. He sees Moshee and the Breschuvine. She backed away, pulled her eyes from the frigid white glare, and snarled at the boulders. Polaris barked and growled, and Aurora yelped. Just then, pebbles and stones clacked against each other and scattered under Mist's big paws, as he came crashing out of the woods onto the bank of the river. He ran to Tundra's side and positioned his grey length between the pile of boulders and his mate. She pressed against him, shielding her gaze from the white eyes that retreated again into the dark.

A deep growl vibrated from the hollow beneath the boulders. A mocking voice followed. "So this is mighty Polaris—First Star of Lone Mountain. And these are your whelps, that squeal and boast. Do you not speak on your own behalf? Where is your song, Land Crow? Sing for me, and I will tremble." The voice rose into a peal of laughter.

Polaris snarled and strode forward. Tundra and the other Wolves stared at him. They were shocked, for they had never before heard any animal openly mock their First Star; even the Grizzlies gave their pack a wide berth for fear of their numbers and hunting prowess. Polaris' lips curled back in a snarl, and though he answered, he could not match the menace of the voice from the rocks.

"I do not suffer the impudence of cowards, Shadow-walker. Come, let us speak tooth to tooth."

"Tooth to tooth?" the voice scoffed. "I have no quarrel with you, Land Crow, or these curs that follow you. You are what you are. I am what I am. This is the north, and you are far from Lone Mountain. Leave me to my own affairs." The low voice was dismissive.

"You track us, coward," replied Polaris. "We have seen your Crows. You stalk the yearling. He has spoken of you. And now you are stretching my patience as thin as life. If you are not careful, it will break, and I will warm your innards beneath the rising sun."

There was a growl and a stirring from below. Bone-white eyes materialized out of the darkness and glared, cold as hate, at Polaris, who flinched. The voice deepened and said, "You are mistaken, Wolf. It is *my* patience that wavers." Then the eyes melted again into the gloom beneath the rocks, leaving only silence and stillness.

Mist left Tundra's side and crept slowly to the heap of granite slabs. He moved his muzzle up and down, then side to side, scenting the air as he approached. Nearer and nearer he crept.

"Polaris!" Aurora called out suddenly. Her bark surprised Mist, and he scrambled back from the rocky outcrop. Aurora's snout pointed away from the river, back into the forest to where Tundra had left the Caribou. The Wolves turned to look. Deep in the wood a brilliant, white light blazed for a few moments, dancing through the Spruce boughs. As they watched, two big Crows climbed up above the forest into the pale dawn sky. The white light softened and was lost from view in the trees.

The First Star swung his head to Tundra. "Go to them, Tundra. Take Mist, and see that Moshee is safe."

The green-eyed Wolf leapt away with Mist running at her side. They plunged together into the shade of the forest.

When the two younger Wolves were departed, Polaris padded fearlessly to the stone pile and pressed his big muzzle into one of the cavernous shadows. His head jerked and tilted as he huffed through his nose, drinking the air and scenting the space beneath the rock slabs. He withdrew his head and peered out at the river. "He is gone."

"It is as Windshim warned," Aurora said simply.

"There is much space beneath the rocks; it is dug out and runs deep. He has grown larger than Blinn suspects, and he hides his new strength from us." Polaris turned to his mate. "You saw his eyes?"

"Yes, I saw them. And we have seen the light of the Tuatha De Danann in the forest. I think he has done something terrible. I think he is hunted. Perhaps this is why he hides." Aurora moved slowly to her mate and peered up at him. "You are troubled."

The black Wolf looked carefully into Aurora's yellow eyes, then peered out at the river. "He leaves no scent trail beneath the stones. We smell his breath when he is near, but we cannot stalk him, there is no track. Windshim told me that he went stealthily upon the land before, and that now he ranges darkly. He is more than he was, and I fear he will become even more than he is."

Aurora nudged Polaris' black snout. "He has broken his covenant; he has assailed the Children of Danu. Now he is hunted by a Faerie. Surely he will succumb."

The big Wolf pressed his face tenderly against Aurora's warm muzzle and spoke softly. "Who can say how long he has evaded the Faerie, or, with any certainty, what purpose guides her? I have seen his eyes, and I have heard the cold hunger in his voice. I fear that soon his cunning will be beyond even the craft of the Tuatha De Danann."

Bou and his mother shook their heads. Their eyes were crowded by darkness in the sudden absence of Faerie light, and it took them a moment to adjust. Bou was upset by the Faerie's words and pressed near to Taiga. He felt a new weight upon him. *Much will be sacrificed for you, Moshee. Do not waver. What did this mean?* He had been chosen by Rahtrum. He asked nothing of anyone. As he was considering the Faerie's message, the sounds of approach crackled through the underbrush. Bou and Taiga backed away from the noise. But then a familiar voice rang out through the Spruce trunks.

"Moshee? Are you there?" It was Tundra, running with Mist at her side, pushing through the scrub.

"We are here, Tundra!" Bou answered, relieved to see the Wolves bounding through the trees. Tundra drew near to the yearling, while Mist stopped a little way from the Caribou, lifting his head to scent the air and peer about.

Tundra looked carefully into the young Caribou's big, brown eyes. "Are you well, Moshee? I should not have left you...but it was Polaris that called, and we are bound to him."

"We are well," Bou answered anxiously. "The Crows came again, but a Faerie blazed out of the twilight and spoke to them, and with only a word from her, they fled into the sky. What is happening, Tundra? We, too, heard Polaris howling."

Taiga stepped toward the Wolf and spoke. "Yes, tell us, Tundra. Why does the First Star howl for you? Why do you leave us without guard? Without warning? There is danger. We see it in you. Speak!"

The black Wolf looked at the old cow. "There is danger, but we do not know its distance or its season."

Mist stared at his mate and spoke urgently. "Tundra, we are not to speak of it!"

She glanced back at him. "They ask, Mist. We are bound to them. If they ask it of me, I will tell them."

The grey Wolf moaned and began to circle through the trees impatiently as Tundra turned again to the Caribou.

"We know little. But Windshim has said there is one called Grotto. One that roamed stealthily upon the land, but that now ranges darkly. The Eagle brought word to Lone Mountain that Grotto has tracked you from the Peel River. He is the frost-eyed shade that came to you in the Eastern Mountains, the one you spoke of to Polaris."

Taiga interjected with surprise. "But you said nothing of this to me, Bou."

"I did not want to frighten you," the yearling said, "and I have seen nothing of him since."

The cow huffed with exasperation, stamped her broad hooves, and shook her antlers.

Tundra continued. "We know little of his purpose, but we know the Crows, Hugin and Munin, are in his service. Even now, Blinn travels the north in search of answers. It was the shadow-walker that Polaris discovered hiding by the river, this is why he howled for us, unsure of the danger. Hoping to track him if he escaped."

Bou's eyes were wide. "But what is Grotto?" he asked nervously. "He is like no creature that I have seen."

Tundra paused a moment, and her pale, green eyes drifted apprehensively. "He is like you, Moshee...he is more than what he was." Then she stared into the yearling's anxious face and her green eyes focused sharply. "It is said that he is a —"

"Tundra!" The First Star's voice boomed through the air. The female Wolf jumped a little, startled, and then hung her head in silence. At that moment dawn broke in the east, and as Polaris and Aurora padded slowly through the Spruce, their long guard hairs were kindled in a halo of pink-orange light. The forest filled with spears of sunlight that leaned steeply through the Spruce boughs. Polaris continued severely. "You are not to speak of him. The Eye of the North is still searching. Let him say what he will when he is ready."

"But we are bound to them." Tundra tucked her tail, and spoke softly as she looked up at the young Caribou.

Polaris approached the green-eyed Wolf menacingly.

Mist moved to his mate's side and stood with his mouth gaping, threatening the First Star to come no nearer. The grey-mane's golden eyes burned fearlessly in the new sun.

The First Star paused and spoke. "There is much we are bound to, Tundra. But Blinn begs our silence on this matter, and I will not second-guess him."

Now the big, black Wolf stared dispassionately into Mist's eyes. "There is much valour in you, Second Star, foolish as it may be. Stand ready for these Caribou, as you do for your mate, and they will be safe. We will cross the Driftwood River together. You and I will travel with the Caribou. Aurora and Tundra must stride west and make for Lone Mountain. It is time."

The Caribou forded the river easily, while the Wolves alternately lurched and paddled to reach the other bank. On the far side, Bou and Taiga simply walked out of the water and stood waiting. But when the Wolves padded onto the shore they shook fiercely in the rising sun, and sheets of rainbow mist exploded from their coats, drifting on the breeze. They broke into pairs to say their good-byes. Aurora stood near to Polaris, who lowered his head and leaned lightly into her. They did not speak, but instead, they leaned against each other quietly, warming their wet fur in the sun.

Tundra and Mist stood apart from the others, near the river. They faced each other, muzzle to muzzle, silhouetted against the sunlight that glittered on the water.

Mist whispered gently to her. "I should not go. My place is with you."

Tundra pushed her snout into his broad neck. "Your duty is to Moshee."

"Then I care nothing for my duty." The grey Wolf's voice was tender and rough.

Tundra turned to look at Bou. "My heart is with you, but it is with the yearling, too. There is much hope in him. Safe-keep him as you would me. Then come home to our den. Your pups will be eager for their father."

Mist raised his head into the sun and stared long into his mate's pale green eyes. "I will dream of emeralds."

Tundra sighed and pressed hard against him. "And I of gold."

Mist and Polaris now stood together. Aurora waited by the edge of the trees that lined the river basin.

Tundra walked to the Caribou and paused before them. "Go safely, Moshee. Perhaps I will see you again when Autumn takes the Summer in her arms, and the land begins to sleep." She looked at the cow. "Keep him well, Taiga." Bou's mother nodded slowly at the Wolf.

Bou spoke quietly. "I will look for you in Autumn, Tundra. I wish you happiness with your litter."

Tundra looked the Caribou in the eye, wagged her tail, then turned and walked toward Aurora.

The yearling called out after her. "I will miss you, Caribou-friend!"

Tundra stopped and turned to face Bou. "And I will miss you, Wolf-friend!" Then she wheeled and sprang away, disappearing into the Spruce trees with Aurora at her side.

chapter 11

Dark Tidings
MAY

Bou and Taiga journeyed with Polaris and Mist. They travelled in and out of days that stretched wide beneath the sun. The bright, yellow orb shone tirelessly now, circling the horizon without rest and coaxing the sleepy land toward wakefulness. Their route passed over the Old Crow Plains. To the east were the Old Crow Flats, a maze of lakes, wetlands, and ponds. Rivers also snaked through the watery labyrinth. The snow, which had ruled all the long months of Winter, now retreated quickly, or clung to waning ice and low riverbeds, no match for the sun's pervasive rays. Plants breathed in the warming Spring air. Waking Sedges, Cottongrass tussocks, Shrub Willows, and Sphagnum Moss had begun to pattern the slopes with greenery and fill the air with the rich scent of life. The land was alive, and Bou drank it in as he marched along with his mother, following the long, black haunches of Polaris. Mist travelled to their rear, and sometimes the yearling stole a glance back at the grey Wolf, who ignored him and pretended not to see. Mist said very little to Bou and Taiga, but watched over them steadfastly when Polaris drifted out onto the land to hunt Muskrat, Lemming, and Marten. The First Star always returned with a catch, stopping a little way from the Caribou and barking to Mist. The Wolves lay at a distance on beds of Moss and ate their kill, while the Caribou grazed. Bou and his mother paused now and then to watch curiously, as the two big predators gobbled their meat.

They journeyed this way for three days, pausing now and again to lie in the cool Sedge grasses and rest. But as they walked in their line on the third day, a Snowshoe Hare, who had been foraging upwind, hopped from behind a tussock to find two of the fiercest Wolves in the north staring down at her. They'd scented her when the light breeze carried her presence downwind to them. Polaris had motioned Mist forward, and the two Wolves had padded stealthily nearer, while the oblivious Hare rummaged among the reeds. The Wolves had separated slightly in case the Hare bolted on instinct before they were able to determine if it bore a message. But when it loped out into the open, it did not bolt. Instead, as the Caribou looked on, the Hare froze in mid-stride with one tufted forepaw held up in front of her nose, and a rear paw raised on its toes. Her small, black eyes stared, unblinking, at Polaris. He held her there with his gaze and pressed deeply into her instincts.

If I do not move he cannot see me, thought the Hare. *But he is looking straight at me. Surely he sees me. No, I am camouflaged in my Summer pelage. He's simply looking this way, but he can't see me. I will stay still until he turns away, or blinks. Blink, Wolf, blink!*

Polaris knew better than to blink, and as he held the Hare by her two shiny eyes, he began to move. Slowly, imperceptibly, like a flower turning with the sun, he closed the final distance, lowering his muzzle to the Hare's nose, taking in her scent and washing her face with his hot breath.

The little Hare's ears lay back and she urinated. *I think he sees me. Is he moving? I think he is moving. He is getting closer. But I cannot see him moving. Why will he not blink? Blink! Blink! Blink! What is that smell? Is that urine? I have peed. Why did I pee? He will smell me now. Should I run? I should run. But the little ones! What about my little ones? Oh my, how did he get so close?*

The Hare began to shake as Polaris spoke calmly to her. "Do you bear a message, Hare?"

A message? Yes, a message. Of course, he is the black Wolf, the one called Land Crow. We are saved! But what is the message? Tell him yes before he eats you. "I...I bear a message for Polaris, Land Crow, First Star of Lone Mountain."

"I am Polaris," the Wolf replied.

The Hare's shaking slowed a little. "Then you are bound, Polaris, Land Crow," she said with visible relief. "Will you receive a message from the Tuatha De Danann?"

"Yes, we are bound. I will receive the message."

He is bound. We are safe. Now, what is the message? The Hare's ears wiggled, and she began to tremble again. *The message. What is the message?*

"Speak, Hare. If there is no message in you we are bound to nothing," Polaris said impatiently.

The Hare's ears waggled frantically.

"She has no message, Polaris," Mist interjected. "She lies to save her kin. Look here, she has Leverets." The grey Wolf motioned to the ground beside the tussock. There, three tiny, juvenile Hares huddled together, shivering in Mist's shadow, each one no larger than a mouse, with soft, brown fur and wide, black eyes.

The First Star replied without taking his copper eyes from the Messenger Hare. "They do not have it in them to lie, Mist. They lack the craft. That is why we trust them."

Mist huffed and lowered his big muzzle to the Leverets. He sniffed at their coats. The miniature Hares pressed closer together and shook with fear.

They have found the little ones. The message, what is the message? Something dark, yes. Something dark makes for the mountain...yes that's it!

"Give us the message, Hare," Polaris growled.

"The dark one," she blurted, "the shadow-walker called Grotto, has turned west and south from your trail. He makes for Lone Mountain."

Polaris backed away from the Hare as though it had stung him.

Mist left the Leverets and charged the Hare with his teeth bared. "You lie!"

The Hare pressed low against the ground and shook terribly. "Y-y-you are b-bound."

Polaris regained himself. "No, Mist. Enough!" He stared at the Hare. "You say your message is from the Tuatha De Danann. Speak then, Hare. I would know the name of the Faerie that sent it. Tell me, and I will release you. We are bound, as you say."

"She is called Ainafare by the Tuatha De Danann — First Light." The Hare looked desperately up at the big Wolf.

Polaris sighed and looked out over the land in the direction of Lone Mountain. He spoke quietly, without looking at the Hare. "Go then, you are released."

The Hare turned slowly at first, watching Mist carefully, then hopped toward her young. She quickly calmed their shaking, and together they leapt away in a little line, disappearing into the Cottongrass.

"We must turn south for the den, Polaris," Mist said.

"Yes. We should go to them," Bou agreed.

The Wolves and Taiga stared at the yearling.

Polaris spoke. "You cannot, Moshee. You must reach the Calving Grounds. Your mother is with calf, and I have given my word to the Eye of the North to take you safely to Babbage River." The First Star breathed deeply. "Mist, you must return to the den, but do not turn west to Lord Creek. Run south, and cross the Porcupine directly."

"But that is Choho territory," Mist replied.

"Yes," Polaris said quietly. "Tell them that I have sent you. Speak to their First Star. Tell him that Polaris pleads for his help, for a war pack to defend Lone Mountain. I will take the Caribou north, then turn back at Babbage River and come with all the speed I can muster. Go now, Mist. Fly. Run as you have not run before."

The grey Wolf sprang away into the south. Polaris and the Caribou watched him disappear into the distance.

Bou and Taiga continued with Polaris. The First Star pushed them hard, setting a difficult pace even for Caribou. He was distracted by the dark tidings the Hare had carried, and he thought only of reaching Babbage River so that he could turn and run, unhindered, for Lone Mountain. He was torn deeply by his predicament. He had promised Blinn he would accompany the Caribou, yet all his instincts fed his desire to be with his pack, and it weighed heavily upon him. They marched on for two days until the Barn Range rose ahead of them, and they climbed over foothills into a valley that ran between high peaks. Taiga watched Bou carefully, and though the yearling did not protest, she saw that his footing grew less sure, and that he could not continue without food and rest.

She appealed to the Wolf. "You are First Star, and I understand your urgency, but even you must hunt and eat and eventually sleep. You make reckless haste, and if you push on too hard, you will be spent when it is time to run for Lone Mountain. How will you serve your pack if you arrive gaunt and exhausted? You know what I say is true."

Polaris stopped without looking back at the cow. "We will pause in the valley ahead. Graze and slumber if you must. I will hunt and return to watch over you. But when the sunlight has crept across the valley and climbs the eastern peaks, we will start out again and will not rest until we reach Babbage River. It is two days through the mountains."

They entered the long valley together, but Polaris soon broke away to hunt, leaving the Caribou to graze and rest as they wished. Much of the day had passed when Polaris finally returned. Sunlight now filled the bottom of the valley and warmed the air. Bou lay quietly near his mother, who was sleeping soundly when the big Wolf trotted up to sit close by and keep watch over them. The yearling observed the predator furtively, with only one eye, as Polaris groomed his black coat in the bright sun.

"You should sleep while you can, Moshee," he said casually, still grooming his forepaws. "We will travel hard these next two days."

Bou raised his head. "How did you know I was awake?"

"The rhythm of your breathing gives you away, as does the glint of sun in your eye."

"You can hear my breathing?"

"I hear a great many things." Now the Wolf paused and looked at the Caribou, his copper eyes weary. "Can you not sleep?"

"I keep thinking of the Messenger Hare. Another came to my mother by the dark path. But the Cargoth came, and he panicked and fell beneath them."

"They are simple animals, and when they are afraid their instinct is to run. They do not care which direction, only that they are running."

"But how is it they have came to be Messengers?" Bou asked.

Polaris yawned and his lips pulled back over his sharp, white teeth. His jaws stretched wide and his tongue lunged out before curling up into his mouth as it snapped shut. He licked his lips. "It was long ago that the first message came deep into the north by Snowshoe Hare. It was sent by the Tuatha De Danann to Gnomes, who held council with Rahtrum. The Hare bore news to him of a war among the Cargoth that raged across the world and of a new power among the Beasts of Shadow to lay waste to the land. It was this message that first stirred the Binder to discover a means of waking the Cargoth from their long dream of hunger."

Bou was fascinated. "And the Hare have carried messages ever since?"

"It served the Gnomes and Faeries well to send messages this way across the north. When the Hare are in the fullness of their breeding bloom, a message given to one is passed by him to his kin, by them to their kin, and so on, until it has spread like wildfire among all of them across the northlands."

"But how can you be sure you'll receive the message?" the yearling inquired.

"You cannot be sure. But if you are not a predator, the Hare is bound by the Tuatha De Danann to seek you out, if he learns you may be near. He must identify you and deliver the message."

"And what if you are a predator?"

"We simply catch a Hare, any will do. If he bears a message for us we give him our name and accept it. Then we are bound by Rahtrum to release him."

"And if the Hare does not carry a message?"

The big Wolf peered into Bou's eyes. "We eat him."

Bou scrunched up his nose and shook his head.

When the yellow sun had drifted west, the Caribou followed Polaris along the floor of the long valley. For two days they pushed on without stopping. The land rolled up and down beneath them and the sun circled. The yearling grew weary, and when at last he thought he must stop to graze and rest, they mounted the top of a foothill, and the Babbage River stretched out before them, running thin and long across the land. Together they descended to the bank of the middling river, and now Polaris became more restless.

"Here I must leave you," he said.

The Caribou looked at him. It suddenly felt strange to know they would be without him. Taiga spoke first. "We understand your haste, Polaris, and we thank you. You have been true to your word."

The Wolf stared a moment at Bou. "We have placed much hope in you, Moshee. Be safe and true." He turned to Taiga. "You know the land here better than I, old cow. I am not foolish enough to counsel you on your route. Watch over him. The dark one assails Lone Mountain, and we cannot know his purpose. But there are other predators that scour the northern ranges: Grizzlies and Wolves that are not bound, as we are."

"I know them well. We will make for the coast and find the herd," Taiga replied.

Now Bou spoke. "Thank you, Polaris, for watching over us. Will you tell Tundra that I think of her, and that I will look for her in the Autumn?"

"I will tell her." The Wolf turned. "I must go. I must run long days to Lone Mountain."

"Polaris," Bou blurted, "I am sorry for what happened to your parents."

The First Star turned his head to look at the yearling. "Do not be sorry, Moshee. But carry their names in your heart. Nightmane and Dawn they were called. If ever you waver, think of them."

Without pause Polaris turned again and took flight, and his long, black legs stretched wide as Ravens' wings over the land.

chapter 12

The Running of Mist

JUNE

Mist ran south, driven by thoughts of Tundra. Never had he run like this. Nor had any Wolf — even Polaris — crossed the northlands this way; unwearying, unflinching, unyielding in his gait. *We are fools. Fools to risk our mates, our pups, our pack for an unproven yearling. For Caribou. Fools to listen to the mischievous words of Gnomes.* His grey legs bunched together and stretched out with every stride. His muscles ached with the incessant motion. His thick coat rippled and shook, and his tail trailed behind him, as he swept across the land like a grey wind. His belly groaned with hunger, and as he galloped on and on, his tongue hung loosely from his open jaw to help cool his labouring body. He was circled by his own shadow as he raced over broad slopes, across the widening daylight. He paused only at streams to drink briefly, and then sprang away again, tireless with fear for his mate.

Twice he scented bull Caribou on the air. They were drifting north to the coast of the Beaufort Sea in small groups or alone, well behind the cows. Mist's instinct to hunt clawed at his thoughts.

His empty stomach seemed to twist within him, but he bared his teeth and extinguished this urge with a determined snarl. On he ran. A group of fifteen bulls spotted the Wolf from a high slope. They panicked and stampeded, but Mist took no notice of them. There was nothing for him now in the north but Tundra, and her pale green eyes burned like emeralds in his mind. *I am coming.*

At the end of two full days of running, the grey Wolf saw the Porcupine River unravelling in front of him. He came to a steep ravine that bordered the river valley. Here the steady flow of water had bitten deeply into the land and over thousands of years had cut a long, open canyon through ice-age sediment to bedrock. Mist wandered along the top of the ravine looking for a place to descend into the canyon and reach the river. His chest heaved for air as he panted.

At last he found an ancient runoff gully with a tapered gravel slide at its bottom. He wound his way through the gully, and as he descended the slide to the riverbed, the loose scree shifted beneath his weight, raising clouds of dust into the sunlight behind him. When he reached bottom, he ran without pause to the wide river and pushed out into the current. He paddled hard with his broad paws, as his fur grew heavy and wet. The cold water felt good against his skin as it cooled his blood, but it also caused his tired legs to stiffen and cramp. The powerful river was swift and swollen with Spring meltwater, and it carried him westward as he struggled for the opposite shore. At last he felt the cold, wet stones of the opposite riverbank beneath him, and he climbed onto the shore, where he shook his coat fiercely. He turned and drank from the cool water, then stared up at the ravine and scanned its length, looking for a quick ascent. A little to the east there appeared to be a more modest slope, which he thought held some promise. Mist struck out for it immediately. As he cantered along the riverbed he did not notice the sudden motion that followed above him, weaving through the shadows of the jagged Black Spruce that grew atop the ravine.

What had looked from a distance like a gentler slope for the Wolf to climb was, in fact, a trick of the light. The river canyon bent sharply, and although there was a scree slide, above it the canyon wall rose steeply. This continued around the bend. Mist paced back and forth staring up at the high ravine. *There is no time to spare. I must continue. There. There is a spot with a slide and a slight gully with some purchase near the top. It is steeper than I would like, but if I run hard, I can charge safely to the top.*

The big Wolf trotted to the place that he had chosen. He shook his wet fur again to release any excess water, and then circled away so that he could build speed for the ascent. He ran at the steep incline from the bank of the river, and his legs pumped hard to propel him up the slide. Dust flew and clung to his wet fur. Gravel slipped and gave way beneath his paws. His legs strained, and his rear haunches burned with the effort. He reached the top of the slide and leapt for the steeper gully. His nails clawed at the loose alluvium, and his rear legs began to shake as they bore his full weight and pushed upward. He scrambled desperately, but the gully grew more narrow and steep as he struggled higher. His paws slid out from beneath him. He clawed wildly, and then he was falling. He flopped down the sharp ravine, turning end over end. His exhausted legs flailed. As Mist tumbled down the gully, his chest struck a large stone. He felt his air pushed out and could not regain it. *Tundra....* His vision fogged as he fell. Darkness came to him, and he sank into it.

Three Wolves watched from the top of the southern ravine as Mist descended to the riverbed and plunged into the Porcupine River.

"Is he lost?"

"He is a Wolf, he cannot be lost."

"Does he mean to cross here and continue south?"

"He cannot cross into Choho territory. This he must know."

"The nearest safe ascent from the canyon is half a day's walk west. He could not continue south here, even if he wished it. Let us follow him."

The Wolves padded lightly along the top of the ridge, weaving through the shade of the Spruce, following the grey Wolf stealthily as he was swept a little way downriver by the current.

"He looks weary."

"Perhaps he is pursued."

"Yes. Perhaps there are Cargoth hunting him."

"The Cargoth stronghold is three days downriver. It would be very strange for them to come upriver hunting Wolf."

"Then perhaps he is in pursuit of another."

"What does he pursue? Where is his quarry? It could not have passed us unnoticed."

The three Wolves fell silent and watched the big, grey Wolf as he clambered out of the river, surveyed the valley walls, and began to canter.

"Now he travels east again. Perhaps he has the madness."

"No, those with the madness fear water."

"And he does not wear a beard of froth upon his chin. The sickness is not in him."

"What if he is a lead scout then? The vanguard of a raiding party?"

"Then he has received poor counsel. It would be foolish to advance alone. Come, we must follow him."

The Wolves tracked Mist and watched from above as he chose a place to try and scale the ravine.

"Why has he stopped?"

"Surely he does not think he can climb out there?"

"He is backing away for a running start."

"He is a fool."

"No. Something drives him. Strange things are afoot in the north."

"Look. There is strength in him yet. See how he mounts the slide? He will make it."

"No, the soft walls of the gully will not hold his weight. Look, his footing is lost."

They watched silently as the big Wolf tumbled raggedly to the bottom of the slide.

"He lies still. Is he dead?"

"Perhaps."

"He will not wander far if he still lives. Let us go to our First Star. He would want news of this."

The three Wolves turned from the river and strode swiftly through the Black Spruce.

At the side of the scree, very near to where Mist lay, there was a tiny hole burrowed into the ravine. From this hole one pointy little nose emerged, and then another.

"What is it?"

"It's a bug."

"You say everything is a bug."

"The only animals I know are bugs. Except for us."

"What are we called?"

"We're called Piggy Shews."

"Piggy Shews?"

"That's what Mom said."

"Well, if that's a bug, it's the biggest one I ever saw."

"It's the hairiest one I ever saw."

Two very young Pygmy Shrews inched out of their tunnel. They were no bigger than small mice and had long, pointed noses with white whiskers. Their backs were brown, but their sides tended more toward grey. They had tiny, inconspicuous eyes and ears, short, thin tails, and small feet with five long toes. They moved a little closer to where the big Wolf lay, still and quiet on the ground.

"Is it dead?"

"How should I know?"

"Mom would know. I wonder when she's coming back. How come she left with that big, flying bug?"

"I don't know."

The big, flying bug had, in fact, been a Red-tailed Hawk, and it had swooped down and clutched their mother with its talons two days earlier, leaving the youngsters alone to fend for themselves. The young Shrews crept closer to the big Wolf.

"Can we eat it?"

"It's too big. It'll take three whole days to eat it."

"But it's a bug, and we're supposed to eat bugs. I'm hungry."

"How do you know for sure it's a bug?"

"I don't know for sure. Maybe we should taste it."

"What if it's not dead?"

"I'm pretty sure it is. I never saw a sleeping bug."

The little Shrews meandered toward the prone Wolf. They tried their hardest to appear indifferent. They sniffed under stones. They scurried to and fro busily. They wound their way closer and closer. Before long they stood beside Mist's big nose, which alone was larger than either of the Shrews.

"It's windy."

"And warm."

"And stinky."

"Well, what are you waiting for? Taste it."

"*You* taste it."

"You're oldest, you should go first."

"Okay."

The tiny Shrew lifted up on its two hind feet and, with its five fingered forepaws, tentatively prodded at the Wolf's black, spongy nose.

"It's *really* windy up here."

"Just taste it."

"And stinky."

"Just taste it!"

"Okay."

The Shrew chose a spot, opened its mouth wide to reveal little, red-tipped teeth, and bit Mist's nose. The Wolf flinched unconsciously, and his head twitched. His eyelids fluttered, revealing slivers of gold. He drew in a deep breath. His chest convulsed, and then he sneezed violently and moaned. The little Shrew that bit the Wolf was blown clear away from the Wolf's muzzle.

"Run!" he squealed.

Together the tiny animals panicked and scurried, squeaking and whistling, straight back to their tunnel. They disappeared inside.

Mist groaned quietly once more and lay still.

The day wore on, and Mist's fur dried in the high, yellow sun. The caked dust made his grey coat look ragged and tawny in the light.

But the sun soon skirted the edge of the ravine and the Wolf was cast into shadow. It was then that a stirring came from the gravel slide above him. There was a clicking of pebbles as they shifted against each other, a tapping and sliding of stones that sounded a little like heavy rain on a still lake. The scree slid and moved, it rose and scattered as a small figure appeared from the gravel. The figure was no taller than a fox. His torso and limbs were short and stocky, and his arms were as thick and gnarled as his legs. His skin was rough, and scaled, like the mottled bark of an old Pine tree and was the colour of red clay. The sinews of his muscles seemed to snake and coil around one another like the roots of a tree. Tendons twisted down his short legs into wide feet, so sure and strong that they could clasp the very bedrock of the earth. His round head was slightly misshapen, like the knot of a tree, with two holes where his deep-set eyes glowed dimly jade. His beard was long, wispy, and Sage-green. It hung like Lichen around his crooked mouth, beneath his knotted nose, down from his chin to his knees.

The Root Troll paused a moment and stared down to where the great Wolf lay unconscious. He examined the predator carefully. He watched for the subtle movement of the Wolf's chest; for the shallow breath that came and went. Then he began to chant. His voice was low and gentle, but it spread out across the river valley and widened. Stone and earth and water seemed to vibrate with it. Even the curious young Pygmy Shrews stuck their noses from their tunnel. The Troll stood alone like this for a short time, chanting softly, and then the gravel slide around him began to seethe and come alive. Ten more like him emerged from the scree. Fine gravel ran from their tangled sinews as they rose up. Some had smooth skin like the bark of a Maple, others deep furrows like that of a Black Walnut. Some had deep green bristles for beards that hung thickly from their jaws like Fir tree boughs. Still others had beards that poured from their chins like Weeping Willow and hung nearly to their feet.

All of the Trolls looked quietly down at the Wolf, and one of them spoke out, addressing the first Troll to emerge from the slide. "Why do you chant for us, Karst? Why do you call us forth into the light from root and stone?"

Karst pointed a long, slender finger at the big grey Wolf and addressed the others. "Because I know this Wolf. He is called Mist, Second Star of Lone Mountain. I spoke of him to The Eye of the North when Rahtrum came into the Wernecke Mountains at the first breath of Spring. When six of our kind were sent in tribute, I was among them. I spoke well of Mist to Blinn, and of his First Star, Polaris. This is not any Wolf, brothers. This is one of four from Lone Mountain. All of them guardians of Moshee."

A deep gasp went up among the other Trolls. They murmured and glanced at each other. Another of them spoke anxiously. "What darkness is this, Karst? Why does he lie here, by the banks of the Porcupine? He should be north of the flats, in the Barn Range, keeping watch over the yearling."

"I do not know. It is unexpected." Karst drew his twiggy fingers through his beard. "I cannot know what drives him south, but it is not well with me." He turned and looked up at the top of the high ravine. "He makes for Choho territory, but I cannot guess why. We must aid him. We are bound." The Root Troll looked around at his brethren, who all nodded in quiet agreement. "Then bring forth your craft, brothers. Let us tend to him."

The Trolls circled the Wolf in the shade of the steep ravine. They laid their tendril fingers upon him and chanted low and steady. At last one of them spoke. "It is his rib. The bone is cracked." Then others talked in turn above the chanting.

"Here there is a torn muscle. It is swollen."

"He has come far without rest or food."

Karst searched in the scree for a sharp stone, and as the chanting intensified, he stood at Mist's head and drew the edge of the stone across his woody palm. His fingers curled into a knot around the cut, as he gently pried the Wolf's jaws open. He squeezed several drops of blood from his fist, which dripped, clear and slow as tree sap, onto Mist's dry tongue. Then the next Troll stepped to the Wolf's muzzle and repeated this process as Karst moved aside, replaced his hands on Mist's big shoulders, and continued to chant. All of the Root Trolls circled the Wolf in this way, and soon his tongue slowly lapped up the clear, sweet blood. Again they spoke over the chanting.

"The bone is knit."

"The swelling has receded."

Karst answered. "Our blood is powerful. He will sleep while it works within him, and gives him new strength. Let us wash him in the river while he slumbers. Then we will carry him to the top of the ravine. I will hold council with him when he awakens."

The Root Trolls held the Wolf gently in the cool waters of the Porcupine. They ran their reedy fingers through his coat and the dust dissolved from his fur, clouding the river and drifting downstream. Next they gathered him securely in their arms and moved to the steep ravine. They grasped the Wolf tightly and began their ascent. The Trolls' feet curled into the loose scree and anchored each of them solidly between steps as they bore Mist slowly up the sharp slide. When they reached the alluvial gully, their root-like feet found easy purchase, and they effortlessly lifted the great bulk of the Wolf to the top of the escarpment. There in the soft Lichen that grew beneath the Black Spruce, the Trolls laid Mist in the shade. Now Karst remained quietly at his side, chanting softly with his eyes closed. His incantation was gentle and ancient, and it disguised the scent of the Wolf's wet fur so it could not be carried by the wind. In this way the Root Troll, Karst, stood watch over Mist until at last the gift of blood they had given him finished its work. The other Trolls moved away and each of them, in turn, burrowed into the earth, or stepped slowly behind a Spruce trunk and was gone.

At last the Wolf stirred and shook his head. He whispered Tundra's name. His eyes flashed gold and opened. He scrambled onto his paws in a panic, turning and backing away from the edge of the ravine. He spotted the Troll, lowered his head and tail, and waved his big muzzle back and forth to scent the air.

"Where am I, Troll?" he growled. The Wolf's golden eyes narrowed and burned hypnotically, but they were no match for the deep, green gaze of the Root Troll.

Karst's voice was soft and warm. "Put aside your stare, I am not your prey. We found you injured at the bottom of the ravine." He opened his gnarled arms and spread his slender fingers. "Now you are whole, and at the top of the ravine. It is well, is it not?"

Mist looked around quickly. "There are others?"

"They have gone."

The Wolf was anxious. "I cannot tarry. But I thank you, Troll, and would know your name. I am called —"

"You are Mist, Second Star of Lone Mountain."

Mist cocked his head.

"You do not remember me, Grey-mane. Long seasons have passed. You were but a pup when I found you then, washed alone onto the shore of the Porcupine River, your lungs heavy with water. Since then, I have only seen you from afar. But today I discovered you, once again, on the banks of the Porcupine. It is the Binder's providence."

The grey Wolf's eyes softened as he stepped nearer. "You are Karst, elder among the Root Trolls?"

"I am."

"My First Star has spoken of you. How you carried me yourself to Lone Mountain. How you chanted softly and entered the den of Polaris and Aurora unmolested. How they watched you come and place me among their new litter to nurse."

"Yes, that was I."

"I do not have words for the thanks that you are owed." The Wolf sighed. "And I do not have time, Karst. Even now, there is a darkness that tracks my mate to Lone Mountain. I have come for the aid of the Choho. I must fly. I have lost precious time."

"Do you speak of Grotto?"

Mist was surprised. "Yes. You know of him?"

"Let us speak a while, Mist. Let us deliberate."

"But there is no time."

Karst drew his long fingers through his beard. "It is said among Trolls that there is great speed in counsel and much folly in haste. It was haste that left you lying helpless at the foot of the ravine. Come, Mist, let us speak." The Troll walked slowly into the Spruce trees.

Mist hesitated a moment, then followed the Root Troll, all the while thinking of Tundra.

Mist raced through the Spruce trees toward Choho Hill. The blood of the Root Trolls still coursed in him, and he ran easily in long, steady strides. There was a pain that throbbed in his ribs, but it was dulled by urgent thoughts of his mate. He ran, and the land unravelled beneath him. Soon he saw the hill rising in the distance. *That is where they are denned. They will have scented my approach already.* As the thought entered his mind he heard the first howl ahead of him, climbing onto the wind. There came another a little to the east and one more to the west. Then another and another. *They have found me. They chorus-*

howl. To them I am a rogue Wolf that invades their territory. They will not allow this affront. I make for their den and they will deny me. They will come for me, and their First Star will lead the hunt.

The howling grew nearer and less frequent as the Choho Pack closed around their prey. Mist slowed his gait, falling into a light trot. Then a howl rose into the air only a little way ahead, and he slowed again, this time to a walk. *They are skilled, this pack, to close on their prey so quickly.* The grey Wolf mounted the top of a small rise. Here there was a low rock outcropping in a clearing where no Spruce grew. He stepped into the clearing and the Choho Wolves drifted out of the surrounding trees. Six of them in all. They growled and snarled with their heads lowered and their teeth bared. Mist stopped and stood his ground as they tightened their circle around him.

He puffed up his chest and spoke slowly. "I am Mist, Second Star of Lone Mountain. I am sent by Polaris in search of your First Star."

"Then you have found him," came a deep voice from just behind the grey Wolf.

Mist whirled. A Wolf, black as night and very nearly as large as Polaris, stood in the light.

He spoke impatiently. "I am Timber, First Star of Choho Hill. Speak to me, Mist of Lone Mountain. Why does my brother send you?"

"The shadow-walker approaches Lone Mountain. He may well have crossed through your territory. Polaris bids me plead for your aid. For a war pack to defend our den and our new pups." The black Wolf looked puzzled. "You speak of the one called Grotto. We have heard news of him. If he had crossed into our territory he would quickly find himself surrounded. Just as you have. He would never arrive at Lone Mountain," the Wolf boasted.

"He is more now than what he was, Timber. He has grown strong. He was stealthy before, but now he ranges darkly upon the land and leaves no trail for Wolves. You would not know that he was here if he did not wish it." The Choho Wolves exchanged glances. "You would not know that he was here if he circled us now."

Timber was thoughtful for a moment. "Where is mighty Polaris? Why does he not come to ask for my aid himself? Why does he send his adopted Second Star?"

"He is nearing Babbage River by now. He guards the yearling called Moshee."

The Choho Wolves whispered to each other.

Timber silenced them. "These are strange tidings you bring. Why should I trust you? It is said that you are the whelp of a Root Troll, is it not?" The other Wolves chortled.

Mist growled deeply and the others fell silent, surprised at his brazenness. "It is said truly. For it was a Root Troll that carried me to Lone Mountain when I was but a pup. That is all the more reason to give us your help."

Timber laughed outright at this boast. "I do not grovel at the paws of my brother, Grey-mane. I am master of this pack. I alone." The other Wolves growled. "Why should we not gut you where you stand? It is you who have invaded our territory. Why should we tolerate your indiscretion?"

Mist did not falter. "Because I am bound by Rahtrum, the

Earthshaker. Because I am a guardian of the yearling, though I, too, question his worth. Because, though I harbour your doubts, I fear for the safety of my mate. Because you are not immune to those that may work beneath you, those that move among root and stone. You would do well to heed me."

The black Wolf became irate and swayed defiantly. "We wish the yearling well, Mist, though we, too, have our doubts. But I do not bow to threats. You are a fool to come to Choho and threaten the First Star. You have been counselled poorly by my brother." The big, black Wolf turned away from Mist and called over his shoulder to his pack. "Leave his bones by the river, let us dissuade others from coming this way."

As the Choho Wolves advanced on Mist, the earth began to move beneath them. Moss and Lichen stirred as though alive. Tendril roots grasped the paws of Timber and his pack. Root Trolls lifted up from the ground and rose, green-eyed and impatient, to halt their movements. A large Troll climbed out from between the roots of a Black Spruce and faced the First Star. He spoke candidly. "You are Timber, First Star of Choho Hill?"

"I am."

"The shadow-walker is our common enemy. It is Karst, elder of our kind that bids you aid the Wolf called Mist. The grey-mane is one of the Keepers of Moshee, and you will send what aid you can with him. If you do not, then we are sent to end the reign of Timber at Choho Hill. We will assail your den and remove you. You know this to be within our power."

Timber bared his white teeth. He flinched and arched his back, but he could not free his paws from the Trolls' sinewy grasp. He turned to Mist. "So it has come to this?"

"Polaris would answer your call if it came."

"So be it." He swivelled his broad head again and looked to the Wolves that were ensnared. "We cannot wrestle with Root Trolls." He turned to the green-bearded Troll that addressed him. "We submit, and I am bound." Then he turned to Mist. "If it is a war pack you desire, it is a war pack you shall have."

Mist nodded to Timber and then sprang away into the west. The Trolls released their granite hold on the others. Timber lunged after Mist and followed him through the Spruce with ease. The Choho Wolves each departed in kind and leapt after their First Star, who called over his shoulder to them: "We are Choho, born and bred. A den all to your own for any among you who fells the shadow-walker."

When at last all the strange bugs had departed from the banks of the Porcupine River, the Pygmy Shrews' curiosity was quickly replaced with a keen awareness of their hunger. Since the gravel slide was again quiet, they decided to leave their tunnel and forage along the riverbank for insects or worms. They scurried here and there, pushing their pointed noses under this stone or that piece of driftwood. The first Shrew caught a juicy beetle, and as he paused to munch on this delicious morsel, he saw his brother foraging nearby. As he watched, the big, flying bug returned, descended quickly out of the sky, clutched the second Shrew with its sharp feet and flew away. The first Shrew sulked irritably as he ate his beetle. "Where is he going?"

Then he had an idea, he decided that he too, would befriend the big, flying bug so that he could be reunited with his mother and brother. He waited patiently out on the bank of the river under the bright sun. When at last he saw the big bug flying overhead, he scurried excitedly in a circle to draw its attention and then stood up on his tiny hind feet. "Hi there, I'm a Piggy Shew!" he squealed. The Red-tailed Hawk dove expertly from the sky. She fell upon the tiny Shrew and clasped it tightly in her deadly talons. The Shrew emitted a short, confused whistle and fell silent.

chapter 13

The Calving Grounds
JUNE

Bou and Taiga watched as Polaris galloped quickly into the
distance and out of view. When he was gone the Caribou grazed
and rested, fatigued by their long march. When they felt some
strength creeping back into their sore muscles they turned
quietly, crossed the Babbage River, and climbed into the foothills
of the Northern Mountains. Taiga was careful to skirt along the
mountains' eastern slopes where foraging was plentiful, and the
way was less strenuous. On they journeyed, toward the Coastal
Plains in the north. Birdsong filled the spring air.

"Is it far now to the coast?" Bou asked.

"We have crossed Trail River already. Up ahead is Tulugay
River, and finally Spring River. It is not far, Little One. But we
travelled hard with Polaris for many days, and we are before the
other cows, so let us walk easy and rest and eat. In three days'
time we will reach the foothills and plains that run down beside
the Firth River and out to the sea. It is there I hope we will join
with other cows who are with calf this Spring."

They walked on together through the long day, stopping often to graze. The sun winked behind rare white clouds and then blazed in the open sky. A warm breeze blew out of the east, carrying the scents of new growth.

Bou lifted his muzzle into the fresh current of air and drank in the smells of Spring. But there was one he did not recognize. *That's a strange scent. It isn't a Lichen, or a flower. Maybe an animal?*

Taiga suddenly lifted her nose into the air and pointed her muzzle to the east. Her eyes widened slightly, scanning the long slopes that stretched out below them. Her body became tense. "Grizzlies," she said in a low breath.

Then a cry rang out above them, shrill and piercing. The Caribou looked up into the sky, and the sharp call came again. There, circling against the wide, blue expanse, were two large Golden Eagles, one slightly bigger than the other. The larger of the two pitched, folded her broad wings, and began to descend toward Bou and Taiga.

"Windshim," Bou said slowly.

Taiga nodded in response and whispered, "So that is Windshim." The old Caribou continued to watch in wonder as the great bird plunged through the sky in a wide, graceful arc.

Her long wings pitched and tilted expertly. Adorned with feathers of black-brown and chestnut, she cleaved the sky. As she glided lower, the primary feathers of her wing tips spread out like slender fingers to filter the wind. The deep brown contour feathers of her body looked like the layered armour of a Spruce cone, flecked here and there with white down. Her tail plumage splayed in a white-banded fan to steady her on the air. She was crowned by golden feathers that lay like flaxen scales down her neck and glowed in the sun. She was immense, and though Taiga had seen Golden Eagles before, she was mesmerized by Windshim. She knew this was the same Eagle that had swept overhead at the Peel River, but now the old Caribou saw the Raptor for the first time in daylight. Windshim approached at great speed, and Bou stepped closer to his mother to press against her flank. The Eagle called out again as she drew nearer. The Caribou flinched and laid their ears back. Windshim spread her wings to slow her speed. Her legs began to lower with her yellow, leathery toes curled back. She beat her wings powerfully, uncurled her toes, and extended her black talons as she touched down on a stony rise before the Caribou. Taiga and Bou felt the wind from the Eagle's outstretched wings brush their faces. As she settled on the rock, Windshim folded her vast wings neatly on either side of her broad chest. The point of her hooked beak was black and sharp. Her mahogany eyes, set sternly beneath her feathered brow, gleamed in the light. The black circles of her pupils focused and penetrated the eyes of the Caribou, who shivered under the intensity of her gaze.

Her voice was high and breathy, like the wind. "I am called Windshim, first among Raptors of the north. That is my mate, Aquila, who circles above. I am sent by Blinn to watch over you, while you await his coming." The Eagle spoke slowly. "Much is said of you, Moshee. That you are chosen of Rahtrum, and that you will wake the Cargoth. We shall see. You have grown since last I saw you. Your antlers reach for the sky." She looked around cautiously, surveying the ground in every direction, while her mate spiralled high above as lookout.

Bou replied nervously. "This is my mother, Taiga."

Windshim stared at the cow with her sharp eyes. "Greetings, Taiga of the Porcupine herd." She looked the old Caribou up and down. "You are with calf. Do not worry. You need not fear us. We are bound, Aquila and I. The Gnome bids us leave the yearling and his kin in peace."

Bou's mother nodded at the Eagle as Bou continued. "It was you who came to my aid on the Peel River. Thank you."

The Eagle's reply was dismissive. "It was a small matter to summon the Tuatha De Danann." Then her eyes shifted to the yearling. "But it is my hope that you have learned from that experience, Moshee. That you have grown less foolhardy." Again she turned her smooth head to inspect her surroundings. "We Eagles are not well suited to the open ground, I cannot tarry here. Know that there are Grizzlies to your east. No doubt you have scented them on the wind. They follow cows of your herd that travel to the Calving Grounds." Her eyes focused long and scanned the horizon as she spoke. "They have left their dens early for green-up. They are gaunt and hungry, and now they come this way, hoping for a taste of Caribou. Stay your course, and you will be clear of them until you reach the others. There is a herd of cows grazing and drifting west on the high plains. We will watch from above." She began to unfold her wings.

"There are two Crows following us," Bou blurted. "They track and watch us for the dark one called Grotto. Their names are Hugin and Munin."

The Eagle considered this for a moment. "There are many Crows in the north, yearling. We will watch for them, but they will be wary of us and hide among their kind. The Crow is shrewd and has some skill upon the wing." Aquila called out from above. "I must go."

"But when will Blinn come to us? Where is the Eye of the North?"

The Raptor called back to her mate. "The Eye of the North? Bah! The Gnome will come when he comes." She unfurled her wide wings and leapt from the rock. "Remember this well, Land-walker, no eyes in the north surpass my own." The air around her hissed as she cut through it and climbed easily into the wide, blue sky to join her mate.

Bou and his mother carried on along the foothills, and the Golden Eagles wound high in the sky above them. The yearling was preoccupied by the thought of Grizzlies and kept a furtive watch to the east. He was haunted by the memory of his dreams, by the Bear that came in his sleep to topple the tall, straight Spruce tree. He shivered as he trotted to catch up to his mother. It was the middle of the third day since they had left Polaris. They skirted the edge of a high ridge and looked out over the Coastal Plains. In the distance, the Arctic tundra was speckled with small brown spots that moved slowly across the open land.

"We have found part of our herd, Bou." Taiga said happily as she looked out at the Sedge meadows at the base of the foothills. The young bull nodded his head up and down with excitement as his mother turned and broke into a run. The two Caribou cantered down the long slope and out onto the wide plains that ran from the Northern Mountains to the sea. There, on the plains, two thousand cows grazed, some with their yearlings, all in loose groups. The slow clicking of their ankles and hooves drifted in the air.

Bou and his mother joined the herd and foraged late into the afternoon. The other cows and yearlings stole furtive glances at Bou. Stories had run through the herd during their Spring migration; it was said among the Caribou that a lone yearling and cow travelled to the Calving Grounds without the herd, and that these two had been seen trekking in the company of Wolves. When Bou and Taiga strode onto the plains to join the herd, it was with two mighty Golden Eagles circling overhead. The other Caribou took this as a sign that these were the Caribou the rumours spoke of. The cows and their yearlings did not reject the two newcomers, but neither did they welcome them. Instead, they stayed a little apart from Bou and Taiga, stealing looks as they drifted toward the coast of the Beaufort Sea.

For two days mother and young bull wandered with the herd, grazing and weaving in broad arcs around lakes still skinned with the thin ice of Winter. On the second day, a heavy fog drifted across the coast, greying the land and blotting the sun. Rain began to fall, wetting molted fur and softening the ground. The musk of Caribou filled the air. Cows and yearlings near Bou moved like strange shadows through the thick mist, some lay on the soft tundra heavy with calf, while others were invisible in the distance and could be heard grunting and huffing with the strain of labour. Occasionally the lonesome, eerie cries of Windshim and Aquila could be heard high up in the sky above the fog, and this sent shivers through the herd.

In the evening of the second day, Taiga lay in the Cottongrass, grunting now and then as the first pains of labour came to her. Bou paced in circles around her, then lay by her side, and then paced some more.

"What is happening? Is it time? What should I do?" he asked.

"I am with calf, Little One, just as I was with you a year ago. The time is drawing very near. There is nothing for you to do. Graze and rest. Soon you will have a new brother or sister," she replied.

"Brother." Bou said simply.

Taiga sighed and laid her head in the Cottongrass as Bou grazed and paced around her. At last the yearling grew weary and settled a short distance from his mother. He rested on his side and tucked his head in among his hooves, his new antlers jutted out like long, arched branches. The mist drifted over him like a dream, and finally their long journey took its toll as a great weariness crept into his body. He slipped into a deep, restful sleep.

Bou had slept for long hours before the sun burned away the mist, and a warm breeze came across the plains to gently wake him.

"Hi," came a little voice in front of him.

Bou's rear leg twitched sleepily.

"Hi," came the voice again, beside him.

His ears flapped lazily at a fly.

"Hi," came the voice behind him.

His eyes fluttered and opened slowly against the brightness of the Arctic Spring. The fog was gone, and the sky stretched out wide and blue from the seacoast to the Buckland Hills in the south and the Northern Mountains behind them. Birdsong filled the air; Widgeons and Pintails and Teals, all flitting here and there with boundless energy. The yellow sun stung the yearling's tired eyes but warmed his coat and body. Suddenly a shadow obscured his view.

"Hi," came the little voice again.

Bou blinked, raised his head, and cleared his eyes. A small calf stood before him with her little, black muzzle nearly pressed against his nose. Her big eyes were ringed with amber, and her dark, oval pupils stared happily into Bou's.

"Hi," she said again.

"Hello," Bou replied, shaking his head.

When at last he spoke, the little calf leapt backward on her long legs, then stepped awkwardly forward again. "Hi," she said cheerfully.

"Hello."

She leapt back again, tossed her head, and ran in a circle around the yearling. Her red coat shone in the sunshine, and her little tail stood up over her white rump and twitched as she ran.

Bou turned to look for his mother. She was a little way away, grazing in the warm sun, weary from her long night.

"Who is this?" he asked Taiga. The little calf raced around him as he spoke.

Taiga turned to her yearling. "That is your sister, Bou. I have named her Beringia, but we will call her Bree."

And with that the little calf did her best to bleat out her name over and over. "Bee! Bee! Bee!"

"I wished for a brother," Bou said simply, as he climbed to his hooves. "Why is she running in circles? Stop that!" he told the calf, who ignored him and turned to run around him in the other direction.

The old Caribou nodded at him. "You too, ran endlessly on your new legs. Have you, with your uncommon memory, forgotten what it was to be suddenly and newly alive? To feel your first Spring? To be Caribou? Look at your sister. One day you will wish you could see and feel the world again as she does now." As Taiga finished speaking, Bree ran in a wide arc around them both, weaving around other nearby cows and their calves and bleating out, "Hi! Hi! Hi!" again and again.

Bou turned in a circle to watch her run. He shook his antlers, then lowered his head to graze.

Days of blue sky warmed the plains, and the last of the gullies and cliffs that were lined with snowpack blazed white under the sleepless sun, even as the world all around turned deeply green, bursting here and there into yellow Mastodon flowers, white Cottongrass petals, or wisps of Foxtail. New calves frolicked and nursed and called out for their mothers.

Bou's sister ran in great, wide circles, chasing moths and racing past other calves calling out, "Hi! Hi! Hi!" and, "Bee! Bee! Bee!" before returning, breathless, with shaking legs, to stand in Taiga's shadow and nurse thirstily. When she stopped nursing to take deep breaths and peer about, warm, white milk clung to the black hairs of her muzzle. A rust-coloured Arctic Fox that had been pouncing for Tundra Vole on a nearby snowpack sauntered past. Bree stared at the Fox and tracked him with her ears, which were much too big for her new, little head. When the Fox had passed over a hill, Bree peered about for her brother. Bou was close by, and she watched him as he lowered his head and pressed his nose down into a patch of budding Cottongrass to tear at it with his teeth. She took a small, excited leap, then ran to where her brother stood, pushed her nose down beside his own, made a small grunting noise, planted her hooves, and did her best to take hold of Bou's Cottongrass with her little teeth. Bou huffed and gently butted Bree. She lost her tooth-hold and stumbled back onto her haunches. Immediately she leapt up again and grunted in a ferocious little voice as she charged in to take hold of her brother's Cottongrass once more. Bou abandoned the grass and raised his head.

"She is persistent. Let me graze, annoying little Mouse," the young bull admonished her.

Taiga's eyes shone brightly at the little calf, who turned in circles in front of Bou, tearing at the Cottongrass and spitting it out. "She is only playing. Let her taste the world. She is your sister."

Bou grunted at the calf. "Go and drink some milk, runt!"

Bree sensed that she was being addressed and stopped what she was doing to stare up at her brother. "Runt!" she said.

Bou huffed and turned away to graze in another spot. His sister ran around him in circles, sometimes charging in to tear at the plants he was grazing on, and sometimes breaking away to nurse with Taiga. This carried on long into the day until a shadow crossed the evening sun, and the Caribou close to Bou and his family scattered.

Windshim descended out of the sky and lit on the ground near Taiga. Bree panicked out of instinct and scrambled underneath Bou to hide. He muttered and tried to dislodge her, but she would not relent, and he took pity on her and the fear that sprang into her dark eyes.

Windshim addressed the old Caribou, speaking quickly. "There are Grizzlies to the southeast, they draw near and know this land. Beware."

"Are there many?" asked Taiga.

"We have seen five at least, hunting together," the Eagle replied. "If there are more, then they are hidden from our eyes in the Buckland Hills."

"And what of the Crows, Hugin and Munin?" asked Taiga.

"What Crow has felled a Caribou? Let us be wary of Grizzlies now and worry about Crows when there is time. Keep your muzzles to the breeze and your eyes to the horizon. They are cautious and patient, these Bears. I will call three times when they draw near."

With a great rush of wings Windshim leapt into the sky. Aquila spiralled above in wide arcs, waiting for her. The other Caribou, who now stood a safe distance away with their calves and yearlings, eyed Bou and his little family carefully. A whispering went up among them.

The sun circled and dipped low over the Beaufort Sea. Bou and Taiga lay in the Sedge grass, and Bree nuzzled against her brother. Just as Bou's eyes began to grow heavy, his sister began, again, to speak in her little voice. "Grizzy?" she asked Bou with her wide eyes.

"Grizz-ly" replied the yearling. "They are called Grizzly Bears."

"Grizzy Burrs?" said Bree inquisitively. By this time Taiga was watching.

"Why is she so slow to learn the names of things?" Bou asked.

"She is not slow, she is like the others." Bou's mother gestured with her head at the many calves standing or running or sleeping on the plain. "They learn by degrees, and in time they know how to speak of their world."

The yearling huffed. "I cannot remember not knowing the world. Sedgegrass has always been Sedgegrass to me, and Grizzly Bears have always been Grizzly Bears."

Taiga nodded at the yearling. "Your memory serves you well, but you seem to forget that you are Moshee, chosen of Rahtrum, and that you are different from other Caribou." Taiga took a long breath as she looked out over the plain. "When you were born last Spring on the plains, you ran in circles for seven days, weaving through the herd with your ears pricked up, watching and listening to the other cows. All the other calves ran and bleated and grunted, but you were strangely silent. Then, on the eighth day, you spoke to me, and though you stumbled a little over your words, already you knew the names of flowers and grasses and animals. By your sixteenth day you knew north from south and Spring from Autumn. I do not have the great memory of Wolves or Gnomes, but still I remember how quickly you learned the world around you." She paused and looked out at the herd. "And still these other cows whisper of it."

Bou looked at the Caribou spread out around them. For the first time he noticed how some of the cows and yearlings stole glances in his direction and spoke in low tones to each other.

Taiga continued. "I do not know what it is to be different, Little One. But I think it must sometimes be difficult. Learn patience for your sister. If you wish her to speak, then teach her."

The yearling stared into Bree's big, waiting eyes and sighed. He tried at length to explain to her what a Grizzly Bear was. He stood over her to show her how large they were. "A Grizzly bear is frightening," he said. "Do you understand? We Caribou are scared of them." Bree tilted her head in confusion. "They are scary," he said. He chased her, trying to show her what scary meant, but she only ran and bucked with glee. He struggled to teach her his name and her own, and though she had little difficulty with *Bou*, she continued to refer to herself as *Bee*.

Progress came very slowly, and each time the yearling taught his sister a new word she ran off in circles bleating it over and over, often incorrectly, before suddenly returning to lie panting at Bou's side and waiting for her lessons to resume. Bou, who's patience was quickly waning, was about to tackle the rather complicated topic of why a cow is different from a bull, when Windshim's distant, piercing call rolled out over the coast three times.

Caribou that grazed nearby stared up at the sky lazily, then peered about to reassure themselves that their calves were close by. But Taiga and Bou scrambled immediately onto their hooves and scanned the horizon to the southeast. Bree copied her mother and brother.

"I do not see them, Bou," said Taiga anxiously.

"They are there," the yearling replied, nodding at the horizon. "Three of them, lumbering over a rise in the south. The low sun is in their tan fur, and you can see them move against the green of the land."

"Yes I see them now. Just barely." Taiga replied slowly. "Your eyes see well, Little One."

"Grizzy Burrs?" Bree offered and squinted out at the horizon.

"Yes, Bree, Grizzlies. Three of them," Bou said without taking his eyes from the horizon.

"But where are the others?" Taiga asked. "Windshim spoke of five."

Bou scanned the horizon. "There are only three."

"Grizzy Burrs," said Bree, as she turned and pressed against her brother.

"The Raptor's eyes do not lie," Bou's mother insisted. "She said there were five hunting together, and so there must be."

"Then the other two must lag behind, hidden beyond the rise. There are only three now on the slope to the south."

"Grizzy Burrs! I'm scary, Bou!" said Bree anxiously, and she pressed closer to her brother's flank.

It was then that several things happened at once. The herd around Taiga, Bou, and Bree grew restless and began to shift. Windshim, who had been circling with Aquila, now flew overhead and called out twice more from high above the plains, and Bou, who peered down at his trembling sister, saw that she stared wide-eyed into the east. He turned his gaze that way as well, and there, coming up out of the gully they had hidden in, were two, big Grizzlies breaking into a canter straight for the herd. Windshim called out again from above, and Bou looked to see that the other three Grizzlies had picked up speed and were separating — fanning out to press the herd toward the sea. Taiga also saw their dilemma.

"I'm scary, Bou!" Bree whimpered.

"We must go!" Taiga called over her shoulder as she began to move with the herd.

"Wait, Mother! We must turn the herd west. If we run north, we will be pressed against the sea, and they will encircle us." He stared into his sister's eyes. "Stay near me, Bree."

The little Caribou shivered.

He pressed his muzzle to her small nose. "Do not be afraid. This way!" Bou sprang away, and Bree ran at his heels, her long, slender legs a blur of motion, her little white tail bumping up and down as she leapt over hummocks. Taiga struggled to move as quickly as her calf and yearling, but she kept up as well as she could and kept a watch on Bree to be sure she was not lost in the confusion. As Bou ran through the herd he called to the other Caribou, "Stampede west!"

Bree, who by this time thought her brother was the most important Caribou in all the north, echoed his every cry with her own little high-pitched bleat. "Stampy west! Stampy west!"

As Bou, Bree, and Taiga cut through the herd, many Caribou joined them in turning west, but others were confused. Pandemonium spread among the animals as the Golden Eagles circled overhead, and the Grizzlies closed from the south and east. Some cows ran erratically and were separated from their calves, and some calves, too confused by their first stampede, became lost amid the thundering of hooves. Some even ran mistakenly in the direction of the bears, while others ran desperately through the herd, bleating for their mothers.

The herd was divided for a time when it came upon a high embankment where the coastal plain, still thick with the last of Winter's snowpack, dropped steeply in the direction of the sea. Deep snow jutted from the slope and fell away in a steep, white cliff. Bou led Bree, Taiga, and part of the herd along the top of this embankment to where it tapered gradually, and the plains lay flat and even again. But as the three Grizzlies pressed north in a wide arc, many of the Caribou felt compelled to descend the embankment and continue toward the sea. It was here that mothers and their calves were separated again. Some of the cows chose difficult, steep snowpack to descend, and their calves would not follow, hesitating instead, on their unsure legs. Then, in their confusion, they backtracked up the embankment to where the bears drew ever nearer. Some of the cows too, returned up the embankment in search of their calves. Most continued on, and eventually the two halves of the herd met again on the western plain. Though calm eventually returned to the animals, the air was filled with the bleating of lost calves and the grunting of mothers who searched for them. Some, who were very fortunate, found each other again and nuzzled tenderly, but many did not, and several cows wandered the herd calling out for their young.

"Grizzy Burrs?" Bree inquired of her brother.

Bou stared into the east. A cow circled a little way away, grunting and anxious, her voice now hoarse from her long search. "We are safe for now, Bree." He stared at the cow. "The Bears have found what they came for."

Taiga, who was grazing beside her calf and yearling, looked up at the cow and said to Bou. "She will give up her search soon."

As they stood together and watched the cow move in long, erratic circles, a tiny runt of a calf was chased out of the herd with her muzzle held up in front of her.

The calf trotted straight toward the lone cow and her little, white tail waggled as she bleated at the anxious Caribou.

The cow cried out again with her rough voice.

As the calf drew near to the distraught cow, she paused a moment. Then, desperate for warm milk, she leapt forward and cantered in to press her muzzle beneath the cow.

But as the little calf charged in, the cow turned and lowered her nose to scent the calf's rump. The cow continued turning and the calf could not reach her teat. Now the cow grunted aggressively and butted the little calf with her forehead. The calf stumbled a little on her hooves and fell back onto her haunches. The cow continued bellowing for her lost calf and moved off to circle the herd once more.

The calf regained her feet and wavered a little on her thin legs as she watched the cow retreat. Flies gathered around her face and she blinked her big eyes and twitched her long ears. It was then she spotted Taiga standing beside Bou and Bree. Her little tail pricked up and she cantered in a crooked line toward the old Caribou.

Taiga stepped toward her as she approached and grunted menacingly, then she lowered her antlers and charged.

The little calf had grown accustomed to this response and turned away. Her white tail was limp as she wandered a little into the distance and then turned to stare back at the herd. She bleated faintly to nobody in particular and then stood quietly, wobbling on her weary legs and blinking in the sunlight.

"So we will leave her to die?" Bou asked Taiga.

The old cow turned to look at her yearling. "That is a strange question, Little One. Would you sooner I gave her Bree's milk? Is it your sister who should die?"

Bou considered this. "But what about the other cow? She had milk and no calf to give it to."

"That is not our way, Bou." Taiga stared out at the little calf. "We cannot abide the calf of another. This one no longer belongs to the herd."

"Then where does she belong? Who does she belong to?"

"She belongs here in the north." Taiga said somberly as she peered up into the sky. "And now she belongs to Windshim."

Bou jerked his head up. The Golden Eagle, who had been spiralling above the herd, folded her wings and fell through the blue sky so quickly that the yearling could not follow her descent. He looked over at the calf and began to call to her. But she was too distant and distracted, chasing a moth that fluttered near her hooves.

As Windshim struck, her wings pumped wildly, and her yellow talons curled deeply into the spine of the little calf, who collapsed heavily onto her side. The calf's eyes widened and her rear haunches kicked uselessly as she appeared and then disappeared under the great flapping wings of the Raptor. As Windshim's wings rose, Bou could see that the little calf tried silently to lift her head. He turned and looked away, but Bree could not, and she shivered as she watched.

chapter 14

First Light and First Star

JUNE

Polaris, First Star of Lone Mountain, turned south from Babbage River and ran. For two days he stretched and coiled and reached with his wide, black paws to pull the green earth beneath him. He did not slow or stop or falter, haunted as he was by the memory of Grotto's frost-cold gaze and by thoughts of Aurora's warm flank and tender, yellow eyes. He passed over the land with the smooth, ceaseless motion of a cloud's shadow. Arctic Hare whispered to each other of the great Wolf's run, for he had been seen leaving the Barn Range when the sun still lingered in the late corners of the afternoon. He was spotted again entering the Old Crow Flats before the sleepless star could circle one full day. For a time across the north, Hares met and shivered as they spoke of the running of the one called Land Crow. They traded their messages and wondered aloud what it could mean to see the mighty Wolf driven south this way.

"It is said he does not stop, not for water, nor for food," some said. "Then he will falter. He must," they agreed.

Others spoke of Hares that had seen him. "My twenty-seventh cousin forages at Johnson Creek. She says he ran right past her. She says he came upon her so swiftly that her heart nearly burst with fright. But he ignored her and was gone without missing a stride."

Still others speculated. "He runs for Lone Mountain. I have heard it said the Earthshaker himself sends him over the land."

"No, I am told he is pursued by the dark one called Grotto."

But whenever this name was spoken, the Hares became nervous and fell silent, twisting their long ears anxiously and sniffing at the air.

Even Polaris recognized that he could not run like this forever, and on the third day, he felt all of his seventeen seasons gather together against him. At first they crept into his mind. *You are old,* they whispered to him, *you cannot hope to run as the Crow flies for such a distance.* But his copper eyes narrowed as he bared his teeth and pushed the seasons from his mind with visions of Aurora.

So the seasons crept down his neck and into his long muscles, where they burned his sinews and whispered, *You must rest.* But the Wolf would not listen, and on he surged. So the seasons climbed over his spine and weighed upon him like water, and he felt the air grow thick and sting his lungs, and his tongue hung dryly from his dark muzzle. Still he would not relent, and in this way he passed into the Old Crow Flats, lapping up water as he crossed rivers and wove around blue lakes.

A cool wind came to ease the weight of his long seasons and bend the Horsetails and Bur-reeds as he ran. When the early evening came on the third day, the lightness he felt in the wind betrayed him. Feeling a fleeting new strength, he turned from the paths he knew well and made straight for Lone Mountain, drawn by his fear and his need and his love. But the way he chose took him between lakes that were too close together. Their Sedge fens nearly touched, and soon the big Wolf found himself caught in a Spring-wet marsh of tussocks that sucked at his paws and made his fur heavy with water and mud. For a short time he coiled and heaved through the wetland, pushing his wide chest over the hummocks and through the tall Horsetails. But his long seasons clung to him, tugged at his legs, and slowed him with an ache he had never before known. Still he would not relent. Carefully and deliberately he pulled his paws from the mire and trudged on. Now his seasons twisted around him like a great snake and squeezed his wide chest. He panted hard and stopped often, searching for his breath. By late evening he made little better pace than a Lemming and his long seasons whispered to him again. *You are not all that you were, mighty Polaris. You must rest or you will falter.*

At last he could not resist. When the land rose before him, he carried his heavy body up out of the wetlands over a hillock. The hill tapered on its southern slope into a short, shallow valley tightly packed with Black Spruce. The Wolf plodded down the hill and found a bed of moss beneath trees that leaned against each other, robed in wisps of Lichen that glowed like tangled green webs in the low sun. Though his tight belly churned and growled for food, his eyes fell closed as soon as he tucked his muzzle in amongst his sore, muddied paws. So it was that Polaris, Land Crow, first among Wolves in the north, met the limits of his strength, and in a land that knows only light all the hours of a Summer day, he slipped into the darkness of sleep.

"Land Crow." The voice was gentle, but edged with impatience. It pierced the gloom of the Wolf's slumber, like a cool shaft of light. "Awaken, Polaris."

He squinted his sleep-filled eyes and lifted his weary chin. A white light shimmered above him as he shook his head and blinked. His legs and paws ached as he stared up. The voice came again. "Do you know me, Wolf?"

Polaris' voice cracked with fatigue. "You are Tuatha De Danann." He blinked several times, and the light came into focus. The Faerie hung in the air before him, glowing softly, her wings a blur. Her frost-white eyes examined him carefully, and her light played strangely between the dark green branches of the Black Spruce. The clouds that gathered in the sky beyond the dark branches were red with the low light of the night sun.

"I have slept too long. I must run." The black Wolf struggled onto his feet, grimacing as he stretched the stiffness from his legs.

"You are Polaris, First Star of Lone Mountain. You are known to me." The Faerie drifted close to the Wolf's muzzle.

"I am known to many in the north," Polaris grunted.

"You are feared by many in the north, Land Crow, but you are known only to a few. There is a difference. I did not learn of you until the Winter took this Spring into its arms." The Faerie's voice hardened, and a hint of red flickered in her eyes. "I did not know the Raptor, Windshim, nor the yearling, Moshee, until the rivers shook themselves free of ice."

The Wolf growled impatiently. "Time is short, Faerie. Say what you have come to say. Lone Mountain beckons, and I must run."

The Faerie's eyes suddenly flashed with wisps of red and her light blazed around Polaris, who was driven to his belly. He shut his eyes and turned his head away. Her voice was like ice. "The time for running is past, Land Crow. Listen and be still. What patience is left in me wavers." Her light diminished a little, and her voice softened again. The Wolf blinked and peered up at her.

"I am Ainafare of the Tuatha De Danann. First Light, I am called." Here she paused. "I bear news from Lone Mountain. It was I who sent word to you of the shadow-walker. By the look of you, it is news you have received." As she spoke a sorrow entered her voice that turned in the Wolf's heart. He closed his eyes a moment, and his breath seeped out in a long sigh. *I have failed. I am too late.* Hope grew cold in him, and he sat quietly and listened. As Ainafare began to speak she spread her arms wide, and the Spruce trees grew tall, obscuring the light of the night sky. Her own strange, white light crept among the branches and coaxed long, thin wisps of green Lichen to life. These undulated out of their tangled webs and wove together in the air above her. The gossamer threads moved slowly and strangely, as though waving in the currents of a river. As the Faerie began her tale the strands of Lichen bent and writhed with her words, making the shapes of trees and mountains and animals. In this way they played out her story as she spoke. Polaris sat mesmerized, watching and listening.

"It is as I have said. I bear word from Lone Mountain — from your den. But I see how you ache for news of your mate. Aurora is well, Land Crow. She awaits your return, as do four new pups."

Polaris' breath escaped and his eyes grew gentle as the Lichen shaped itself into Aurora's familiar silhouette. The green strands arched over to show that she stood guard at the entry to their den, and four fluffy little Lichen pups bounded in slow motion out of the dark entrance to play at her paws.

"But that is not the story I have come to tell you." Ainafare waved a hand. The Lichen wavered, and Aurora's image was lost. New shapes began to materialize, echoing Ainafare's words as she continued. "I too, came to Driftwood River, Land Crow. I have followed the shadow-walker since the first breath of Spring — over hill and dale, across rivers and mountains, where he wound his path in great circles for fear that I persued. He was stealthy then, but still he left a bitter scent upon the Spring. This I followed carefully, though it cloaked itself in shadows and spiralled upon the wind. I tracked him through day and twilight without rest. He gave no respite, stopping only occasionally to hunt; such is the nature of his hunger. As we travelled, his skill grew. Sometimes he was lost to me, but always I found a dim trace of him and followed, until his craft grew beyond my own, and I could scent him no longer amidst the perfumes of Spring. But I knew he sought the yearling, so it was then I searched for the one called Moshee. I found him and his mother in the company of Wolves from Lone Mountain. I picked up your trail at Berry River and found you skirting the Porcupine, heading west. I followed far behind and watched as two black Crows tracked you, flying high to shroud themselves in the sun. When you came to Driftwood River I was nearby, seeking my quarry. But it was you, Land Crow, who sniffed him out, hidden beneath the stones. You have tasted the stink and the coldness of his hunger."

Her voice faltered for a moment. "You have seen his eyes. You have guessed why I hunt him." The Faerie paused as a flicker of red flame gathered in her eyes and welled. "The wind was still when he crept from his hiding spot, and though he ranged darkly, the stink of his breath hung lightly upon the motionless air. In this way, using all my craft, I tracked him slowly and with great difficulty. He moved in wide circles across the land, fearing that I followed. He circled carefully south past Choho Hill and then on toward Sharp Mountain.

"On the second day I began to close on him and his trail zigzagged in a kind of panic. Just as I began to draw near, the wind came up and scattered his stink across the foothills. By then it mattered little, for though his trail was lost to me, I had seen that his wandering route veered west. I knew then that he made for Lone Mountain."

The Lichen swirled and changed and molded into the shapes of the things Ainafare spoke of. "It was on that second day that I stopped a Messenger Hare and sent forth word to you in the north. And it was then that I too, struck out for Lone Mountain, hoping to encounter my prey there, before his strength could grow further."

The Faerie paused and looked up toward the sky, which was obscured by the Lichen and Spruce, and by the strange glow of her light. "The clouds gather," she said plainly. "The rain has come." Raindrops began to patter through the trees. It fell thin and cold and dampened the Wolf's thick, black fur. Ainafare's glow cast a strange halo in the rainfall, but she, herself, was untouched by the water.

Polaris blinked the rain from his eyes and spoke quietly. "The shadow-walker follows the yearling. We know he seeks the Breschuvine. But why should he make for our den? Why turn south when Moshee travels north? What could he hope to find at Lone Mountain?"

"He is more than he was. His hunger grows like a madness in him and little room is left for patience." Here the Faerie paused. "He scented the she-Wolf Tundra at Driftwood River, as she stood her ground with you and your mate. There the young Wolf, made foolish with bravery, peered into the shadow-walker's eyes. And can you guess what she saw there, Land Crow?"

Polaris hung his head.

"Look at me, Wolf."

He raised his muzzle slowly.

"She saw eyes, frost-white as a Faerie's. Eyes like my own."

Silence passed between them as the Wolf considered her words.

"But you have seen them too, Land Crow. You already know how his craft has grown. You have guessed at what cost." "We saw that you hunted him." His voice was quiet. "Aurora feared it might be so. I am sorry for you, Ainafare."

"Save your pity, Wolf. You will have need of it." Ainafare's light flickered. "The she-Wolf, Tundra befriended the young Caribou. When she met the shadow-walker's eyes he knew at once that she had knowledge of Moshee, and of the Breschuvine. That is why he made for Lone Mountain. He was seeking a shorter path to his goal. He went there seeking her knowledge. He went there to consume her."

This alarmed the big Wolf. "What news from Lone Mountain, Faerie?" Polaris growled. "Speak to me, or I must run."

The Lichen gathered around the Wolf and the Faerie, suspended in her light, jeweled and dripping with rain.

"The north is awake with whispering. With stories of a Wolf who has out-flown you, Land Crow."

Polaris whispered his name. "Mist."

"He passed south over the land like a grey wind, to the Porcupine. He is stronger than you, Polaris, but he is still young and untested. Desperate to reach his mate he refused to stop. Though his belly twisted, and all his instincts bent his mind to the hunt, his heart ached for the she-Wolf, and he would not turn from his path. He ran as no Wolf has ever run before him. He very nearly ran to his doom but for the Root Trolls that rescued him on the banks of the Porcupine River."

The green Lichen shifted into a circle of Root Trolls that moved slowly around Mist, who lay prone, floating in the rain-filled air above the Faerie and the Wolf. "Time was lost, but you must not fault him for it. Though he can be impetuous, and his mood as sour as standing water, his heart burns as bright as the Summer sun for her. He could see nothing but the land that lay between him and his mate, and so he sought to swallow up the distance with his broad paws and long legs. Even you, before you were burdened by the seasons, could not have reached Choho Hill more quickly, mighty Polaris."

The black Wolf stared blankly at the Faerie. "Mighty no longer."

"Did I not counsel you to save your pity? You will have need of it." The Faerie waved an arm through the air and the wet Lichen shifted. "Aurora and Tundra left you at Driftwood Valley. They passed easily across the Porcupine and circled safely around Choho territory to Lone Mountain. There, Aurora had her litter, Land Crow, and Tundra whelped one black female and two grey male pups. Like all mothers she was filled with their light." Here the Faerie faltered and turned her gaze away for a moment before continuing. "Your packmates rejoiced. For it is not often that food is plentiful and the Second Stars may breed. Soon all the pups' bright eyes were open and they stumbled like little Bears into the light. There was much play under the widening sky."

Polaris allowed himself a gentle tail-wag.

"But Wolf-pups grow like Fireweed, and always their bellies cry out for more. So the pack was often set to the hunt by your mate. And when they ranged out upon the land seeking prey, only Aurora and Tundra remained by their dens. So it was when the shadow-walker came." The rain intensified and the Faerie's light seemed to dim.

Watching the Lichen, the black Wolf rose onto his long legs as though ready to spring away. He huffed a deep breath and bared his teeth. The damp hair on his back stood up.

"Dark clouds rolled in from the west. An unnatural fog drifted over Lone Mountain. Aurora was curled in her den when the one called Grotto came creeping up the slopes with all his craft. But Tundra knew his stink from Driftwood River and nudged her pups into shelter before she rose up in front of her den to meet him. Filled with a mother's fearlessness, she stood her ground and howled for her pack. It was the she-Wolf's call that I heard through the fog, and so I raced for Lone Mountain. When I came upon them, Aurora, newly roused, stood at the entrance of her den, teeth bared and hackles raised. Tundra, filled with the light of her pups, made reckless by love and fear and rage, charged down the slope at the shadow-walker, white fangs glinting as though she meant to haul him down. I have not seen such bravery in an age. Such fearlessness."

Polaris turned in circles and growled deep and low as he watched the mysterious Lichen. He listened to the Faerie as the rain fell heavily through the spruce.

"But he has grown, Land Crow." Ainafare's voice softened. "He fell upon her as though she was but a pup." The Faerie seemed to speak to herself. "With such strength. With such speed as I have not seen. In only a moment her light was gone from the World."

The big Wolf growled at Ainafare. "And what of Aurora? What of our pack? Why did you do nothing, Faerie? Are you not Tuatha De Danann?"

"I came too late, First Star. Aurora, wise with her seasons, stood guard between the two dens as the shadow-walker slouched over the fallen she-Wolf. She barked at Tundra's pups to retreat when they came to the mouth of the den to look for their mother. There, as I drew near to Aurora with my light, she made ready to stand her ground to the last, and I with her. But we were not alone in hearing Tundra's call. Laboured howls rose through the fog as Mist arrived, too late, with your brother, Timber, and a war pack from Choho. Eight menacing Wolves and a Faerie stood before the one called Grotto." She paused. "And still he rose slowly, undaunted, from the fallen she-Wolf and fixed us with his stare through the haze. He seemed to waver like a shadow as wisps of fog wreathed him. The others did not yet know the she-Wolf had fallen, that she was laid out on the ground behind the bulk of the shadow-walker. Mist looked to Aurora, and his gold eyes began to search desperately for his mate. It was then that Grotto let loose a growl as I have not heard from Wolf or Bear. He lunged forward a little through the fog, and in that moment, his eyes were plain to all of us. Frost-white, but for a lightning streak of green."

Polaris hung his head low, as though he could not stand to hear any more. Rain dripped from his fur.

The Faerie looked softly upon the Wolf. "It was too much for Mist to bear, and he charged forward with the war pack. But the shadow-walker, unwilling to test his new strength against eight Wolves and a Faerie, snarled and turned, quick as an Ermine, and slipped away into the fog. His scent scattered on the fog, and though Timber and the Choho Pack ran forward into the haze, they could not track him. Even I, with all my light and all my craft, could find no trace of the one called Grotto. He ranges darkly, Land Crow. It was as though he had never set claw upon Lone Mountain." Ainafare drifted closer to the big Wolf, whose head still hung low. "Do you hear me, Wolf?"

Polaris' voice was gruff and low. "I hear you, Faerie. Finish your tale."

"I was first to return to the dens. There I found Aurora gathering all of the pups into a single burrow. A little way down the mountain stood Mist, still as stone, over the broken body and bloodied fur of his mate. He stood that way as his packmates returned from hunting, too late to answer Tundra's call. He stood that way as the Choho Wolves, unable to track the shadow-walker, drifted back out of the fog to stand in a semicircle around him. He stood that way when gentle Aurora padded close and licked his muzzle, though he seemed not to notice her. He stood that way as the fog broke, and the pale moon rose, and the sun burned low in the sky. But at last, as all the others lay watching, he left her and climbed silently to the big rock atop Lone Mountain. Then at last it came; the howling of Mist.

Long and high and mournful, until it filled all the northern sky." She paused here as the Lichen writhed.

"I am Tuatha De Danann, Land Crow. Much have I seen, and still it stung me to hear his pain ring out. I know something of his loss. I cannot howl, but I wished to. I wished to call out into the wind and the wild for some answer to this darkness. I was comforted when the Choho and Lone Mountain Packs raised their voices and howled in unison. If ever you were uncertain that another Wolf would rise from your long shadow, ready to become First Star — think no more on it. He has risen."

The big black Wolf raised his head slowly. "It is not how I wished it to come to pass — not with darkness in his heart."

"And what of the Cargoth, Land Crow? Is there not a shadow upon us all?"

Polaris looked at her. "That is why I have answered the Binder's call. It is why we have sacrificed so much to guard the yearling, Moshee. Why all our hope is in him. We, all of us, are bound and bent against our nature because we fear the Cargoth and their reckless slumber. But we did not think the cost would be so high."

"The cost will grow dearer still. And where is the yearling called Moshee? Why is he without his company of Wolves?"

"I turned south at Babbage River. The Eagle, Windshim and her mate, Aquila, watch over the yearling while they await Blinn."

"And what of Blinn? Where is the meddling Gnome now?"

"Who can say for certain? When last we saw him he made ready to range north and east. He spoke of Rat River but said little else. He does not answer to Wolves, not even Polaris."

Ainafare seemed to consider this. With a wave of her arm the Lichen retreated back into the branches of the Spruce trees where it once again hung in stillness. Grey light filtered down through the branches with the rain. "Go then, Polaris, Land Crow. Make for Lone Mountain. Your pack has need of its First Star. I will seek out the Eye of the North that he might help me find my quarry."

The Wolf padded several steps into the Spruce trees before he stopped and turned. "Thank you, Ainafare, First Light. You are Tuatha De Danann, and it is known to me that you did not need to seek me out — to break from your path to bear this dark tale — to ease my heart with news of Aurora. If you hunt the shadow-walker, call upon us, and we will answer. He is beyond us, but teach us to scent him, and we will pursue him through seasons without end so that he may never again sleep or feed."

The Faerie drifted close to Polaris. "There is something I have not told you, Wolf. Before I departed your dens to seek you out, I visited your Second Star atop Lone Mountain. There, in his season of darkness, I came to him with my light, as I come to you now." The Faerie's light began to grow as she pressed her little palm to the big Wolf's muzzle. "Like this, I pressed my hand to his face and broke faith with Rahtrum and my kind." Now her light blazed, and the Wolf's eyes narrowed. "These words I spoke to him." Her voice grew hard and cold. "Hear me, Mist, Grey-mane. We are bound by loss, you and I. It is true the shadow-walker has grown — that he is more than he was — that he is beyond our craft." A strange red flame flickered for a moment over the Faerie and lingered in her eyes. "But know this; I will kill him. I will hunt him across the world, and I will watch as he dies." And then her light went out.

Polaris blinked his eyes and shook his black mane. Ainafare was gone. The big Wolf turned slowly and padded between the Spruce trees. He peered back once and then sprang away for Lone Mountain.

chapter 15

The Warble and The Nosebot

JULY

The warmth of the high Arctic Summer brought with it an abundance of food for the herd. Young Willow and white, fluffy Cottonsedge blossomed everywhere. But the yellow sun and wide, blue skies also brought a new misery for the Porcupine Caribou: flies.

The Mosquitoes came like a grey mist across the plains, accompanied by the horror of the Warble and Nosebot Flies. The Caribou gathered together by their thousands for shelter and to seek out the wind. They stampeded in fits of anxiety, running this way and that and finally into the low hills. They were made mad by the Botflies that assailed their noses. There the Botflies released larvae that crawled deep into the poor animals' nostrils to stay warm and feed on mucous during the Winter, until being sneezed out in the Spring. The Caribou were driven to panic by the buzzing of the Warble Flies that dove from the air in an attempt to lay their egg packets on the hair of the Caribou's legs and bellies. These eggs then hatched into larvae that burrowed into the warm tissue of their hosts, tunnelling painfully through the flesh to their spines, where they carved holes through the afflicted animals' backs to reach the air. So the Caribou ran and twitched and shook and gathered together, desperate in their search for cool, strong winds that swept up from the ice floes out at sea. These gusts of cold salt-wind helped to clear the Flies from the air around the herd and provided the weary animals with a chance to graze.

Bree pushed her little snout up into the wind and blinked her big, wet eyes. "I'm hungry." She had grown a little in the time since they had left the Calving Grounds, and she was sure upon her hooves. The little calf was pressed close between Bou and Taiga, desperate for relief from the Flies. They stood together at the edge of the great herd, a sea of Caribou stretched over the Buckland Foothills. They had tried to take their turn sheltering deep at the centre of the herd as it moved erratically across the land, but the other Caribou, unsettled by Moshee and the two Golden Eagles circling relentlessly above, always shunned them. The torturous buzz of the insects and the incessant movements of the herd made grazing difficult for little Bree, and she was becoming tired and frustrated.

"Why can't we leave this place? Why can't we go away and leave these Flies?" She stamped her small hooves.

Taiga looked softly at her new calf. "There is much food here, Bree. You must eat all you can. The Summer is short and the Autumn shorter still. Soon the Flies will be gone and we will turn south. Then the Winter will spread her arms wide, and you will have your first taste of snow."

"I hope snow is better than Flies."

The old Caribou rubbed her muzzle against Bree's flank. "When there are Flies, there is much food. When there is snow, food is more difficult to find. Who can say which is better? Perhaps you should ask your brother what he prefers."

The little calf stared at Bou, who had wandered a short way away from them to stand alone on a small, rocky rise. He stood still and alert, staring into the southeast, down a long slope that ended in a creased valley. A cloud of Flies circled his head and haunches but never seemed to land. He remained strangely unaware and unperturbed by the insects. Bree shook her head and huffed Flies from her nostrils. "I don't think the Flies bother him at all."

Twitching her ears, Taiga watched the young bull carefully. *I believe you are right, Little One. He moves with us and with the herd, but the Flies will not touch him.* She looked up into the sky to watch mighty Windshim circling with her mate, Aquila. *It is no wonder the other Caribou turn away and whisper. He grows more different from us with every season.*

Suddenly Bou turned to his mother and sister. "They are coming!" A piercing call rang out from Windshim above. The sound sent a nervous shuffle through the herd. A few cows began to stampede a short distance and the rest followed. Bou paid no attention to the movements of the herd. He returned his gaze to the southeast and watched intently.

Bree bounded to his side to look on with him. She peered in the direction her brother was looking as carefully as she could. "Who's coming?" she asked, as Taiga wandered to her side.

Bou spoke slowly. "It is Blinn, Eye of the North. He makes straight for us, and there is a Faerie with him."

"What's a Blinn? What's a Faerie? Mother, what is he talking about? I don't see anything!"

Taiga stared down the long slope and blinked. "Nor do I. We cannot see as Bou does. His eyes are different from ours. But we will know soon enough."

Bree looked up at her brother and then again into the southeast. She shook her head and ears and shivered the skin on her haunches in an effort to clear the Flies away, but she did not take her eyes off the slope, hoping to catch a glimpse of what Bou could see. Her eyes strained against the bright sky until Bou said, "They are here." She saw the Gnome first and her eyes widened. His tawny, grey coat and bushy tail suddenly moved among the rocky scree, his black eyes glinting in the sun. It was as though he wasn't there, and then he was, only a few strides from where Bou stood, moving deftly between the Crowberry and Shrub Birch.

For a moment Bree forgot the Mosquitoes buzzing around her. She cocked her head and watched as the Gnome approached Bou. Then she saw the Faerie. It moved silently in the air above the Gnome, cast in a strange white glow that shimmered in the sunlight. Bree gasped, scrambled backward behind Taiga, and then peeked out from behind the cow, full of wonder. As they did with Bou, the Flies circled the Gnome but never landed. The Flies did not approach the Faerie at all, and the globe of luminous air that surrounded her remained clear and bright.

The Gnome stood up on his rear legs in front of Bou, his keen black eyes wide and searching. But the Faerie hovered in the air at a little distance and would come no closer. The Gnome seemed to pay her no attention.

"It is plain you are no longer a yearling, Moshee," the Gnome said playfully. "The Summer Cottongrass has been kind to you. The rut will call to you early."

"Where have you been, Blinn?" Bou was full of concern. "I have not seen you since we crossed the Peel River. It has been two moons since news reached us that the shadow-walker made for Lone Mountain. We have had no news of our friends, the Wolves."

Blinn looked quietly into the young bull's eyes for a moment, and then, ignoring Bou's questions, turned to his mother. "You must be Taiga. It is good, at last, to make the acquaintance of the mother of Moshee. I regret it could not be sooner. Time was short upon the Peel River, and I am sorry I could not pause to ease your worry. I left that to my companion." The Gnome looked over his shoulder at the Faerie, but she would not acknowledge him. She hovered in the air indifferently, silently, her light slightly dimmer, her arms crossed, her frost-white eyes distant and unblinking. "Forgive her, she is not herself," he said.

Taiga rolled her head to one side, stared at the Faerie, and blinked her eyes as though struggling to remember. "First Light she is called. She was there, at the Peel...and again when the Crows came at Driftwood River."

Blinn's eyes widened. "It is well you remember, Taiga. What you say is true. She is called Ainafare, First Light by the Tuatha De

Danann." He peered again over his shoulder, but the Faerie remained oblivious. "It is as I say, there is a weight upon her, and she is not as she was. Forgive her." Now the Gnome leaned to one side to look around Taiga's flank. "And who is this who hides behind her mother's legs, like a Fox among the Spruce?"

The two older Caribou both looked back at the little yearling. She crept forward a little. "My name is Bree."

"It is well to meet you, Bree, sister of Moshee."

The little Caribou was confused. "Who's Moshee?"

Blinn cocked his head, and his tail twitched. "Your brother, Bou is called Moshee by us, Little One."

"Why?"

"It is the name given to him by Rahtrum." The Gnome now approached Bree slowly, his mesmerizing black eyes wide and kind.

"Who's Rahtrum?"

Blinn placed his paws on either side of the little yearling's muzzle and stared deeply into her eyes. "Answers will come in time, Bree, daughter of Taiga, yearling of the Porcupine Caribou herd." The little Caribou nodded her head quietly, and Blinn left to stand again before the young bull.

"You seek news of the Wolves of Lone Mountain, Moshee. You wish for light when I bear only shadows. Time is short, so I will give what little light I can. In these seasons of plenty the Lone Mountain Pack is grown stronger by seven new pups."

Bou blinked and sighed. "And Tundra? Her cubs are well?"

"Three she whelped, Moshee. One black female and two grey

male pups. All are well and safe."

"Will we go to see the pups?" Bou looked at Blinn and then his mother. "When the Autumn takes the Summer into her arms, and we turn south again? Will Tundra come to guard us, with Mist and Polaris and Aurora?"

Blinn stood quietly a moment.

Bou implored. "When we've found the Breschuvine, surely then we can visit Lone Mountain?"

"Tundra has fallen, Moshee."

"What?" The young bull stared at the Gnome. "What do you mean?"

"Tundra has fallen." The Gnome repeated softly. "Struck down by the shadow-walker as she defended her den."

"I don't understand. Surely Mist — he ran for Choho territory, for a war pack to defend Lone Mountain!"

"And he ran as no Wolf ever has, Moshee, but the shadow-walker was before him by the breadth of a twig. Tundra is no more."

Bou hung his head low. "I don't understand why this is happening." A tide of clouds swept up from the sea and crossed the sun.

"The shadow-walker would have the Breschuvine for himself. I have ranged far and wide to learn what I can of the one called Grotto. The Crows that track you are in his service. We must be wary. The Cargoth cast their long shadows, but now another darkness moves in the north. The danger is real, Moshee."

Bree watched her brother as the young Caribou turned from Blinn and strode away to watch the cloud-shadows skirt the long valley and race along the green and grey slopes before he turned again to face them. "Then let us make for the Breschuvine now. Tell us the way, Blinn."

Taiga stepped forward. "We cannot leave the foothills. The Sedges are in bloom, and we must have our fill before the herd turns south to the mountains. Your sister is still weak, and the Flies only hinder her. She must grow fat if she is to survive the Winter."

Bou continued looking at the Gnome. "Where is the Breschuvine?"

"For everything a season."

Bou huffed suddenly and charged at Blinn. He seemed to grow broader and taller as he moved. Small stones scattered as the Caribou stopped before the Gnome, who stood his ground and watched Bou with great interest. Bree scrambled behind her mother. A sliver of light broke through the new clouds and for a moment the young bull cast a long shadow. "Enough of your riddles, Blinn!" His voice was deeper. "How will we seek the Breschuvine, if you will not tell us where it grows?"

The Gnome stood still and met Bou's stare. The Faerie glanced down curiously at the Caribou.

The young bull huffed as he looked into Blinn's black eyes. As Bree watched, her brother hung his head low and seemed to shrink to his normal size.

"We are all saddened, Moshee."

"She was my friend," The young bull said simply, and then he turned to wander alone up the slope.

Bree left her mother's side and followed behind her brother. Bou stopped and turned to look at the yearling, and she paused too. He looked down the slope at Taiga and Blinn then turned again and climbed high into the foothills. Bree trotted along behind him as quietly as she could and then, carefully, stood closer and closer to him, until she was pressed against his flank.

Taiga turned to the Gnome. "The Flies do not assail him. He is not like other Caribou. She stands close to him to be free of them, but still they beset her."

The Gnome looked up the slope at the young bull standing in the wind with Bree at his side. "No, he is not like other Caribou, Taiga. Like the shadow-walker, he is becoming more than he was."

The yellow-orange sun circled the strange little group. Bree, her mother, and Bou were on their own now, standing apart from the rest of the Caribou. The strange company that Taiga and her offspring kept had spooked the herd. Though Blinn would not allow the other Caribou to see him, Ainafare hung silent in the air and seemed not to care who took notice. A few of the calves from the herd were curious and wandered away from their cows to sniff at the air in the direction of the odd little band, but the shadows of Eagles and buzzing Flies always chased them back to the safety of the herd.

Bree was miserable. Separated from the other Caribou, she could find little shelter from the Flies when the wind did not blow, no matter how close to Bou she tried to stand. Since the arrival of Blinn and Ainafare her brother seemed distant and distracted. From time to time he spoke with the Gnome, who was kind to Bree and eased her fear with his wide, black eyes whenever the great Eagle descended to perch on a rock and keep council with him and her brother.

Bree was fascinated by the strange beauty of the Faerie. When she asked Blinn about Ainafare, she was amazed to hear that the Tuatha De Danann, though winged and very tiny, were in form and feature very much like the Cargoth.

"Are they kin, like the Eagle and the Crow?" the yearling asked.

The Gnome's eyes brightened and he reached up to scratch the calf's chin. "We are all of us kin."

At least once every day Bree wandered furtively in the Faerie's direction. Grazing quietly until she stood, blinking and twitching in a cloud of Mosquitoes, Warbles, and Botflies beneath the strange little figure that hovered effortlessly in the air. Bree looked up with wonder at the tiny white Faerie and tried to speak with her.

"Hi. My name is Bree. That's my brother, Bou." But always the Faerie remained silent and motionless. So each day the little yearling tried again.

"I wish I could fly."

"Do you like snow?"

"How come you don't eat?"

"I don't think I like Flies very much."

But each time the Faerie only stared quietly into the distance until Bree could no longer keep still, and the tormenting Flies chased her away.

Taiga gently and constantly encouraged Bree to eat. The yearling did as her mother instructed and foraged as best she could when the wind whistled across the foothills. But always the winds would falter, and the Flies came again to chase her. It was agonizing. She ran in circles around Taiga and her brother, and sometimes she kicked and bucked. As the days passed she began to feel strange, and a weakness crept into her little legs. She huffed and sneezed, and the skin on her back ached and itched.

On the sixth day after the arrival of Blinn and Ainafare, the Eagle called Windshim circled down out of the grey sky and alighted on a stone. She spoke at length with the Gnome, constantly turning her head this way and that as her gold eyes searched the horizon. Bree watched the Eagle nervously. She stared in awe at Windshim's sharp, black-tipped yellow bill, golden feathers, and powerful black talons. Her brother stood a little way uphill. He was disinterested in another visit from the Eagle, but Bree, who was at once frightened of the Raptor and immensely curious, hung on to Windshim's every word.

"...We have scouted for the meddling Crows called Hugin and Munin. If they are here, then they are well hidden. Crows are plentiful on the plains and in the foothills this season. They seek out the many spoils left by Bear, White Wolf, Fox, and Eagle. The Tulugaq Murder surrounds us, but they are insolent and will not speak to us. Be wary. Any among them could be those you seek."

Bree watched as Blinn considered the Eagle's words, then leaned in close and whispered something to the big Raptor that the calf could not hear. The Gnome then turned from the Eagle and moved gracefully over the rocky ground on all fours toward Bou. Windshim spread her great wings, called out with her high-pitched voice, and strode upon the wind into the sky. Aquila, hearing his mate's cry, circled wide and flew at her side as they turned together and disappeared into the distance. Bree watched them go, then grunted out of frustration and rubbed against her mother. The skin on her sides and back was sore and maddeningly itchy, and it seemed almost to move on its own. Her little body felt wobbly, her nose felt strange, and she huffed and sneezed. Still she did her best to forage at her mother's side as the Gnome stood a little way uphill with her brother. Together Bree and Taiga tore at the young Willows with their teeth and occasionally raised their heads to watch Bou and Blinn. The young bull seemed to listen intently as the Gnome spoke. Bree turned to look at Ainafare. The Faerie still hovered in the air, perfectly still but for her wings, her arms folded, her white eyes staring into the distance. The little yearling did not understand how the Faerie could remain in one place for so long. She wondered if, perhaps, Faeries could fly while they slept.

The next day, Bou came to Taiga and Bree and said simply, "It is time. We will turn west tomorrow and make for the Firth River Valley."

Taiga looked at Bree with concern. "But it is too early."

"The way is long, and we must begin," he said simply.

His mother huffed. "Where is Blinn?"

"He is gone."

"Where?"

"I do not know. He said only that the darkness deepens in the north, and that he must leave us to seek counsel with Rahtrum."

Taiga stared up at the sky. "And the Eagles?"

"He has sent the Eagles to circle south and keep watch with their keen eyes for the shadow-walker — to learn where he ranges."

Bou looked at the ground. "It is a slim hope."

"Then who will watch over us?"

Bree saw her brother's gaze shift. She turned her head along with Taiga to look over her shoulder. There, hovering silently where she had been for seven days, was Ainafare.

"She will watch over us?" her mother asked. "A Faerie, who does not move and who will not speak to us? How can you be sure that she will?"

Bree continued to stare at Ainafare as her brother answered.

"Blinn says there is a weight upon her; that we must not mistake her silence for disinterest. Wherever we go, she will travel with us."

"She is no company of Wolves." Taiga huffed.

"I think she's beautiful," Bree said.

Taiga ignored the yearling. "Look at your sister, Bou. See the pestilence that is upon her. Standing alone as we have without the herd, the wind coming and going, she has had no escape from the Flies. She has not eaten as she should have. Her nose is home to

Botfly. Her skin fairly moves with the young of the Warble. She is weak. See how her legs tremble?"

The little calf looked down at her own legs. *That's strange,* she thought, *my legs are trembling.* Though she was tired, she had taken no notice of her legs because her skin was sore all over.

Her brother considered her for a moment with a gentle look. "I must turn west tomorrow, mother. I am bound. The Breschuvine will bloom again in the first breath of Winter. Let me go alone, if I must. If I am late, all is lost. Tundra will have fallen for nothing."

"We will go together. But she cannot go as she is. She will not make it out of the coastal mountains."

"I can do it, Mother," Bree implored.

Her brother nudged her gently. "Of course you can, Bree. We will help you." He looked up at the Faerie and said quietly. "Make ready. Tomorrow we turn west."

That evening Bree rested beside her mother on the stony ground and watched as her brother went to stand before Ainafare. He was silhouetted by the sun as it burned low and orange. She could not hear what Bou said to the Faerie, but Ainafare did not appear to answer or to move. After a time her brother turned slowly and strode away. The little calf shivered and watched the Faerie glowing softly as the Warble larvae tunnelled beneath her skin.

The next day Taiga urged Bree to eat her fill. She foraged as best she could, though she felt weak and sore and had begun to notice that her legs were shaking again. Still, she was excited to be leaving the foothills, and as she had done every day since the

Faerie's arrival, Bree slowly made her way to where Ainafare hung effortlessly in the air. When at last she stood just below the Faerie, she peered up at the tiny white figure and shook her head to try and clear the Flies from her muzzle. She tried to ask Ainafare a question, but instead, she sneezed, and her legs buckled beneath her. The little Caribou crumpled to the ground.

As Bree blinked her eyes and sneezed again, something amazing happened. The Faerie moved. She descended until she hovered just in front of Bree. The yearling's eyes widened, and for a moment she forgot how her body ached. She marvelled at Ainafare's long, white legs and slender arms; her little paws, each with five slender fingers, and her tiny feet, each with five little toes. The Caribou could not tell where the little creature's light came from. It seemed at once all about her and within her. As Bree looked on in wonder, she heard the clicking of her brother's and mother's hooves drawing near, and then Bou's voice.

"Do you see how she suffers, Ainafare?"

To Bree's amazement, the Faerie spoke. Her voice was firm and cool. "Is it not the way of Caribou to suffer the Warble and the Nosebot?"

"Not like this," her brother replied. "Not to stand apart from the herd in the morning of her first year, assailed by Flies. We are cast out because of the company we keep."

"Is it my fault that she suffers as she does? That is deep snow you tread through, Caribou."

"Yours in part."

"In part? Or wholly? None may see the Gnome, but whom he chooses, and the Eagles — they are departed."

"You spook the herd. They will not come near while you hang in the air. Though you could hide yourself as Blinn did. She would have shelter otherwise."

Now the Faerie's eyes glowed brighter. "It is *your* company she keeps, Moshee. It is *your* company I keep, though I wish a thousand times each day it were not so."

"Then why do you —"

"Enough!" The Faerie glowed brighter. "Do you remember the words you spoke to me beneath the evening sun?"

"I do."

"And you will be bound by them?"

Bou paused a moment before responding. "I will."

"Then you are bound to me, Moshee. There will come a time when I call upon you, and you will answer me first; before your kin, before the meddling Gnome, before even Rahtrum himself, you will answer me first."

"Then I am bound. It is done."

The Faerie looked deep into Bree's wide eyes and with surprising gentleness said to her, "Close your dark eyes, Little One. Close them tight. Think of the Summer sun, warm breezes, and the wide Coastal Plains. You will feel better soon, but first..." Ainafare placed her little palm on the calf's muzzle, "...there will be pain." A pulse of white light enveloped the yearling, momentarily blinding Taiga and Bou.

It came and went in a flash but the Faerie's light seemed to cling to the hairs of Bree's coat and run up and down her back. The light felt warm as it washed over her body and the Caribou's eyes flickered open. Ainafare had descended to the rocky gravel in front of Bree.

"It feels warm. It feels wonderful," the calf whispered.

The Faerie knelt gracefully upon one knee in the scree, her wings strangely still. She carefully placed a palm to the ground, and as she did so, she looked up at Bree once more and said, "It will pass, yearling. Brace yourself."

Then Bree felt the first stab of pain, like a dozen black Flies biting her in one place. Then another and another. She squeezed her eyes shut and the pain spread along her back, sides, belly, and legs. Her breathing grew heavy, and in a panic she tried to stand, but her legs would not move from where they had collapsed. She shook and grunted and mewled where she lay. Her skin seemed alive, and as her mother and brother looked on, two thousand Warble larvae burrowed and chewed their way, one by one, to the surface of her flesh and burst through her skin. As each one surfaced, it came in contact with the Faerie glow that still clung to Bree's coat and erupted into a soft white flame. They fell, each one wriggling and burning to the ground, leaving small, round holes in Bree's skin that bled and oozed. Soon Bree was crying out so loudly that the Caribou in the valley below stopped grazing, raised their heads, and sniffed the air.

Bou hovered over his sister, terrified. "What have you done?"

The Faerie ignored the young bull and, with her hand pressed firmly to the ground, whispered a soft incantation. When she was done, she stood and took again to her wings. She hovered before the yearling's nose, and moving one arm in an arc, cast Spring Dust into the calf's labouring nostrils.

Through the pain Bree felt a warm sensation spreading in her muzzle, but soon it moved down into her throat, and she felt as though she couldn't breathe. She convulsed several times, and a great sneeze welled up in her. She huffed and sneezed, and a ball of mucous filled with Nosebot larvae was expelled onto the ground. The little Caribou stared at it through half open eyes, her body in anguish, her breathing shallow and difficult. She watched as Ainafare waved an arm, and each Nosebot larva was shrivelled and consumed by gossamer white flames. She seemed to hear her mother calling out, "She will die! What have you done?" But a fog was upon her, and weakness crept through her little body. As Bree lay her head down, the gravel where the Faerie had knelt seemed to stir and move. A strange creature, gnarled like the roots of a tree, scattered pebbles in every direction as it climbed out of the rocky ground before her. *I must be asleep and dreaming*, she thought, before the pain closed in upon her, and everything was dark.

chapter 16

Hugin & Munin

JULY

Hugin rasped and barked at the young Crow from the Tulugaq Murder. The fledgling chortled back at him and took to wing.

"We are their guests, Hugin. Do not antagonize them." Munin pleaded. "They are the only reason we have not been plucked from the sky by Windshim or her mate."

"Do you not see how they whisper, Munin? Word has travelled from branch to tree, on the wind, of two Crows who fly in service of the shadow-walker. They shelter us because they fear us," Hugin cooed and trilled.

A gust of wind ruffled Munin's feathers as she stared up the foothills to where the Caribou called Moshee grazed with his mother and sister. All three of them were now guarded by an unsleeping, unmoving Faerie and two Golden Eagles that seemed to circle endlessly above. "These Crows do not fear us, Hugin. The shadow-walker ranges darkly, and all the north now whispers and trembles. These Crows hide us because they fear Grotto. They too, know they cannot fly forever. Eventually they must come to land."

Hugin chortled dismissively. "What is the difference? They shelter us all the same."

Munin stared at him. "You are right, Hugin. There is no difference between us and these Crows we hide amidst. We all fear the shadow-walker." She turned to peer up the hill at the Caribou and the Faerie. "But I do not think that *they* fear him. And I am certain they do not fear us."

Hugin shifted from one foot to another. *Kek, kek.* "Why must you sulk, Munin? Has he not cached and shared his spoils with us? Have you forgotten how cruel the Winter was? We might have starved like the others. We serve him, and he will protect us." He, too, looked up at the hill. "They are fools if they are not afraid."

"Will he?"

"Will he what?" Hugin was exasperated.

"Will he protect us?" Munin warbled. "Go then. Fly, brave Crow, fly to the Caribou they call Moshee. He is just there, a cloud's breadth away. Demand of him the location of the Breschuvine as we did in the Driftwood River Valley. Go! Pay no mind to the Faerie or the Eagles. Tell them that the shadow-walker has sent you, and see if they shudder."

"What would you have me do, Munin?" He turned to look at her. "Abandon our purpose?"

Munin turned away, but Hugin continued, a new coldness in his song.

"Shall we return to our Murder? Beg our kin to take us back? They will tolerate us, but only out of fear. Or shall we join another Murder, where they too, brook our presence when, in truth, we are unwelcome? We are marked, Munin. He is in our thoughts as we are in his. Do you think he will just forget us? That he will not find us? That he cannot track us? *Ark!* What would you have me do?"

Munin sat still and silent in the wind for a few moments. "I do not know." She peered up at the great Golden Eagles who circled high upon the wind. "I only know that I do not want to be afraid anymore."

Hugin and Munin flew and roosted with the Tulugaq Murder, hidding within it. They kept their watch over the Caribou and the Faerie, always careful not to draw the keen eyes of the Raptors. But on the sixth day, after the Faerie arrived, they watched as Windshim came to ground to hold council. With whom she spoke, the Crows could not be sure. But when she was finished, she rose up into the sky and flew south like the wind, her mate, Aquila, on her wing.

"They fly south in search of the shadow-walker. He is hunted from the sky because none may track him upon the ground. It is as he said it would be," said Munin.

"Then we must keep our watch," Hugin replied. "We must know by what path the Caribou will travel and send word to the Fox."

"Why do we follow them, Hugin?"

Hugin stared at her. "That is a foolish question."

"No, it isn't. He is Grotto, the shadow-walker. Why does he not stalk his quarry himself, if he has the craft?"

Hugin puffed up his feathers. "I do not know his thoughts, Munin. But I know that as long as we do as he asks, he will keep us fat when the Winter spreads wide her arms."

Munin rattled at Hugin. "You do not know his thoughts. But you are certain he will be charitable when Winter comes?" She looked up into the foothills. "I think he fears the Tuatha De Danann."

Hugin chortled. "Nonsense. Why should he fear the Faeries? The Children of Light keep to themselves. They are long-lived and aloof. What notice will they take of the shadow-walker, or anything that transpires in the north?"

"You are a fool sometimes, Hugin. Think on it. Do you not remember his eyes when last we saw him near Driftwood River? You yourself remarked on it. 'Frost-white,' you called them."

Hugin blinked at her.

"Do you not remember the Faerie that rebuked us in the woods when we assailed the yearling? How easily she dismissed us with her light?" Munin spread her wings and cawed up at the hill where the Caribou were. "That is her, there, with the Caribou."

Hugin stared up to where the Faerie's clear, white light twinkled. "You cannot be sure."

"But I can. I have thought long on it. His eyes, his craft. Grotto has done something terrible, Hugin. He has broken his covenant with the Children of Danu."

"Think on what you are saying, Munin. Even Grotto would not, could not, do such a thing."

"He fears this Faerie because he has wronged her, and that is why he leaves us to track the Caribou in his stead. That is why he bids us seek out the Fox to set his trap."

Hugin ruffled his feathers in silence and considered Munin's words for a moment. "Do you know the mind of Grotto?" he asked. "You cannot be certain."

Ark, wok! "You are like the Cargoth, Hugin. Filled with hunger but asleep with your eyes firmly shut."

On the eighth day, the entire Tulugaq Murder clicked and gurgled nervously when there was a bright flash of light upon a nearby hillside. The Crows scattered into the sky and circled, made curious by the light. Hugin and Munin took this opportunity to circle with the others and to spy on Moshee and his kin. They saw the Faerie at work upon the yearling and heard her mewling in pain. They watched with great curiosity as the Faerie summoned a Root Troll out from the rocky scree. All of this they considered as they spiralled into a nearby valley and perched together in the low branches of a Spruce tree.

"The Faerie's craft is unlike anything I have seen," Munin clicked quietly.

Hugin agreed. "She is an elder of her kind and possessed of great skill. It is well for us."

"How is it well for us to have such an adversary? How can this serve us?"

"The yearling was feeble with Fly larvae," Hugin cooed. "The

Faerie has cured the calf and summoned a Root Troll to heal her wounds. When she awakens, she will be strong enough to travel. They ready themselves to leave the foothills. That is why the Eagles have departed — to watch for the shadow-walker. It is time. Moshee will turn south in search of the Breschuvine."

"Then it is as you have said," Munin sang quietly. "We must discover by what route he will travel."

Hugin clicked. "We will track them until we are certain. Then I will fly in search of the Fox."

Munin stared at Hugin and tilted her head. "Let us fly east," she cooed gently. "Let us leave this place together and follow the coast, past the mountains, across the great delta. Let us fly, Hugin. Let us fly east without rest before the sun is lost, and the dark, cruel Winter is upon us. Let us pass the plateaus, cross the stone lakes, go to the great inland sea. Are we not Crow? Let us fly!"

Hugin paused. "He will find us," he cawed softly.

"He will not!" Munin protested, her song rising. "He seeks the Breschuvine. Why would he care where two Crows roost?"

Hugin looked into her eyes. "If what you say about the Faerie is true —"

"Then you believe me?"

"If what you say is true, then we cannot know what craft the shadow-walker wields."

"Then let us try, Hugin. Let us leave this Caribou to wend his path and not tempt the Binder."

"The shadow-walker will find us."

Munin leapt closer to him and bobbed her head slowly. "But we must try."

"I cannot."

"Why, Hugin? Why will you not try?"

Ark, kek, kek! "Have you not looked upon him, Munin? I am afraid!"

Ark, wok! Hugin spread his black wings as he leapt into the air, and they cut the wind in whispers as he climbed into the broad sky.

Munin sat silently in the Spruce and watched him circle the hill where the Faerie's light shone.

chapter 17

The Gwich'in Faerie
AUGUST

Bou felt light as he watched Bree canter ahead of them on the age-old Caribou path. The worn trail wound its way steadily through the steep slopes of the barren Northern Mountains near the Firth River. Though Bree had buzzed for days with Root Troll blood and new strength, Taiga had insisted they move slowly and graze often so the little Caribou could fatten up. The red sun settled lower in the sky each night, and the first cold frosts of Autumn had cleared the insects from the air. The new relief from the Flies had lifted all of their spirits, save for Ainafare, who had not spoken again since saving the yearling's life. But this did not discourage Bree. She was content to trot along for hours beneath Ainafare and speak to the Faerie at length. The yearling seemed resigned to Ainafare's silence.

Bree had only a dim memory of her ordeal, and she was mesmerized by the story of the Root Troll, who was summoned forth by the Faerie and had risen out of the stony earth before her. How he had cut his sinewy palms with the edge of a stone and squeezed his clear blood into her mouth to heal her. How, when Ainafare dismissed him, his strong, root-tendril feet had curled into the scree, and his body had swayed and undulated eerily as the stone and pebbles and sand swallowed him up. How his deep, green eyes had watched Bou and Taiga carefully before he sank into the earth and was gone.

Bree made Bou repeat the story often, and she watched the land with a new care and curiosity as they travelled over the mountains. Whenever a distant Dwarf Willow cast strange shadows in the low sun, or a rock tumbled down a steep slide and made the scree click and move, the little yearling cried out, "Root Troll!" and charged forward to investigate.

On they went, wending their way slowly through the mountains and stopping for long periods to graze on the exposed Lichens that grew in abundance on the treeless slopes. Sure-footed white Mountain Sheep with great curved horns wandered the high ridges. Always the Caribou and the Faerie kept the Firth River Valley to their west, and as Bree grew ever stronger and plumper, they drifted south. When at last the first dusting of snow frosted the Spruce Trees and Sedge tussocks that huddled in the valleys, the little group wound their way down from the windy slopes of the northern coastal mountains and into the foothills.

One morning they mounted a low peak to meet the yellow sun. Before them the land stretched out flat and wide. It was green with peat, Willow, and White Spruce as far as the eye could see. The three Caribou stood together and stared out at the endless green expanse. Ainafare hovered behind them, silent as ever.

"What is that?" the yearling asked, her mouth hanging open slightly.

Taiga replied quietly. "That is the Old Crow Basin, the vast lowlands that rest at the heart of all the mountain ranges."

"At its heart are the Old Crow Flats," Bou added. "A tangle of lakes and rivers that stretch on for days."

The yearling looked up at her brother. "Is that where we're going?"

"Yes," he said.

As they descended the foothills, a cool wind followed them. Upon the wind, low clouds, heavy with rain, drifted silently and cast green-black shadows across the lowlands, their misty underbellies burnt orange and red by the morning sun.

The light grew while the little family travelled along a ridge that looked out over the basin. It was Bou that saw him first, long before his sister or mother could hope to. Well out in front of the Caribou, atop a large stone, sat a strange figure. It was so still that at first Bou was certain it was part of the rock. The young bull stopped in his tracks. Taiga and Bree stood by him.

"What is it, Bou?" the cow inquired.

Bou blinked his eyes and sniffed at the air. "There is some manner of...animal sitting atop that stone in the distance."

Taiga and Bree stared hopelessly in the direction of the stone. Before the little yearling could complain that she couldn't see anything, Ainafare grew suddenly brighter and flew over their heads directly toward the big rock. Bou cantered forward to follow her, his mother and sister close behind.

The Caribou slowed as they approached the tall stone. The big rock stood at the top of a rise that looked over the broad green splendor of the Old Crow Basin. Bou, Bree, and Taiga stared up at the strange animal. The figure sat atop the stone, facing south, and had an unobstructed view of the wide horizon. It was hairless but for its head, where a tangle of wiry, grey hair, streaked with black, fell over its shoulders and down its back. Its hide was tawny and weathered, tanned by long seasons of sun, though still it appeared soft and warm. Like a Faerie, the creature had two long legs, but these were crossed, and it sat upon them. The forelegs hung at its sides with the paws resting in its lap. It seemed too small to be a Cargoth, though it was very much like one, and too large to be a Faerie, though it had features like the Tuatha De Danann. As the Caribou drew closer, a stream of sunlight stabbed down between the clouds and illuminated the figure. Ainafare hovered in the air beside the animal, watching it carefully, being sure to avoid obstructing its view. As the Caribou rounded the front of the stone, they looked up at the animal. Its face was peaceful and strangely beautiful. Its small mouth was nestled between fleshy cheeks with lips that curved up slightly at the corners. Its eyes were dark, upside-down crescents, surrounded by fine wrinkles. They gathered up the light of the morning and twinkled. The creature did not stir or blink. In fact, it seemed oblivious to their presence.

Bree was first to break the silence. "Hi. My name's Bree." Taiga, Moshee, and even Ainafare looked down at the yearling. "This is my brother, Bou, and my mother, Taiga, and this is Ainafare. She's a Faerie!"

The figure remained still and quiet. Bree huffed.

Bou looked up at Ainafare. "What is this creature that sits upon the stone?"

To everyone's surprise, the Faerie answered. "He is Cargoth. He is called by the Children of Danu into the light." She drifted closer to the figure. "Once in a very long while, a Cargoth here in the north becomes known to some among us." The Faerie slowly circled the creature's head. "Usually it's an elder, one who has not forgotten the old ways, one who still treads softly upon the earth, or who has done some great kindness. One who is not wholly consumed by the long dream of hunger. When the Autumn of life spreads wide its arms and Winter creeps close, then one of our kind may go to to that Cargoth with our song." The three Caribou listened intently to the Faerie's words. She hovered in the air beside the figure, glowing softly, staring out across the plains. "This we offer them; to be like us, to look upon the world as we look upon it. To see as we see, and in time, to live as we live. To become one of the Children of Danu; to join the covenant of the Tuatha De Danann."

"But why does he remain silent? Does he not see us or hear us? Is he sleeping?" Bou asked quietly.

"He is not asleep, Moshee. He is awake. Far more awake on this day than when he was but a Cargoth, lost in a grey dream of the world." Ainafare studied the creature. "He may yet hear us, but we are like the beating wings of a Waterthrush beside the roar of a great waterfall. Look upon him, Caribou, for he is a wonder of the north; a Cargoth made Gwich'in Faerie and granted great vision."

She raised her arm and pointed a slender finger at the horizon. "He is seeing the world as it is for the very first time. Your kind may visit the Coastal Plains in Summer again and again, forage the southern forests for Winters on end, and still he may rest here, unmoved by the seasons, drinking in this new world, overwhelmed by what he sees."

Bree's eyes were wide. "But what will he eat? What will he drink?"

"He will not," Ainafare replied. "He is not yet Tuatha De Danann, but he is no longer Cargoth. See how he has grown smaller? Already he has sat here upon this stone for long seasons. What he once was will be consumed and distilled until, like the Children of Danu, he grants that he will do no harm and kicks himself free of the earth. The Chrysaling it is called."

"Then let us leave him," Bou said plainly. "He is wondrous, but we must carry on." The Faerie did not answer. Instead, she turned slowly in the air to scan the horizon in all directions. The young bull looked up at her. "Something troubles you, Ainafare. What is it?"

The Faerie returned the Caribou's gaze. "There are none of my kind as far as I am able to see, and there are none here with him. A watcher should have come to greet me as we approached. He has been abandoned here without his Keeper. It is not well. Something is amiss."

"What need has he of a Keeper," Bou asked, "when he has no need of food or water?"

Ainafare did not answer. She flew in a slow circle around the Gwich'in Faerie, singing softly and scattering Spring Dust all around him on the stone.

Twice she went 'round before she hovered at a slight distance from the figure and spread her arms wide. Her song became louder, and though Bree could not understand it, she was mesmerized. At last the song came to an end, and Ainafare began to glow brighter. The Spring Dust rose up around the Gwich'in Faerie and began to circle him in a whirling wind, until he was obscured by white mist. When at last Ainafare's arms fell to her sides the mist dissolved in the sunlight, and the Gwich'in Faerie was gone. Bree was beside herself.

"He's flown away!" She turned in circles. "Bou, look, he's gone! He's gone!"

"What do you mean, Bree, who is gone?" Moshee stared at the figure and then at Bree.

Taiga wore a confused look on her long, dark face. "The creature on the stone is gone."

The Faerie flew down to where Bou stood beside his mother and hovered before him. "You see him still?" she asked.

"He is there, upon the stone where you left him, looking south," Bou replied.

This seemed to surprise the Faerie, and she gazed curiously at the Caribou for a moment. "Do not be deceived, Moshee. Though you may see him still, others cannot." She turned to Taiga.

The old Caribou looked up at the stone and nodded. "He is gone, as surely as he was never there."

The Faerie continued. "We have the craft to conceal ourselves. We may hide others too, but only for a time. He will remain unseen for now, but in the passing of a few days he will again become visible.

It is no trifling matter to call a Cargoth into the light. Whoever among us is moved to grant the Chrysaling must be prepared to stand watch as the new Faerie's Keeper. Until the Chrysaling is complete, he is vulnerable to animals in the north, who forage and hunt."

She looked up at the top of the stone. "Most will avoid the Gwich'in Faerie. He is strange, and the scent of Cargoth lingers. But some may fall upon hard seasons and be driven by hunger or simple curiosity. The Lynx or the Grizzly, the Golden Eagle or the Gyrfalcon, the Marten or the Wolverine. Any among them may do harm without realizing that they have stumbled upon one who is to be Tuatha De Danann. For this reason a Keeper is appointed." Again the Faerie scanned the horizon. "But here there is none, and it is not well with me."

"What does this mean, Ainafare?" Bou asked. "Perhaps the Faerie has been called away and will return?"

"No," Ainafare said. "I fear another reason drives this Keeper from her vigil." She drifted close to Bou and stared into his eyes. "I must leave you, Moshee. I must fly east to Skull Ridge. There is a Troven there, a council of the Tuatha De Danann. There I will seek another Keeper."

Taiga huffed and shook her head. "You cannot leave us! The Gnome said wherever we go, you would travel with us."

Ainafare ignored the cow. "I will not be long. Two days, three at most. I will convene and address the Troven, summon a new Keeper, lead her here, and then find you again."

"Blinn will not be pleased," Bou stated.

"I do not answer to Gnome or Caribou," she replied coldly. "This I must do."

The young bull paused for a moment. "We will skirt the high ridges and follow Timber Creek into the Old Crow Flats."

The Faerie rose slowly into the air and glowed more brightly. "Be watchful for the Crows, Hugin and Munin." She sang a few words and cast an arm out before her. A mist of Spring Dust fell upon the Caribou. "This will make it difficult for the shadow-walker to scent and track you if he is near. Do not fear an attack, Moshee. Grotto will not assail you until he is sure you know the location of the Breschuvine."

"Why?" Bou called out. "Why does he seek the Breschuvine?" But now Ainafare was too high up to hear him. Her light flashed in the sun, and she raced off into the east.

chapter 18

Cordillera

AUGUST

The dark of Winter nipped at the edges of the day. Every evening since Blinn had departed from the Northern Mountains the skies of Autumn had grown more dim, bruised blue and red and purple by the brooding twilight and speckled by stars. At last, one evening, the mighty sun blazed behind the mountains before sinking beneath the horizon, and the first whisper of night fell across the land. It seemed only a little while until the twilight returned, but every night the darkness grew a little longer, a little deeper.

The three Caribou followed an old hoof-worn path that wound down into the basin until they reached Timber Creek, which ran south through the lowlands. Taiga was skittish. She had not realized how accustomed she had become to Wolves and Eagles and Faeries. Travelling alone, apart from the bulk of the herd, she felt strangely vulnerable. Only one night had passed since Ainafare had left them, but Taiga and Bou both felt the absence of the silent Faerie and her craft, though perhaps not as much as Bree. She asked Taiga again and again where Ainafare had gone and when she would be back.

In spite of feeling vulnerable in the Faerie's absence, both Taiga and Bou were heartened to find the Spring Dust was doing its work. As they followed Timber Creek, they passed into the Old Crow Flats. It wasn't long before they passed between two bull Moose who were making their way to their Wintering Grounds. Neither of the immense animals seemed to scent or notice the Caribou. This eased the old cow's mind.

On their second evening travelling through the flats, they followed the winding Old Crow River, keeping it always to their west. Muskrats busied themselves eating reeds and Horsetails at the marshy edges of the lakes, occasionally chased by lithe Mink. Birds and Fowl were everywhere. The sky and water were alive with their sounds and movement: Widgeons, Pintails, Yellow Warblers, Tundra Swans, White Geese, and Loons. Higher up, all across the flats, Bald and Golden Eagles, Gyrfalcons, and Osprey flew watch for their prey. Crows perched and preened and called to each other across the land. In fact, since they had entered the flats, a single Crow seemed always to be nearby. But Hugin and Munin travelled as a pair, so Taiga paid it little mind.

The deep, blue sky was empty of clouds, and the air was still over the flats. The low, Autumn sun burned red and warmed them as they walked. Taiga followed Bou as they wandered through a stand of Black Spruce. She watched as the uneven, peat-laden ground passed underneath his sure hooves. Suddenly he stopped. When Taiga looked ahead, she saw the reason why. There, directly in their path between the trees, sitting upon a mossy hummock, was a Red Fox. Her black-tipped ears were turned forward toward Bou. Her rust-red face, with white chin and piercing eyes, was cocked slightly to one side. She vigorously scented the air in the direction of the Caribou.

Bou kept still. The Fox sat confidently on her haunches and twitched her bushy tail. She cocked her head to the other side and sniffed the air again. Bou took a tentative step forward and a dead Spruce branch cracked beneath him.

"Hello?" said the Fox, coolly.

Before Bou or Taiga could respond, Bree trotted forward. "Hi, my name's Bree. This is my brother, Bou, and my mother, Taiga. We have a friend called Ainafare, but she isn't here right now, and she's a Faerie!"

Suddenly, it seemed the Fox could see them all clearly. She addressed Bree first. "Hello, Bree. I am Cordillera." Then she spoke to Bou and Taiga. "And you must be the very Caribou I seek. Who else could have such craft for stealth?"

Bou strode forward, slightly impatient. "You seek Caribou? For what purpose?"

"I have no purpose," the Fox replied. "My purpose belongs to another. I am bound by his resolve."

Taiga was confused, but Moshee stepped closer. "To whom are you bound?" he asked.

"I am sent here by your unlikely friend at Lone Mountain; the black Wolf called Polaris. Land Crow, some call him."

This surprised the young bull. "Sent for what reason?" he inquired.

"Polaris fears the shadow-walker awaits you in the lowlands, where the old Caribou trails empty out of the flats with the Old Crow River. He sends me to lead you to him by another route." Cordillera watched the Caribou intently as she spoke. Her eyes shone like auburn gemstones in the evening light, made more arresting by the thin line of black skin that ringed them.

"Why?" Bou asked. "What does the shadow-walker want with me? He seeks the Breschuvine, but I do not know where it is. The Eye of the North sets me on one path, and now Polaris sends you to set me on another. *Why?* Am I an Autumn leaf, adrift, fallen from the tree only to be pushed wherever the wind may blow?"

The Fox considered this carefully before responding. "You seek the Breschuvine?"

"I seek it, but I do not know where to find it." Bou seemed strangely calm to Taiga. "Do you know of it?"

"I have heard only stories."

"Tell us then. What stories have you heard?"

At last the Fox blinked. She eyed the Caribou warily. "That it blooms for but a Hare's breath, once every fifth Autumn, under the first new moon of Winter. That none but Rahtrum knows which Autumn is the fifth. That if plucked by its root from the earth it will wilt to dust in an instant. That is, if any could find it. For none in the north know where it will bloom, but those the Binder himself may choose to tell." Cordillera paused a moment. "That if consumed, the Breschuvine flower may make any animal something much more than what he was."

Bou stepped closer to the Red Fox and Cordillera seemed to lose some of her poise. "You have much lore for a Fox."

The Fox's tail curled around her black paws. "I have only stories." Her eyes thinned. "But we should not tarry. Let us turn from this path. Polaris awaits you in the southeast, near the foothills of the Old Crow Range."

The young bull stepped closer still to the Fox. "I have told you already, Cordillera, I do not know where the Breschuvine is. Why should I fear the shadow-walker if I do not have what he seeks?"

The Fox seemed to grow uncomfortable. "Where does the Eye of the North send you? Perhaps that is where the Breschuvine blooms. Who knows what is in the mind of the shadow-walker?"

Before Bou could reply, a large Crow lit in the high boughs of a Black Spruce. The Caribou looked up at the Crow, and the Fox rose up onto all fours. *Ark, kek.* "She lies, Moshee. She knows what is in the mind of the shadow-walker. I am Munin. I am known to you. I come to warn you that Cordillera is foe, not friend. It was Hugin and I who followed you to the flats from the Northern Mountains. When the Faerie left you, Hugin went in search of the Fox to put her in your path. Like us, Cordillera is in the service of Grotto," the Crow gurgled.

Taiga was perplexed and instinctively retreated a few paces. "The Faerie should not have left us," the old cow said gloomily. She watched Bou intently, and he seemed unruffled. Bree looked back and forth between the Crow and the Fox.

Cordillera dismissed Munin. "Sing your tales elsewhere, Crow.

You are also known to me. Polaris spoke of you." She implored Bou. "Do not be fooled by this Crow."

The young bull stared up at the Crow for a moment and then stepped closer still to the Fox. The two were now almost nose-to-nose. As the Caribou did so, he seemed to grow in stature. "And you are known to me, Cordillera. The Eye of the North warned me of a Red Fox, bent by long seasons to the will of the shadow-walker; snake-tongued and shrewd, aged by some dark craft beyond the normal years of a Fox."

The Fox's tail slunk between her legs and the hair on her back rose.

Bou continued. "You were known to me before we set out for the Firth River Valley. It was Blinn who sent word to Lone Mountain. I have known where I should seek out Polaris and Mist for the passing of a moon, just as they have known where to look for me."

Munin cooed. "You see, Fox? Some in the north do not tremble before the shadow-walker."

"Foolish Crow!" The Fox barked up at her. "Have you grown weary of your life?"

"I have grown weary of fear," Munin spat back.

Cordillera stood tall suddenly, and all of her uneasiness fell away. Her eyes, already bright with the evening sun, now glimmered with their own light. Bou was surprised and stepped back a pace. The Fox stared at each of the Caribou in turn, which sent a shiver down Taiga's back. Cordillera then glowered up at the Crow with her bright eyes. As she glared at each of them, she spoke words they could not understand, and something strange began to happen. The black colour that tipped the hair of her ears seemed to run and move from one guard hair to the next, faster and faster, until it flowed across her fur, down her face, muzzle, and chest, along her back, and down her legs to join with the blackness of her paws. A sudden, unnatural mist rolled through the stand of Black Spruce. Cordillera's tail waved in the air, and every hair, from base to tip, turned black. The Fox's new black coat only made her glowing copper eyes all the more striking.

The Fox spoke to the young bull, her voice full of derision. "You seek to awaken the Cargoth, Moshee, chosen of Rahtrum? You think them truly asleep? You are as foolish as the Crow. You asked me a question only a few moments ago. Here is my answer. Yes. You are but a leaf in Autumn, adrift, fallen from the tree only to be pushed wherever the Binder may blow you. Before the end, you too, may discover that you have been asleep."

Cordillera then addressed Munin. "Is your bravery well spent, Crow?" Munin shifted back and forth nervously as the Fox growled at her. "You think you are grown weary of fear? Soon you will be exhausted. The shadow-walker will haunt your dreams. Even the Crow must come to land." She whispered another incantation before turning quickly and disappearing in a wisp of fog.

Taiga stared after the Fox as a light wind began to carry away the mist. Bree pushed anxiously against her flank. The low sun sent a strange, orange light crisscrossing through the Spruce boughs.

Bou turned to the Crow. "What is she?"

"I do not know. She is known to us only as Cordillera, the Red Fox. That is all we know. I am as surprised as you to see such craft in her."

"And what of you, Crow? Am I to trust you now? After Rock River? After the Driftwood River Valley? When the shadow-walker has stained your mind with fear?" The young bull huffed.

"It does not matter, Caribou. Trust me, do not trust me. My time here in the north is at an end. Cordillera is right. The shadow-walker will not let this pass. I must fly before the deep of Winter. Across the great delta, over the plateaus, past the stone lakes, to the great inland sea." She clicked softly to herself. *Kek, kek.* "Let us see how far his spite will carry him."

"And what of your mate, Hugin?" Bou asked.

The Crow ruffled her wings and stretched them out as she stared directly at the Caribou. "He is not what he was. He is afraid, and I can no longer wait for his fear to pass." Her breast dipped low as she thrust her wings high into the air above her and leapt into the sky.

The three Caribou carried on into the widening darkness of the Arctic night. They walked beside the Old Crow River as it wound like a snake down into a wide valley and led them out of the Old Crow Flats. Bree had many questions about the Red Fox for her mother, and Taiga did all she could to answer them. Bou walked ahead in silence.

When at last the first blush of deepest blue rose in the south-eastern sky to dim the stars, Ainafare appeared out of the night. As the Faerie approached, moving brightly out over the water, the old cow had a fleeting memory of her night by the Peel River, when the Tuatha De Danann had come to Bou's aid. She looked ahead at her proud young bull. His antlers, now fully grown, silhouetted in the early dawn. *What must it be like to remember as he does?*

When the Faerie came at last to the shoreline, Moshee halted the little procession, and Ainafare hovered before him, her white light framed by the twilight sky. She looked the three Caribou over. "You are well, I see."

"We are well," Bou replied. "But we came upon the Red Fox called Cordillera, as Blinn warned we might. She sought to lead us west."

"Then it is well that you were warned."

"It is. The Crow Munin came to us as well, to warn us of the danger."

"She will pay dearly for it when the Fox returns to the shadow-walker," the Faerie said.

"She has flown east, to the great inland sea, where she hopes to hide." The Caribou paused a moment. "I do not think Cordillera is a Red Fox. At least, it cannot be all that she is. There is lore in her and strange craft."

This the Faerie considered carefully for a moment as she hung, silent in the air. Taiga watched them as Bree took advantage of their rest to forage.

"You know nothing of her?" Bou pressed.

"I know nothing for certain," Ainafare said.

"And what of the Gwich'in Faerie? Did you find a new Keeper?"

"Yes. The Troven has granted him a new watcher," she answered.

"Was there news? What became of the first Keeper? The Faerie who first called the Cargoth into the light?" Bou was frustrated by Ainafare's terse answers.

"You are deeply curious for a Caribou, Moshee. Do not concern yourself with the affairs of Faeries," she said dismissively and turned to look south. "There are Cargoth ahead that make their dens where the Old Crow River empties into the mighty Porcupine. We will turn southeast."

The Faerie fell into her usual silence as the Caribou climbed up a steep ravine and out of the river valley. Bou tried again to wring more information from Ainafare, but she paid him no attention, and in time he strode ahead of them into the dawn. Soon Bree had taken up her familiar position. The yearling trotted along beneath the silent Faerie and talked at length about all she had seen upon the Old Crow Flats. Special attention was paid to the Red Fox called Cordillera, and Bree recounted their meeting in great detail while it was still fresh in her memory. Taiga couldn't be certain, but it seemed to her that during this part of Bree's story, Ainafare drifted ever closer to the little yearling, intent on hearing her tale. As they turned toward the Porcupine River, the skies darkened and the early snows of Winter came heavily out of the sky.

chapter 19

Sky-mane and the Rising of Mist

JULY - SEPTEMBER

In the Summer, after he left Ainafare, Polaris ran south out of the Old Crow Flats and forded the Porcupine River, filled with dark news of the fall of Tundra and the howling of Mist. When at last he climbed the steep slopes of Lone Mountain it was evening, and the sun was low in the sky. He found three Wolves from the Choho Pack standing watch on the mountainside. The Wolves parted for him in silence as he passed and clambered up to the dens, his body sore from his long exertion. Deep inside the warmth of their stone den, he found Aurora nursing seven pups at her breasts. The she-Wolf's eyes shone in the twilight of the cave, and her tail thumped the ground. The black Wolf drew near and licked her muzzle before scenting and licking the pups.

He looked at her. "Where is he?"

Aurora's voice was a whisper. "You are weary. Rest, mighty Polaris."

Mighty no longer. Polaris hung his head. "The Faerie, Ainafare, came to me upon the Old Crow Flats. I know that Tundra has fallen, I have heard of the howling of Mist."

Aurora's eyes softened, her ears lay flat, and her tail was still. After a short silence she stared at the roof of the den and spoke gently to him. "When he is not at the hunt he stands up upon the high stone. Always he surveys the land, searching, like an Eagle. There he sleeps alone, curled up in the wind with no thought of shelter."

The black Wolf looked away. "I will go to him."

"No. Rest, my First Star," she insisted. "Sleep by your pups. He can wait. There will be time."

Polaris looked into her sun-yellow eyes, then turned his long body in a circle beside her and curled up as he collapsed onto the den floor. Two of the pups squealed and grunted as they crawled out from beneath the bulk of his legs. They flopped across his dark fur with heavy eyes and milk-fat bellies. In an instant their little chests heaved with sleep.

In the days after Polaris had returned to Lone Mountain, there was no sign of Mist. The First Star held council with the three Wolves of Choho Hill. He thanked them for their service to the pack and bade them carry his gratitude back to his brother, Timber. Before he released them, the First Star inquired what they knew of Mist and where he might be. The Wolves glanced at each other.

"The grey-mane is out upon the land, hunting," one of the Wolves offered. He looked ready to say more but held fast.

"Speak," Polaris encouraged them, and the Wolves again looked at each other.

The largest of the three stepped forward. "He hunts at length and alone. There is a fierceness in him. He brings generous kills to the den as tribute to your mate and First Star, Aurora. But he spends long days out upon the land hunting to feed himself." Here the Wolf paused. "For still he grows in stature."

Polaris was confused. "What do you mean?" He eyed the Choho Wolf. "He is young for a Wolf, but he is far beyond his time for growing."

Another of the Choho Wolves stepped forward. "It is the truth. Since the she-Wolf Tundra fell to the shadow-walker, he has been out upon the land hunting, and he has grown. It is not by much, but it is enough. You will not recognize him. He is —" But here the Wolf stopped.

"He is what?" Polaris growled.

"He is grown greater even than you, Land Crow." The Wolf lowered his head and tucked his tail.

The big black Wolf considered these words in silence for a moment. "Lone Mountain thanks you. Go to your pack. Stand watch over Choho Hill. The shadow-walker still moves in the north."

The Wolves seemed relieved to be dismissed, and they turned quickly and trotted down the western slopes of the mountain. The other Wolves of Lone Mountain seemed equally uncomfortable when Polaris inquired after their Second Star, Mist.

"He is not as he was," they said. "The Winter has come early for him, and we fear he may never again feel the Spring."

Aurora, too, padded softly around the subject. "Tundra was his light, Polaris. She was his sun. Whatever she tamed in him is tame no longer. We treat him as a packmate, but we must remember, we do not know where he comes from. We do not know by whom he was whelped and left at the banks of the Porcupine River for the Root Troll to find."

On the evening of the seventh day since his return, the First Star climbed up to the high stone atop Lone Mountain and stood in the red glare of the night sun. He looked out across the northlands, lifted his muzzle to the sky, and sent up a rallying howl. *If you are yet a Wolf of Lone Mountain, then you will come.*

As the sun crept along the horizon they came, all the Wolves of Lone Mountain, alone or in pairs. All of them save for Aurora, who would not leave her pups — and the grey-mane, Mist. After a time, seven Wolves stood quietly in a circle around their First Star. They exchanged glances, tails gently wagging. But Polaris stood in silence and waited. Onward the sun crept.

At last they heard a stirring upon the stones below. Mist came padding slowly up the mountainside. As he approached, the other Wolves parted to let him pass. Polaris watched him come. It was true, he had indeed grown in stature. He stood a full ear's length above the largest among the seven, and as he approached, it was clear that he was a little broader and stood an eye taller than the First Star. They stared a moment at each other before the black Wolf spoke.

"I am sorry, Mist. I came south from Babbage River as soon as I was able. The Faerie, Ainafare came to me on the flats and told me of our loss."

"For this you call me from the hunt?" Mist asked bitterly.

Polaris bristled. "Am I not First Star? What reason do I need to call upon Wolves of my pack?"

The other Wolves look furtively at each other with lowered postures and sleeked hair.

The grey-mane's tail rose and quivered a moment before he replied slowly. "You are First Star, Polaris, and yet Tundra is fallen while the bull Caribou and his kin are well. You are First Star, and yet the shadow-walker roams free across the north."

Polaris dismissed the other Wolves with a glance. They turned and drifted back down the Mountain. With his tail raised, the black Wolf addressed Mist. "I have said to you that I am sorry. All of our hope is in Moshee, Mist. He is the chosen of Rahtrum, and that is why I put him before us, before all. Tundra, too, saw hope in him. Have you forgotten?"

Mist huffed and stared out over the land. His eyes smoldered in the low light. "Do not speak her name to me."

"I implore you, Mist. Come down to be near your pups. Be Second Star to your kin. What can you gain up here, alone upon the high stone, apart from your pack? You have seen the shadow-walker, you know he is beyond us."

The big, grey Wolf locked eyes with Polaris. He wrinkled his nose and curled his lips into a snarl. "He is beyond *you*, Land Crow." He turned to leave but paused a moment and looked out at the circling horizon. "We are not kin, you and I, and I am Second Star no longer. I have but one purpose in this world, and you will not keep me from it. When I return again from the hunt I will leave food by your den. In return you will leave me to my vigil atop Lone Mountain. This, at least, you will grant me in exchange for my loss." Mist broke into a run and disappeared.

Polaris began to bark after him but stopped and thought better of it. He watched the grey Wolf go, and then he too, descended the mountainside, bathed in the red light of the night sun.

During the Summer, days full of light passed on Lone Mountain, and the pups played outside the den, pouncing on each other and stalking the adult Wolves whenever they were nearby. But even the bright Summer was occasionally dimmed by shadows, and during this time two of Tundra's three whelps fell ill and wasted away. Aurora sent Wolves up to the high stone to summon Mist, but he would not come. At last, the two male pups would not feed or drink, and their eyes closed quietly and would not open. Their sister, forlorn, watched over them, and curled beside them until they were as cold as the earth. The pack was saddened terribly by their passing. It was harder still to bear in a year of plenty. For days the mood was black, as the pack mourned its loss.

But five pups remained, and when the second moon of Summer was past, their legs were longer and more sure, and at last their blue, juvenile eyes began to turn yellow and gold and copper; all but one, whose eyes remained blue. The Wolves rejoiced and gathered together, for when the new pups' eyes turned, it was called their Sunrise, and it meant names would be given to each.

Under the high sun, the five pups lay obediently on their bellies as the pack looked on. Polaris strode before them, and all of them followed him closely with their eyes. He stopped before the first, a black-and-grey male with bright, yellow eyes. Polaris looked around at the other Wolves of the pack. Each had grown fond of the pups, and all of them wagged their tails and barked their choice for a name. With a nod from Polaris they grew quiet, and he looked down at the first pup.

"You will be called Dusken."

The pup jumped up on his two hind legs, his tail wagging, and licked Polaris' face. The old Wolf growled playfully at Dusken, and the pup ran in a little circle, barking before joining the pack to watch the others. One by one, Polaris stood before the pups.

"Rockpaw, you will be called." He said to the tawny-grey male with copper eyes.

"And you are Stalker," he told the grey-black female with yellow eyes.

"Tussock, you will be called," to the grey-and-tawny male with gold eyes.

Each pup in turn jumped and ran and barked before standing with the pack. Finally, Polaris stood before the last. She was a black female with eyes of blue. Of Mist and Tundra's three pups, she alone had survived to her Sunrise. When the First Star looked down at her she wagged her tail gently. He turned to the pack, but it remained silent.

Aurora stepped forward to stand beside her mate. "This one I have named," she said gently to Polaris.

He wagged his tail and turned to join the other Wolves.

Aurora lowered her head. "Hello, Little One," she whispered. The Wolf pup's tail thumped the ground, and Aurora stood tall and said clearly, "Sky-mane, you will be called."

The little black Wolf sat up on her haunches and barked at the sky with her high-pitched voice. Soon the pack joined her, and all the Wolves were at play under the Summer sun.

Another full moon came and went, and Polaris set a watch upon Mist. Still the big Wolf went out often upon the land for long stretches of time to hunt alone, and whichever of the Wolves tried to follow, they could not keep pace. For the grey-mane always seemed to grow a little larger and stronger, they said. When he did return, he stood or slept atop the high stone of Lone Mountain. There, Crows came often to visit him and bring news, but no one could say what they spoke of. As the Summer grew late and the sun crept low, several of the Wolves carried news to Polaris that they had seen a Root Troll upon the high stone with Mist. *It is Karst, the elder, come to keep counsel with his whelp.* Of this, Polaris was certain. *But what can it mean?*

At the last turn of Summer, Windshim came alone to Lone Mountain bearing news for the First Star from Blinn, Eye of the North.

"The Caribou will come south through the flats by the Old Crow River. The Faerie travels with them. They must turn to avoid the northern stronghold of the Cargoth and come to an old crossing on the Porcupine River." She watched the horizon with her keen eyes as she spoke. "This news is for you alone, Land Crow. When the Autumn grows dark, and the first black nights of Winter devour a third of the day, then Blinn bids you go to look for them by the river and once again take up your watch."

"I am bound," the Wolf replied. "But where is Aquila, your mate?"

"He circles east. We hunt any sign of the shadow-walker, though we have not seen him, even with our keen eyes." The Eagle looked up toward the top of Lone Mountain. "Other things we have seen, though. A great grey Wolf that moves over the land, swift as a cloud's shadow."

Polaris ignored the Raptor's account of Mist. "If you speak again with Blinn, tell him Polaris answers his call. I will look for Moshee on the banks of the river."

"It is well," Windshim said simply and leapt into the air.

Slowly night came again to the north, first as a lengthening twilight and then as a short flash of darkness. Finally, it began its slow bloom over the land, like a black flower sequined with star-dew.

The pups grew ever bigger and soon ventured farther and farther from the den, eventually following the adults out on short hunts during the ever-waning daylight.

Mist, too, had grown, and as the Winter began to spread wide her arms, he came to the den carrying the entire hind leg of a Mountain Sheep in his jaws. The pack looked on silently. He padded in among them and dropped the Sheep's leg upon the ground. He was immense now, standing a full head above mighty Polaris. He said nothing and turned to leave. But the black pup with blue eyes trotted up before him and sat on the ground in front of his wide paws. Mist stopped and looked down at the youngster. She let out a high-pitched bark and lay down on all fours with a playful growl. Her tail wagged gently.

"My name is Sky-mane," she said to him. "I am your daughter."

The grey Wolf hung his head low. He scented her and squinted his eyes. "You cannot be mine, Little One," he said gently. "You belonged to another." He stepped over the Wolf pup to leave. "And all that was his was taken from him. Now he is no more."

Aurora could not bear it. "Mist!" she barked.

The grey-mane paused and looked at her a moment. Her yellow eyes pleaded, but the enormous, grey Wolf padded away slowly and climbed up the mountainside to stand alone upon the high stone.

When the first black nights of Winter cast a third of the day into darkness, Polaris stood with Aurora on the windward side of Lone Mountain. A cool breeze ruffled their new Winter coats, as they stared out over the lowlands with their long flanks pressed together. Aurora spoke first. "The shadow-walker seeks the Breschuvine." She licked his muzzle. "I have seen his new strength. Keep your nose to the wind and your ears to your back."

"I do not fear the one called Grotto," Polaris said gently.

"This I know," she replied. "It is what frightens me."

He nudged her. "Do not worry. I will not be alone, the Faerie travels with the Caribou."

A low voice came from behind the two Wolves. "I too, will travel with you."

They turned to find Mist standing in the wind.

"Did you think I would not know when to seek out Moshee, Land Crow? Or where? I have been out upon the land. You have seen the Crows that come to me upon the high stone. There is much I know."

The grey-mane and First Star stared at each other. Aurora broke the silence. "It is well that he goes with you, Polaris. It will ease my mind."

The black Wolf looked into her eyes. He touched her muzzle with his own, then turned and started down the mountainside.

Mist moved to follow Polaris, but Aurora stood in his way. She growled low. "When Karst brought you to us, Grey-mane, we kept you as one of our own. Your three pups have suckled at my breasts while you have mourned alone upon the high stone. I have raised Sky-mane as my own flesh and fur when you have been out upon the land plotting vengeance. Selfish fool."

She looked down the steep slope to where her mate descended on his sure paws. "He believed you would be First Star. He wished for it." She stared at Mist with her bright yellow eyes. "Be sure that Polaris returns to Lone Mountain. If a drop of his blood falls in the north, and it is not accompanied by a river of your own, Sky-mane will not see her second Summer."

Mist drew close to her, unmoved by her gaze. "It is plain that you fear for him. He is no longer all that he was." He looked down the mountainside. "But please, do not say such things. I will do as you wish because you ask it, Aurora. Because you too, are First Star of Lone Mountain, and you have been as a mother to me. You need not bark empty threats. I have watched you with Sky-mane; seen your eyes shine to look upon her. Like Tundra, you would cast your life away before letting harm come to her." The mighty Wolf turned and slowly padded away to follow Polaris.

chapter 20

Cargoth

SEPTEMBER

Mist stood at the top of a high ridge above the steep embankments of the Porcupine River. He looked west and scented the air. Polaris watched the big, grey Wolf from below. *How he has grown.* A cool wind blew light snow and ruffled Mist's new Winter coat against its grain. The grey Wolf stood tall on his forepaws with his long haunches stretched back over the uneven stones. His ears strained forward and his gold eyes surveyed the land. *The Faerie spoke truthfully,* Polaris observed. *He has risen. Never before has the north seen such a Wolf.* Polaris climbed the ridge and stood near Mist in silence.

The two Wolves kept up their watch for Moshee by the Porcupine River. One Wolf stood atop the high ridge, while the other made a great sweeping arc through the surrounding White Spruce forests looking for Caribou signs. On the third day the skies darkened, and the early snows of Winter came out of the northeast.

As Polaris gazed over the flats, he saw Mist break from the forest below into the glade of Shrub Birch that surrounded the bluff. The old Wolf's copper eyes followed the grey-mane as he widened his stride and swiftly crossed the open ground to the foot of the ridge. There he disappeared from view until, what seemed like only a few short moments later, he came bounding up the ridgeline with hardly an effort. He did not pant or steam in the cold but stood calmly at the First Star's side.

Mist spoke. "There is a group of Caribou to the west. They are coming toward us, following an old trail to the river crossing. Moshee and his kin are not among them. But there is danger. Farther west a pack of Cargoth has set out on the hunt from their northern stronghold. They too, come this way."

Polaris stared at Mist. "This you saw?"

The immense grey Wolf looked west. "This I saw."

Then you have run far in a short time. "We must find them."

Now the grey-mane looked at Polaris, his gold eyes impenetrable. "Fear not, Land Crow. The Faerie is with them. We will find them before the Cargoth."

Another short, dark night passed, and at dawn Polaris went out upon the land to search, while Mist stood watch at the ridge. Twilight had come when at last, the First Star mounted the ridgeline once again, his tongue loose and his breath short. They stood there together on the bluff in silence, and the wind came hard out of the east. Eventually Polaris curled up in the rocks and wrapped his tail over his muzzle, wearied by his day's run. He peered up at Mist before closing his eyes. The massive Wolf stood watch, unmoved by the first breath of Winter. *Who are you, Mist, Grey-mane? Who did the Root Troll leave in our den?* This Polaris wondered as he fell into sleep.

Out of the darkness came Mist's call. "Polaris!" The Wolf's growl was deep and urgent. Mist nudged the First Star, and Polaris scrambled up onto his paws to stretch. The blue twilight of morning clung to the sky. Flurries of snow moved on the light wind. Mist stared over the endless range of Spruce forest. Polaris followed his gaze.

"There." The grey-mane said.

Below in the forest, a short distance from the ridge, obscured by the thick Spruce, a white light flashed briefly through the snow-rimed boughs. Once more, it glimmered, and then again.

"Ainafare," Polaris whispered. "It is the Faerie. She seeks to hide the Caribou and to draw our eyes if we are near."

There was a smaller flash in the half-light, a little farther away, followed immediately by a crack of thunder.

"Cargoth!" the black Wolf gasped, and he sprang away.

But the great grey Wolf remained a little while, standing in the wind, staring out over the forest as though searching for something. Then another small crack of thunder echoed up the hill. He blinked his golden eyes, turned, and followed Polaris. The First Star scented the cool September air as he crashed through the White Spruce forest. He turned his ears back as he ran, but he could not hear the grey-mane following. *He will come. Go to them Polaris, you are still a Wolf to be reckoned with.*

A light twinkled ahead, and Polaris caught the briefest whisper of Moshee's scent. *The Faerie has concealed them well.* He leapt over a fallen tree, bending and splintering saplings as he burst into a tiny clearing where the Caribou pressed together behind Ainafare who hovered in front of them, facing the forest with her little arms spread wide, as though ready for a fight. There was a new yearling with Taiga and she scurried in a panic behind the old cow, terrified of the big, black Wolf.

The Faerie spoke without turning. "You are slow in coming, Wolf. I began to think I would have to come myself to find you." Another sharp crack of thunder cut through the forest, closer now. "There are Cargoth to the west. They are hunting."

"Make for the river crossing." Polaris barked. "Watch our flank, Faerie, keep them hidden, the Cargoth will be close. This way, Moshee." He sprang away southwest followed by the young bull. *Run, old Wolf, the only safe descent to the river valley canyon is west of here. We will pass right before the Cargoth.*

Bree was petrified by the big predator and at first refused to follow the Wolf, but another blast of thunder rang out, and her instinct to run leapt up in her. Taiga galloped after Bou, and the yearling bounded after her mother, eyes wide with fright, never more than a nose from Taiga's rear hooves. The Faerie moved easily with them through the forest, weaving through the trees, chanting an incantation as she kept watch for Cargoth.

Thunder cracks came in succession. *It is close, but the Faerie's craft will keep them safe if we can only reach the river.* Poplaris' ears turned back, and he could hear the Caribou moving swiftly through the forest behind him. *The fear is in them, they will overtake me.* He lifted his muzzle and scents came to him on the wind as he ran. The smell of other Caribou, of Cargoth and their thunder, and at last, the river. He wove at full stride between the Spruce trees, and suddenly his nose was filled with a new scent. Blood. He crashed into the Caribou with all his weight. She was a mature cow, wide-eyed with fear. She stumbled and went down and he tumbled beneath her. Moshee came upon them first. Taiga was next, the yearling at her flank.

Polaris tried to struggle onto his paws, but his rear legs were caught between the fallen Caribou and a Spruce stump. The cow huffed and shook. Ainafare hovered above with her light. Snow twirled through the air. The Wolf's black hair glistened, slick with the Caribou's blood. The hunted cow lay still now, splayed out on the forest floor. The thin, red trail of her life led away through the trees upon the new snow. Polaris trained his nose and ears in the direction of the blood and they all heard the heavy crunch of underbrush.

"It is near," the Faerie said calmly.

"Run!" the First Star growled at the young bull. "The crossing is not far." The Caribou seemed frozen. The Wolf bared his teeth in a deep snarl. "Run!"

Moshee blinked and then leapt away, followed by his sister and mother. Ainafare hovered low, near to the Wolf.

"Do not be foolish, Faerie. Go. Keep him safe or much will have been lost for nothing." She stared at him a moment then rose and streaked off after the Caribou.

Polaris pawed at the ground and tried to twist his way free, but the dead cow's weight only shifted and pinned him where he lay. A crack of underbrush made his head whip around to look west. His ears strained, and he scented the air. The pungent smell of Cargoth filled his nostrils. The sounds of the Beasts of Shadow drew nearer and nearer. *How clumsy they are, how slow and weak without their thunder.* Polaris' copper eyes grew wide, his lips curled back and his nose wrinkled.

The Cargoth came noisily through the Spruce trees following the cow's blood. When it saw Polaris with the Caribou it stopped in its tracks and stood a little way away. It seemed surprised to find the big Wolf there, uncertain what to do. *It is a young male,* the Wolf thought. He had not seen many, but this one was not full-grown, of this he was nearly certain. It was covered in strange, coloured skins and furs and carried a long branch, polished like a stone in a river. *That is what makes the thunder. That is their tooth and claw.*

Polaris struggled violently again against the weight of the cow, but could not move. Seeing that the Wolf was trapped, the Cargoth took another step toward him. The Wolf snarled and let loose a deep growl. The Beast of Shadow stopped again. It raised the polished branch to its shoulder and stared down the length of it at the Wolf. In the distance other Cargoth called out. Their strange barks drifted through the forest. The First Star stared into the dark brown eyes of the Beast of Shadow and growled again. *Make your thunder, Cargoth. No Wolf runs forever.*

The sweat of the Cargoth stank upon the cold air. Mighty Polaris closed his eyes and thought of Aurora: remembered how they had run together between the Spring tussocks; how they had hunted side by side during the long Winter; how warm she felt when she would come close and lean against him; how their first litter had made the Summer sun live in her eyes. The black Wolf breathed deeply, and the air seemed full of her scent. *I have lived well for a Wolf.* He prepared himself.

But no thunder came. Polaris opened his eyes. The Cargoth lowered the polished branch from its shoulder. Its eyes were wide, and its paws shook. The scent of its fear filled the air. *Urine.* The Wolf cocked his head, confused. The Cargoth faltered. It stepped back. Stumbled over a log and collapsed. The polished branch fell to the ground. Thunder exploded. The Wolf winced but was unscathed. The Cargoth rose onto all fours. It stared past Polaris, frozen. The black Wolf turned his head to follow the creature's gaze.

There, in the twirling snow, stood Mist. His teeth gleamed, and his growl was as deep and wide as a valley. His grey mane stood high, and his piercing gold eyes were fearless. The Cargoth was frozen, caught in the Wolf's eyes like a Hare. The grey Wolf lunged forward and snarled so fiercely that even Polaris ducked his head. The Beast of Shadow barked and scrambled up onto its two legs, turned, and ran. It howled with its strange voice. The barks of the other Cargoth answered, nearer now. Mist turned and seized the dead cow's hind leg in his jaws. He planted his four great paws, growled, and in a single, powerful motion, he freed Polaris.

chapter 21

The Breschuvine
OCTOBER

Bou watched Bree as she trotted along between Taiga and Ainafare. She kept all the distance she could between herself and the Wolves, glancing warily at them when they were near and only truly relaxing when they galloped off to circle ahead or behind their little group. If the yearling had been frightened when Polaris appeared in the forest, then she was stricken with terror when Mist climbed out of the cold river alongside him.

The Caribou had fled to the Porcupine River as the First Star instructed, panicked by the barking and the thunder of the Cargoth that were closing in around them. The river ran wide and cold but their fear drove them into the water. As they swam against the current, a crack of thunder rang out from the forest on the northern bank. They crossed the river steadily, wide-eyed, their ears trained behind them, terrified the Cargoth would sight them from the shore. But Ainafare hovered over the river as they swam, flying above each of them in turn to hide them, glowing softly and reciting her gentle incantations. Even Bree, who had leapt into the water beside her mother, moved confidently through the current, though this was her first fording of a truly great northern river. When they reached the riverbank they rested, and the Faerie bade them wait and keep watch. Ainafare hung, still, in the air at the edge of the river and stared over the water, until at last she said, "The Wolves are coming."

"And Polaris?" Bou asked urgently. "He is among them?"

"There are two." The Faerie did not turn. "The mighty grey-mane is first into the water, but Polaris is upon his tail." Moshee almost collapsed with relief. The snow flurries twirled around them as they waited.

At last, the two great Wolves strode up out of the water and each shook their Winter coats in an explosion of spray. As Mist padded slowly up the stony beach, Taiga stepped back nervously. Bree's deep instincts welled up in her and she bleated and trotted away a distance, hardly able to restrain a run. She looked back at the Wolves, wrestling with her nerves to stop her hooves for a moment. But again the fear rose in her, and she skittered off in a new direction, always keeping a safe distance.

Bou stood his ground to greet the Wolves, but Mist had no greeting for the Caribou. His hackles bristled, and his golden eyes narrowed. His gaze held Moshee, who stood frozen, as the enormous Wolf walked past in silence.

It cannot be. Never have I seen such a Wolf. Mist now stood above Moshee's eye line. Only the young bull's antlers reached above the Wolf's ears as he passed. The grey-mane quickly broke into a run, bounding across the open ground and mounting the southern ravine with ease. Bree was startled. She ran back to Taiga's side and huddled behind her, as Polaris walked up the beach to stand with Bou.

"You have grown, Moshee. The Summer has been kind to you." The First Star looked up at the Caribou's towering rack. "You will be first among bulls by the look of it."

"I am not alone, it seems." Bou glanced over his shoulder in the direction Mist had run. "It is well you are here, Polaris. We feared for you. When we heard the thunder —"

"I am here, Moshee. I am bound." The black Wolf nodded at Taiga. "There will be time for us to exchange news soon enough, but now I must follow Mist. We must mark the dale and scent the land to be sure the way is safe." He moved to pass.

"I am sorry, Polaris," Bou said suddenly. "Blinn brought news of Tundra."

Polaris paused and turned his head a little. "We are all of us sorry." The Wolf sprang away. He was not as big or as swift as Mist, but he moved with a steady grace that growled in the face of his long seasons.

The Caribou, Wolves, and Faerie travelled together from the Porcupine River. As they trekked through the southern lowlands of the Old Crow Basin, their path led them across the wide plains that lay between Lone Mountain and Choho Hill.

The middle of the day opened above them, and the sun streamed through the breaking clouds. On a high, rocky bluff they saw Wolves of the Choho Pack, standing silently in a line to watch the passing of the one called Moshee. When Bou turned back to look once more at the ridgeline, they were gone.

The young bull tried on several occasions to speak with Mist. He wished to share in his sadness over Tundra, but the great Wolf would not have it. Always he sprang away on his long legs to survey the land in great ranging circles. Polaris, too, kept watch, but returned to the Caribou more often, sometimes travelling by Moshee's flank, or walking apart and speaking quietly with Ainafare.

As they passed west of Sharp Mountain, the First Star strode at Moshee's side.

"He will not speak to me," Bou said, looking ahead to a distant rise where the great, grey Wolf stood alone.

"You are a reminder of what he has lost," said Polaris. "He does not wish to hear her name."

"He blames me for her loss."

"He blames himself," said Polaris.

"I am not so sure," Bou said. "This task was set upon me. I did not seek it out. Surely he knows this. I am *sent* to search for the Breschuvine, and who can say no to the Earthshaker?"

Bou stepped in front of Polaris and stopped. "I do not know why. I do not know how. Only that Rahtrum asks it of me; that the shadow-walker pursues me; that a Gnome and Eagles and Wolves come to aid me." Bou looked to where Taiga and Bree wandered ahead with Ainafare. "That a Faerie goes everywhere with us, but will tell me nothing of her purpose, or my own."

The Wolf's copper eyes were gentle. "We are all of us bent from our nature, Moshee. Myself, you, Mist, Ainafare, Windshim — Grotto, most of all. The Cargoth have risen. Their long shadow disturbs the seasons. Their hunger bends all of Nature. They have disturbed the still surface of the Binder's careful balance. We are the ripples." He sighed. "I fear this is but the beginning."

"And Tundra?" Bou asked gloomily. "Was she a ripple?"

Now the Wolf drew his muzzle near to the Caribou's. "Do not be swallowed by the shadows in your heart, Moshee. That is the sickness that assails the grey-mane."

The bull turned away and looked ahead, but Mist was gone from the rise.

Polaris regarded Ainafare hovering above Taiga and Bree. "Tundra was not the first to fall to Grotto, and I do not think she will be the last." He raised his muzzle into the air. "The first bite of Winter is in the eastern winds. Whatever the Earthshaker's purpose, the Breschuvine cannot be far. Ready yourself, Caribou."

They walked again, side by side. "And why do you come, Polaris?" Moshee was solemn. "Why do you not remain with Aurora and your pups at Lone Mountain?"

The black Wolf stared ahead. "Because I have heard the whispers that come into the hinterlands. Because I have held council with Blinn, Eye of the North. Because the Winter's teeth are dulled, her arms weakened. Ground that has been frozen for ages upon ages thaws into the late Autumn. Strange bubbles rise in the lakes of the Old Crow Flats. Ice vanishes from the sea."

His copper eyes drew thin in the afternoon sun. "I come because I fear the Cargoth and their long dream of hunger. Because I am bound by Rahtrum. Because I believe you will find a way to wake them from their slumber." He looked at Moshee. "Because you must."

The dream was of a Bear; the same Grizzly who came in the night to topple the towering White Spruce. But now the dream was different. The tree already lay upon the forest floor, its trunk splintered and broken. The Bear was calm. It stood over the fallen spruce with the hushed silence that follows a storm, but it did not turn to find Bou with its eyes. Instead, a mist drifted through the forest. The Bear lifted its wide, brown head and sniffed the air. The fog thickened, and the Grizzly became agitated. It growled and bared its teeth, but the mist enveloped it, and it disappeared from sight.

The Caribou squinted his dreamy eyes. Now a new shape moved in the fog. Moshee stood tall, and his antlers rose into the damp night air. *I am not the yearling you haunted in the Spring, Shadow-walker.* Fog curled around the figure. Bou lowered his head, huffed, and stamped the ground. A familiar voice came like a whisper to the young bull.

"Moshee?"

The Caribou was startled. A black she-Wolf with Lichen-green eyes stepped out of the mist. She cocked her head and stared at him.

"Moshee, do you hear me?"

Tundra? He lifted his head and stepped forward. But the Wolf stepped back, away from him. Her tail sunk low and her scruff hair stood up. Her ears turned back, straining to hear something behind her. "Moshee, if you hear me, I beg of you, run."

A blackness lunged out of the fog and swept the she-Wolf aside. White eyes, each one streaked with green, glared at the Caribou. A growl rolled across Bou's dream, deep and wide as the Arctic night. He shivered and was awake.

The Caribou raised his head. Bree was curled next to him, her head upon her rear hooves. Ainafare hovered silently overhead. Taiga stood nearby, grazing. Polaris sat on a little rise nearby, watching the horizon. The young bull scrambled to his hooves. Bree raised her sleepy head, huffed, and lay back down. Bou stood quietly beside Polaris.

Their little group was resting in the crook of a long valley. High, rocky mountains towered in the west, and these burned vermillion at their peaks where the sun touched them. To the south, at the end of the valley, a mountain stood alone, with a thin spire of rock at its top jutting into the sky. The morning light spilled orange and yellow down its eastern flank. Behind the mountain, in the distance, there rose the roots of the great southern mountain ranges.

As he stood beside Polaris, Bou remembered how Ainafare had surprised him the previous day. She had hovered beside him for a moment when they first glimpsed the mountain in the distance.

"Bear Cave Mountain, it is called," the Faerie had whispered. "That is where you will discover what you seek. Say nothing of it to the others." She leaned in close to his ear. "You alone can find the Breschuvine. It is hidden even from me. You will know it by its sweet scent and by its four, white flowers, one for each season." She looked into his dark eyes. "Whatever may happen between this valley and the mountain, Moshee, seek out the flower, and consume it. Do not waver."

Now, as the Wolf and the Caribou stood together and stared down the valley, there was no sign of the grey-mane.

Polaris turned to the young bull. "Mist came to me in the night. He is certain the shadow-walker watches the valley, but he cannot track him."

"But surely we are safe, protected as we are by you and Mist and the Faerie."

"We will not fail you. But the grey-mane is concerned. He does not think that Grotto is alone," the Wolf said.

"Does he think the Crow Hugin travels with him?" Bou asked.

"Mist has cultivated a bond with the Crows. They came to him with counsel on the high stone atop Lone Mountain. He would know if Hugin was watching. No. It is another, nearly as stealthy as the shadow-walker and possessed of great craft."

"Cordillera," the Caribou said. "The Red Fox who turns black. Blinn warned me of her before he left the mountains in the north. She came to us upon the Old Crow Flats. She wished to draw us out to the Old Crow Range."

"That is not well," the old Wolf said. "Be wary, Moshee."

The day was old when the Caribou and the Faerie mounted the low slopes of Bear Cave Mountain. The Wolves had run south to circle the mountain and search the low plains that lay beyond it. The light was failing when a strange fog drifted in quickly among the White Spruce trees that ringed the low slopes.

"I know this fog," Bou said.

The Faerie stopped in front of them, and her light grew a little brighter. "Be still Caribou. I, too, know this fog, and it is neither Autumn nor Winter that breathes it."

She waved an arm through the air and a little of the mist stirred and cleared from the forest in front of them. Sitting on the forest floor, just beyond the trunk of an old, fallen tree was a Red Fox with bright, copper eyes.

"You have some craft, Faerie," the Fox said casually. Her bushy tail was curled around her legs.

"It is Cordillera," Moshee said. "She is not what she seems."

The Faerie lifted her small hand with splayed fingers to silence the Caribou. She addressed the Fox. "You are known to me, Cordillera, by your craft, but also by another name."

The Fox cocked her head. "Why should a Faerie know a simple Fox?" Cordillera paused to lick her front paw. "Tell me, by what other name do you know me?"

Ainafare began to glow a little brighter. "I know you by the name that was given to you by your Troven. I have been to Skull Ridge to hold council with your elders."

The Fox stopped preening and sat up straight. She stared at the Faerie.

"You are Tuatha De Danann, though by some strange craft you wear the skin of a Fox. You are called Dorchafare by your kin, the Darkling. It was you who called the Cargoth to its Chrysaling. You are the Caller and the Keeper of the Gwich'in Faerie. It was you who left him sitting alone, unguarded, at the foot of the Northern Mountains." Her voice was cold. "You are known to me and to your Troven. You have been called upon by the shadow-walker, and you have answered his call. You have turned your back on the Children of Danu."

"Are you so sure that *he* was not called upon by *me*?" The Fox stood up and with a flick of her tail, her hair began its transformation to black. "To whom among our kind do I have the displeasure of speaking? What Faerie is this, who concerns herself with the affairs of Caribou?"

"I am Ainafare, First Light." The Faerie slowly continued to brighten as the mist and the evening twilight closed in around them. "This is my counsel to you, Darkling. Go now, and take your fog with you. I am the Keeper of these Caribou."

"Save your counsel for one who asks it of you. You are also known to me, Ainafare." The Fox stared, unblinking. "How is it that you are the Keeper of these poor beasts, when you could not even safe-keep your own?"

Ainafare was shaken by Cordillera's words, and her light faltered a little.

"Did you think I would not know, Faerie?" The Fox padded the ground with her limbs coiled. "That is why you travel with the Caribou, is it not? It is a deep wound you carry. The weight of your loss must be terrible. Why do you not rest, Ainafare?" Cordillera sprang forward in a dark blur, jumping onto the fallen tree trunk and leaping toward the Faerie. In the air the Fox was lost in a cloud of dark vapour, and from the cloud emerged a Faerie that glistened as black as obsidian. In an instant the Darkling Faerie was directly in front of Ainafare. With a flourish of her arm a little shower of dust fell over the white Faerie like ash.

Ainafare coughed and struggled to hover in the air. Her light flickered.

"Sleep, Faerie. I have not forgotten our spells. Lay down your heavy burden for a little while." Dorchafare glowed with a strange, deep blue light, and her sable wings were a shadowy blur.

Ainafare's tiny body went limp. Her gossamer wings slowed, and she fell through the air to the earth, like an Autumn leaf. Bree pressed close to her mother. Taiga stamped her hooves and looked to Bou. Moshee stared at the little Faerie, lying on the ground, pale as a Wintergreen flower, her light dimmed until it glowed no brighter than Winter starlight upon snow.

"Did you think your Faerie invincible?" The Darkling hovered near Bou. "Do not be afraid for her, Moshee. She is only sleeping. Save your fear. You will soon have need of it." Dorchafare rose up in the air and moved aside.

The young bull Caribou peered forward into the mist. A figure began to emerge, and Bou instinctively took a step back. *It is like the dream.* He bumped into Taiga. "Go," he said quietly to her. But the cow and the yearling stood still, too frightened to move.

The creature in the fog drew closer, and its outline became clearer. The dark shape was enormous, and at first Moshee believed it to be the Grizzly from his dreams. Then he saw the figure's frost-white eyes, each of them streaked with green. *The shadow-walker. He is here.*

"Go," Bou said again to his mother as he took a step forward. He stood protectively over the fallen Faerie and brandished his antlers. Still, the cow and the yearling did not move. He turned his head to them. "Run!" he bellowed. At last their instincts rose up above their fear, and Taiga and Bree turned and fled wildly into the mist.

Moshee huffed the cool, wet air, stamped the ground with his broad hooves, and turned to face the figure in the fog. A familiar tingling sensation ran along his spine. He stood tall and felt suddenly bigger and stronger. The shadow-walker loomed from out of the mist. For the very first time, Moshee could see his pursuer clearly, and fear welled up in his heart like a Winter storm.

The Wolves stood together on the low slopes of Bear Cave Mountain, surrounded by White Spruce trees.

Polaris spoke first. "The day is old, and the light fails. I cannot scent the shadow-walker or the Red Fox that Moshee spoke of. But I have scented the Bear."

"I have also scented the Grizzly," Mist replied, "and two cubs that follow at her paws. The Autumn is old. Winter spreads wide her arms, but the Bear, Arktikos does not sleep. She circles the mountain with her cubs, grazing. It is too late in the season for her."

"Something keeps the sow from her den," Polaris said. A light fog began to drift through the trees. The Wolves sniffed the air.

"It cannot be a search for food that keeps her awake. The summer was plentiful." The grey-mane looked up the mountain. "It is the shadow-walker. He is here. What else could keep mighty Arktikos from her slumber?"

"Then the Breschuvine is also near. Fool of a Faerie! She has known all along where to look for the flower. Now Grotto's trap is set. Moshee is in danger. We must find him." The black Wolf sprang away, and Mist followed easily.

Taiga and Bree ran recklessly through the fog, turning this way and that, weaving around trees and leaping over fallen trunks, terrified that they might be pursued. They ran uphill at first, on the forested slopes of the mountain, and then downhill again. The mist made it difficult to see, and on a few occasions they stumbled as they ran. Eventually they slowed, wide-eyed and panting, and then stopped altogether. *We are simple Caribou,* the cow thought. *We are not suited to such a journey.*

The yearling pressed near to her mother. "Where is Bou?"

"I do not know," Taiga replied, as she turned to survey their surroundings.

The Caribou stood at the edge of a small, open glade that was obscured by fog. Willows, Blueberry, and Shrub Birch lined the ground near them. As they stared together into the mist, Bree stepped on an old, dead Spruce branch, and it cracked loudly under her weight. The sound spooked the little Caribou, and she bolted into the glade. Taiga followed after her, but the yearling stopped almost as quickly as she had started, and the old cow nearly crashed into her. There, grazing in the mist were two brown Bear cubs. They seemed as surprised by Bree and Taiga as the Caribou were by them. The animals all stared at each other for a moment.

Then there came a loud popping sound from out of the fog, just a little up-slope from the cubs. A large female Grizzly lumbered into view. The Bear was inhaling to scent the Caribou, while clicking her teeth and moving her cheeks to make the strange popping noise that alerted her cubs to danger. She had a thick, brown coat that shook with each step and two deep, forest eyes that watched them carefully.

"Arktikos," Taiga whispered to herself.

The cubs reacted instantly to the sounds their mother made. They whirled around and ran toward the far side of the glade, disappearing into the fog. As the big Bear drew near, blowing and huffing, the Caribou could hear the cubs in the distance. Their claws scratched for purchase as they each scrambled up a Spruce tree.

Bree began to shake with fear and to bellow. This only seemed to alarm the Grizzly and she bluff-charged the Caribou with unnerving speed. She stopped her massive bulk just in front of the yearling, grunted, and swept the earth with her great paw. A Shrub Willow was tossed aside in a cloud of humus and soil. The yearling was frozen where she stood, dwarfed by the Bear. Urine dribbled to the ground, and she cried loudly. Arktikos turned away and circled. She blew and huffed and swept the earth with her paws. The Bear made ready to charge again.

She is going to attack. Taiga leaned quickly into Bree and bit the yearling's flank hard to wake her from the terror that had seized all of her limbs. The little Caribou jumped and scrambled away from the Bear, toward the Spruce forest. But the Grizzly had already begun its charge and Taiga sprang forward to meet her.

The sunlight was gone from the sky and Dorchafare's deep blue light hung in the forest mist. Bou stared at the shadow-walker then peered down at Ainafare, who glowed dimly where she lay on the ground. The young bull fought his instinct to turn and run. He stood over the little Faerie, determined to protect her, and raised his antlers into the air.

The shadow-walker moved slowly, fearlessly. Its massive, clawed paws were sure and steady. Bou imagined the immense animal could move at great speed if it so desired. Its wide black head moved back and forth rhythmically to scan the darkening forest and scent the still air. It stood as high as a Grizzly on all fours, but its body was longer and wider, and it had a bushy tail that trailed low behind it. All the likeness of a Wolverine was upon it, but one that had grown beyond all reckoning and was shrouded in gloom.

What are you? Darkness seemed to cling to its long, black fur and drag shadows with it through the air. Its small, rounded ears stood up to listen for enemies. At last the Caribou could clearly see the creature that had haunted his dreams and followed him across the northlands: a Wolverine that by some dark craft had grown into a nightmare. *We are doomed,* he thought. *I am sorry Ainafare.*

"Do not come any closer, Shadow-walker." Bou was so frightened he almost whispered. "I will allow no harm to come to the Faerie." His haunches were shaking but still he lowered the spiked arc of his rack toward the creature.

The dark beast ignored the Caribou and came nearer, until the two animals stood almost muzzle to muzzle. "Grotto, I am called by my kin, though I grow fond of *this* name," he said it slowly, "Shadow-walker." He looked down at Ainafare where she lay, asleep and defenseless. "She looks well-served by you thus far, Caribou." His voice was low and mocking. It shook the night air and made Moshee's belly quiver. "I wonder — were she awake, would the Faerie do the same for you?"

"Ainafare, she is called, First Star of the Tuatha De Danann." Bou was surprised by the sudden daring that rose in his own voice.

"Hope that she does not awaken, or you will have your answer."

The black creature was amused. He looked up at Dorchafare. The Darkling shook her head slowly. Grotto turned again to the Caribou. "The Faerie will not stir again until the sun has risen. She cannot help you." Lightening streaks of green shone in his white eyes. "But you should take care with your tone. The rut calls to you, Moshee. It courses in your blood and clouds your judgement. It makes you foolish with bravery, like the she-Wolf upon Lone Mountain. Do not be foolish, Caribou. We, both of us, seek the same thing. Let us help each other."

"I do not know where the Breschuvine is," Moshee said defiantly.

"This I believe." Grotto's white eyes narrowed and he leaned close. The stink of his breath crowded the Caribou's nose. "But you do know that it is here upon the mountain. Already you know that its scent will call only to you, and that you alone can find it. This your precious Faerie has told you." His voice deepened with impatience. "This I already know."

"I do not know how to find it," the bull whispered.

"Then let me help you, Moshee." The shadow-walker's voice softened. "We have guessed where it blooms; where Rahtrum has hidden it for safekeeping. But although I scent the ground again and again, it remains in the shadows, only to appear for the chosen of Rahtrum. Come with me up the mountain, and I will show you. Come, and we will find it together."

Bou looked down at Ainafare. "Tundra fell to you," he said

solemnly. "It was you who put out her light. She was my friend." His eyes nervously met Grotto's. "I will not lead you to the Breschuvine. I am bound to those who watch over me."

The shadow-walker's mouth gaped wide as he growled. His white fangs glistened in the Darkling's strange light. The ground seemed almost to shake, and Moshee scrambled backward instinctively.

"Do you think I have come to play games with you, Caribou?" The black creature moved forward, placing each of his enormous, clawed paws on either side of Ainafare. He lowered his muzzle and scented the sleeping Faerie before peering up at Moshee.

The Darkling interrupted from above. "Time is short, Grotto. They will not be far."

The shadow-walker held Moshee in his gaze. "Let us strike a simple bargain, you and I. Lead me to the Breschuvine, and I will spare the Faerie." His tongue traced his muzzle and a calm came over him. "Refuse me, Caribou, and I will extinguish your First Light here, before you. Hesitate again, and you will hear her little bones crack between my jaws before I swallow her. Utter one word against my generous overture, and after I have consumed the Tuatha De Danann we will sit here, the two of us, and await your beloved Wolves. They will come, as surely as the morning star. The guts of Land Crow I will spill first. This I promise." He lowered his broad head and nudged the Faerie with his nose. "Think hard on your next words."

Bou stared down at Ainafare. *Where are you Blinn? Where is the Earthshaker? So many you have sent to aid me, and yet, at the end, I am alone. How many must be lost?* He squeezed his eyes shut and pictured Tundra's soft green eyes in his mind. *I cannot bear it.*

The Darkling Faerie spoke again. "The Wolves will scent the Grizzly and know that something is amiss."

"Silence!" Grotto hissed at Dorchafare. He curled up his lips, bared his teeth, and snapped at Ainafare.

"No!" Bou bellowed. "I will come with you. I will lead you to the Breschuvine, but you must leave the Faerie unharmed."

The Faerie was lost in a dream. In it she raced alone over the Peel River and through the night to rescue the yearling. *Where are the others?* She peered back as she flew. Behind her the northlands fell into darkness. Shadows swarmed in the west, swallowing the moon and the stars, the sky and the world. She turned and fled east with all the speed she could muster. Pursued by the darkness, she streaked through the night. But the blackness came swiftly behind her, and a thick fog rose before her. The air became heavy. She strained against the weight of it, and soon her wings were weary.

The river below called to her. "Sleep," it whispered.

No. I cannot. I must not.

Ainafare looked back once again, but now the gloom was upon her. She fell into the murky waters, sinking and tumbling in the wild current. Her light flickered in the torrent and grew dim. Her eyelids became heavy, and soon they slid closed. Thus it was that she fell into a dream within a dream.

Now she was suspended in a vast ocean of darkness, but for a tiny white light that shone in the distance like a star. The light was clear and warm and familiar. It filled the Faerie's heart with hope. But as she watched the star, a black shadow drifted in front of it. A dark, boundless creature swam in the depths.

Ainafare reached out her arm toward the distant light as the long shadowy beast undulated, turned, and then dove deep beneath it. She tried to scream out a warning, but cold water rushed into her mouth. As the creature ascended, its great jaws opened wide and swallowed up the little star. The light was gone. The creature raced toward the Faerie, a monstrous black shadow in a sea of darkness, save for two specks of light — the beast's eyes — frost-white as Faerie's wings.

The Faerie clenched her fists. Her light blazed. The dark ocean boiled and writhed around her. Suddenly, she was once again in the dream of the river. Then breaking its surface. Then rising into the night air. And finally, awake.

Ainafare struggled to stand. She stumbled once before she was fully upright upon her slender legs. She blinked her eyes and peered about the dark, foggy forest. She shook her head and fluttered her wings. Grey ash fell from her body to the ground, and her light leapt up into the night mist. Her wings began to move, slowly at first, and then faster, until at last they were a blur of moonlight. She rose carefully into the air and hovered there, peering at the ground. There she spied the tracks of the Fox, where Cordillera had leapt up onto the tree trunk. There, too, were the clear hoofprints where the Caribou had stood and where the cow and the yearling had fled. She circled the area and lingered over the Fox's tracks. The Faerie dropped from the air to the ground. She crouched low like a Lynx, supporting herself with one palm pressed to the earth. Her still wings stood up straight above her. Her neck craned as she peered left and right and drank in the air, searching for signs of the shadow-walker. With the fingers of her free hand she scooped up a little handful of loam and spruce needles. These she held to her muzzle and scented deeply. Her head shot up, and she stared at the mountain. A line of tracks appeared to her through the fog. It was Moshee's steady gait. And there were faint tracks of another, much more difficult to see. One who was much larger, with wide paws and long claws. *My prey.* She stood and tossed the loam and spruce needles to the ground. Her wings blurred and glowed as she leapt into the air, and her beautiful, white eyes flickered with flame.

Bree had backed away from the Bear as quickly as she could, to the edge of the glade and into the forest. She had seen the Bear making ready to charge again and had felt a sharp pain on her flank. As she fled the glade, her mother galloped past with antlers lowered toward the Bear. She glimpsed the Grizzly rearing up on its two hind legs just as the twilight and the fog swallowed them both from view. Bree cowered in the Spruce trees and listened helplessly to the terrible sounds of struggle and the loud, prolonged growling of the Bear. These sounds were soon followed by an eerie, more troubling silence.

Bree stood alone in the forest. She was shocked and confused. So much was happening, so quickly. After a few moments the little Caribou called into the silence for her mother. In answer she heard a slow movement from out in the misty glade, and her heart leapt up. She called again, and the movement seemed to come closer. She called once more, and the Grizzly lumbered out of the fog. There was no sign of Taiga. The yearling shook where she stood. "My name's Bree," she offered desperately. "Please don't eat me." The Bear roared, its muzzle was darkened with blood. It was then the Wolves came upon the yearling. Rushing out of the forest, Polaris, who was kindest and least frightening of the two, stopped to stand in front of Bree. He turned to face the Bear.

The big, frightening grey-mane crashed forward to the edge of the glade and confronted the Grizzly. There, he planted his paws with his tail held high, his scruff hair raised, and his ears trained forward. Bree could hear the Wolf's low continuous growl, broken only by quick, deep breaths.

The Bear was startled by the Wolves' sudden arrival and immediately bluff-charged Mist. The grey-mane did not flinch, and the Grizzly skidded to a sudden stop in front of him. She backed away and paced in a circle. She turned sideways to show the Wolf her great size. The Wolf remained unperturbed. He understood the sow's body language and knew that she was afraid. He ceased his growling, raised his head, and dropped his tail. He covered his teeth and took a slow step backward to show the Bear he meant her no harm. The Grizzly stared at him a moment, sniffed the air, and then turned and trudged off in the direction of her cubs.

Polaris turned to Bree. "Are you unharmed? Where is Moshee, Little One?"

Bree did not answer. She stared forward through the Spruce trees into the fog of the clearing.

Polaris turned to follow her gaze and watched as Mist strode into the glade and disappeared. His voice was gentle. "Bree, where is your brother?"

She stepped forward toward the clearing.

The black Wolf blocked her way. "You must tell us, yearling. Where is Moshee? Where is the Faerie, Ainafare?"

The Caribou looked past the Wolf. "The Red Fox came."

"Cordillera?" Polaris demanded.

"She's not really a Fox." Bree's voice was almost a whisper. "She turned into a Faerie and put Ainafare to sleep." Bree's eyes would not leave the place where the grey-mane had vanished. "Bou told us to run, and we ran and ran and ran."

"From which direction, Bree? Where did you leave Moshee and Ainafare?"

"Where's my mother?" she asked.

Polaris' lips curled, and he let out a little snarl to capture her attention. Bree's gaze shifted to him, and he held her in the copper of his eyes. Once again, his voice was gentle. "Tell us where you left your brother, yearling. From which direction did you run?"

"The north," she replied. "From the foot of the mountain."

Polaris whirled around and barked at Mist. "We must go north and scent Moshee's trail. They came upon the Fox, Cordillera. The shadow-walker could not have been far behind."

Mist padded out of the fog and stopped at the edge of the forest. His muzzle glistened in the twilight.

"Taiga?" Polaris asked.

Dark liquid dripped from the grey Wolf's muzzle. "Fallen," he replied.

Bree watched the grey-mane silently and then turned away and bleated quietly to herself.

Mist stepped forward into the forest and licked his muzzle. "I will watch the yearling. Go, Polaris. Feed. It is foolish to waste it all upon the Bear and the Crows."

The black Wolf glanced at Bree and then strode into the fog.

The fog that wreathed the low slopes of the mountain thinned and lifted as the Wolves and the yearling moved quickly through the night forest. The moon had risen. It shone silver light among the trees, and their trunks and branches, in turn, cast black shadows.

When the Wolves had first made ready to turn north, Bree was still in a state of shock. She had stood in a kind of daze, confused by the loss of Taiga. At first she refused to go with them, and though he tried, Polaris could not compel her. But Mist had only to tell the yearling that the Grizzly would not sleep while the shadow-walker still stalked the mountain. Arktikos, he told her, would come again in the night with her cubs, drawn by the fallen cow. At last Bree had relented, more afraid to be alone with the Bear than to travel with the Wolves.

It was not long before they reached the place where the Caribou had encountered the Fox.

"The Faerie lay here, asleep." Bree pawed the moonlit ground with her hoof. "She is gone too, like my mother."

Mist padded in slow, deliberate circles, scenting the Caribou and Fox tracks. "Moshee was here. The Fox too. But I cannot say by which path they departed or in what direction."

"It is Faerie craft," Polaris said. "Cordillera conceals them from us. The shadow-walker has come for Moshee. It is certain." He sniffed the ground where the white Faerie had lain. "But what of Ainafare? If Cordillera cast her into sleep, then why is she not here?" A sudden wind swept through the Spruce forest and up the mountainside.

"Because the Fox has underestimated her," Mist replied, as he sprang away into the woods. He crashed through the undergrowth and climbed the mountain slope.

Polaris barked after him. "Mist! Where are you going?" The black Wolf growled in frustration and turned to the yearling.

"Come, Bree, we must hold together."

The Caribou ignored the Wolf. She was staring up through a break in the Spruce trees at the high eastern slopes of the mountain. A strange light played on her face and in her eyes. "What is that?" she asked softly.

Polaris stood at Bree's side and followed her gaze. High up in the distance, a shaft of rotating flame rose from the side of the mountain and burned into the sky, scattering light down the mountain and into the surrounding valley. The First Star was dumbstruck for a moment. "Ainafare," he whispered, and then he leapt away after Mist.

The yearling was mesmerized; she had never seen such a light. But soon she noticed the strange wind and the gloom that was around her and realized that she was alone. She called out for Polaris and ran as fast as she could after him.

Dorchafare, the Darkling Faerie, chanted a strange incantation when they began their hike up the mountain. She showered Bou with an ashen dust to hide him and his tracks from any who might follow. They climbed in silence. Bou could not take his gaze from Grotto. Though he was massive, he moved quietly, with ease and stealth, through the mist-laden forest.

When, at last, they broke through the treeline and stood upon the open rock of the high mountain, the shadow-walker halted and turned.

"We are close." Grotto looked up at the Faerie. "You have done well, Dorchafare. Go, seek out the Crow, and bring word to me."

"What of the fog?" she asked. "What of the grey-mane?"

"What of them?" He looked down the mountain with his strange eyes. "The Faerie sleeps. The Wolves cannot track us. Go. Find the Crow."

The Faerie blinked her black eyes and rose higher into the air. "Beware the Faerie, Ainafare. You have wounded her deeply. I surprised her. She will not be deceived again."

"The Tuatha De Danann has sought me without pause for three seasons, and always I have evaded her." Grotto turned to look at Bou. "Even now she only lives because this Caribou has begged her life in exchange for his service. Do not worry, Darkling. I am grown strong, and she is weak, still bound by her covenant with the Children of Danu."

Dorchafare's deep blue light pulsed brighter. "Nevertheless, be wary, Grotto." She streaked off into the mist.

The black creature watched the Faerie go. "Come, Moshee. The place we seek is not far."

They walked along a high ridgeline. The fog that had ringed the mountain began to lift, no longer anchored there by the Darkling's craft. Moonlight bathed the stone and the forested slopes that descended into the valley below. But it seemed not to touch the shadow-walker, for still the darkness clung to him.

"Why does Ainafare chase after you?" Bou asked. "No other Faeries pursue you."

Grotto looked over his shoulder at Moshee. "Has she not told you, Caribou? Have you not guessed?"

"I believed she was sent by Rahtrum," Bou said quietly. "Or by Blinn, on the Earthshaker's behalf."

"Do you think that the mighty Binder may compel the Faeries? They are Tuatha De Danann, the Children of Danu. They do as they please." He spat his words. "They are bound only to each other, to their Troven, and to their covenant to do no harm. Gifted with long life, they have kicked themselves free of the earth. They are no more concerned with the ascension of the Cargoth..." He looked again over his shoulder at Moshee, "...than they are with the affairs of Caribou. For they have seen other creatures rise and fall."

"Why, then? Why does she pursue you?"

"Truly, Caribou, you do not know?" The shadow-walker stopped and turned to face Bou. "I will tell you, then." A sort of delight entered Grotto's voice. "Do you remember your night upon the Peel River? In the Spring, when you were but an untested yearling?"

"I could not forget it," Bou replied. "Blinn and the Faeries came that night to save me."

"So they did," Grotto agreed. "An entire Troven, perhaps two, summoned by that fool of a Gnome, and the Raptor, Windshim. And did you know that Ainafare was among them?"

"Yes. She came to my mother, Taiga, upon the banks of the Peel."

"Did she, indeed? And has Ainafare told you what she left behind upon the banks of the mighty Peel River that night?" Grotto was almost gleeful. "Tell me, Moshee, is there ice in her heart when she remembers it? Does hate burn in her eyes when she speaks of answering the Eagle's call?"

Moshee said nothing. Already he had begun to regret asking the question.

"Oh, poor Caribou. Do you begin to see?" The shadow-walker callously teased the bull. "Do you think my eyes were always frost-white like a Faerie's wings?"

The Caribou hung his head.

"I followed you in the Spring, Moshee. It was known to me that Rahtrum had sent you to seek the Breschuvine. I stalked you along Wind River to the Peel. And when the Tuatha De Danann flew east over the river to your aid, I turned west so they would take no notice of me. It was then that a sweet smell came to me on the wind. It made the warmth of my hunger call to me. I followed the scent, drawn like a Warble Fly to warm flesh. I found a large Poplar tree that stood beside the river, and I scaled the trunk, drawn up by the scent." Grotto paused to search the Caribou's eyes. "What do you think I found there, Moshee? At the end of a high branch, wrapped up carefully in a leaf, powdered with Spring Dust?"

The Caribou turned away from the shadow-walker to look out over the lowlands. "I am sorry that I asked."

Grotto loomed close and hissed. "But you did ask. And you will hear my answer." His breath was foul. "I found a fledgling Faerie there. A tiny female, white as untrodden snow, brand new to the world. Beautiful, even to me." His voice brimmed with excitement. "A kind of perfection: eyes sealed shut, carefree, asleep, defenseless." The shadow-walker leaned in to speak softly at the Caribou's ear. "She was abandoned there by her mother,

Moshee, who left the fledging that she might answer the call of the Eagle. A mother, who in her haste to save you, cast no spell to conceal her treasure. Poor little Faerie. She was deserted that night by Ainafare, First Light of the Tuatha De Danann, that she might fly to your aid."

"Stop! I do not wish to hear any more." Bou felt ill.

Grotto ignored the bull and continued matter-of-factly. "I have grown much larger since then, but still, the Poplar branch was much too thin to support me. No matter. Hunger can make one fearless, Moshee, and I would not be denied my prize. I leapt from the trunk and swallowed the leaf and the Faerie together, as I fell toward the rushing river. Did you know a fledgling's bones are soft as Spring shoots of the Buckbean?" The shadow-walker closed his eyes and licked his lips in a moment of reverie.

"When at last I climbed from the water downstream, I discovered that an uncommon stealth and vision had been bestowed upon me by the youngling. I fled east then, to find your trail again, unsure when Ainafare would return. So you see, Caribou, that is why I am pursued by the Faerie. And it is why she travels with you, though no one bade her do so."

Moshee walked in silence behind Grotto as they climbed. He thought of the Faerie, Ainafare, asleep and defenseless in the forest below, just as her little fledgling had lain. *It is no wonder she would not speak to us. It is no wonder her heart is grown hard and cold.*

As he and the shadow-walker rounded the edge of a high, stone wall, a strange scent came to the bull on the wind. It was like sweet, Spring Cottongrass and the warm salt winds of the northern sea combined. *The Breschuvine.* Without thinking, Bou stopped and huffed the air.

Grotto peered over his shoulder. "It calls to you, Moshee." He turned. "It is true, then. You alone may scent the Breschuvine. We are close now. Come."

It was not long before the shadow-walker stopped upon a rocky plateau at the foot of a craggy, stone rise that continued straight up to the peak of the mountain – all of it lit by the moon and crowned by stars. A wide, black cave opened in the rock wall before them. *The Bear's den.* The scent of the Breschuvine filled the air around the Caribou until he was almost dizzy. *It is here.* He recalled Ainafare's entreaty. *Whatever may happen between this valley and the mountain, Moshee, seek out the flower, and consume it. Do not waver.*

Grotto stood before the Bear's cave and watched the Caribou carefully. His head drifted back and forth, scenting the air. He watched Bou's eyes without blinking. "Tell me, Caribou, where is the Breschuvine?"

It is there, at the corner of the cave entrance. A single plant with four white flowers, each as large as one of my hooves. It glitters strangely in the moonlight. How is it you cannot see it, Shadow-walker? Moshee did his best not to stare directly at the Breschuvine, though it called to him.

"I do not see it," he lied. "I have its scent, it fills the air, but I am no Wolf. Perhaps if we wait for the morning sun?"

The shadow-walker lunged forward, snarling. "Do not test me. It is here." Rocks scattered beneath the big animal, and Bou scrambled backward.

"Then I will have to look for it," the Caribou insisted.

Grotto stepped close and stared into Moshee's eyes. "Show me where the Breschuvine is, so that I may see it," he growled. "Say that it is there and it will appear. So says Dorchafare. But move slowly, or I will put you on your back, Caribou." He snarled and saliva dripped from his jaw. "Touch just one of the flowers, and I will fly down this mountain to where the Faerie lies sleeping and put out her light. Do you understand?"

"I understand," Bou replied nervously.

The shadow-walker stepped aside slowly to let the Caribou explore.

Bou moved carefully to the other side of the wide cave, his head down, pretending to scent the ground. He moved his muzzle back and forth, pausing now and again to lift up his head, as though to look around. Ainafare's words rang over and over again in his head. *Whatever may happen between this valley and the mountain, Moshee, seek out the flower, and consume it. Do not waver.* Slowly he made his way across the front of the cave entrance until, at last, he was facing the extraordinary white flowers. The Breschuvine was only a stride or two away. It filled his senses and made him shaky. *Do not waver.* He staggered and quickly steadied himself.

Grotto's eyes thinned and he began to growl, sensing something was amiss.

I am sorry, Ainaþare. Moshee sprang forward. He lunged at the Breschuvine flowers as quickly as he could. He clutched two of them in his teeth before the shadow-walker crashed into his flank. Then Bou was on his back, sliding across the stony ground. Pain flared up his side. *Do not waver.* He chewed the flowers and they seemed to burst and run like cool water on his tongue. His mouth began to lose feeling, and he swallowed desperately. A strange heat moved through his body. He tried to scramble onto his hooves, but he could not find his balance. The shadow-walker hovered over the place where the Breschuvine was. Moshee could only see the creature's great, black bulk and writhing tail. He tried again to stand and failed.

Grotto turned and faced the bull where he lay. The shadow-walker was also unsteady on his wide paws. A glittering white liquid dripped from his chin.

The Breschuvine ran hot in the Caribou's blood, it swam in his head. He blinked his eyes and panted. *Do not waver.*

Grotto stepped toward Bou, his teeth bared. "You are a fool, Moshee. It seems Rahtrum has chosen poorly."

It was then a familiar voice, filled with ice and disdain, rose from behind the Caribou. "*You* are the fool, Shadow-walker. Some in the north may tremble when they hear your name, but I am not one of them."

Moshee shook his head. A bright, white light suddenly shone over him.

"Get up, Caribou," the voice commanded. "Do not waver."

He struggled up onto his shaky legs.

The shadow-walker had stopped mid-stride, his eyes were narrow, and his lips curled back. "You are too late, Faerie," he hissed.

The light around Bou grew brighter, and Ainafare, First Light of the Tuatha De Danann, drifted before him. She hovered, radiant, in the air between the Caribou and the giant Wolverine.

"Go, Moshee. He will not stop you." Her voice was hard and sure as she drifted to the middle of the stone plateau. "Descend the mountain the way you came. The Wolves will be looking for you."

Moshee's legs were unsteady. He carefully tread around the shadow-walker to the ridge they had climbed. Grotto watched the Caribou. His hackles stood up, and his ears lay back. He snarled and hissed and snapped at Bou as he passed.

"Enough, Wolverine," the Faerie warned.

Grotto's massive head swung around to face her. His tail twitched in the air, and he took another tentative step forward. "I did not expect you until morning, Ainafare, you are awake early." His eyes glowed white and green in the Faerie's light.

"So I am."

"No matter. Now that you have found me, what will you do?" The Wolverine's voice was calm and low, his immense body coiled, ready to strike. "You cannot hope to stand against me. I with the Breschuvine within, and you, bound as you are by your covenant. Come to me, Child of Danu," he mocked her. "Let me end your suffering. Come. Join your fledgling." He stepped slowly forward.

Ainafare held up a single fist, and her light blazed into the night. Grotto squinted and snarled and pressed low to the ground.

Moshee scrambled backward. He blinked and looked up at the Faerie, mesmerized.

"Hear me, Wolverine." A sadness entered Ainafare's voice. She seemed to look through the shadow-walker, through the stone, through the entire mountain. "It is true that you are more than what you were." Orange flames flickered in her wide, white eyes. "It is true, you have the Breschuvine within; that you are strong, Grotto; that you range darkly. Perhaps now you are even beyond the craft of the Tuatha De Danann." The flames that gathered in her eyes swelled and overflowed. Slowly she shook her head. "It is true that you have slain the she-Wolf, Tundra." Droplets of fire rolled down her face and fell to the stony ground. Her voice grew soft and she wrapped her arms around her chest. "And it is true that you have taken from me all that there was to take." Her tears made a little pool of flame on the ground.

Grotto cocked his head and looked at the fire. "There is one more thing I will take from you, Faerie." His bluster seemed faded.

She ignored his threat. "All of this is true," she continued in a whisper. "But you are wrong about one thing, Wolverine." Her light began to grow.

The shadow-walker growled and rose up on his haunches. He winced in the face of Ainafare's light.

"About one very important thing, you are mistaken." She grew brighter still. She raised her head and stared into the shadow-walker's eyes. Once again, her voice was hard and cold. "I have broken faith with the Children of Danu." Her tears fell upon her breast and her body leapt up in flames. "I am bound by no covenant." The fire danced on her body and mixed with her light. "I am bound only by loss. Only by hate." A conflagration of flame erupted in the air around her. "Only by vengeance."

Bou was driven backward by the heat and the sound. A great wind rushed up the mountain, pulled upward by her fire.

Grotto was caught in the edge of the Faerie's sudden inferno. He snarled, screamed, and recoiled. The left side of his muzzle burst into flame. He turned, ran, and disappeared into the blackness of the Bear's cave.

Moshee watched helplessly as Ainafare hung in the air alone, lost in a corona of fire and light. Her arms were thrown wide and her shoulders seemed to shake. Her tears burned and fell, and her flames rose high into the night. The Caribou tried calling to her, but his voice was swept away by the winds that rushed up the mountain, drawn in by her turning column of fire. Again and again he called to her, but it was no use. Her fire rose higher and higher, twisting and roaring in the night wind.

As Bou watched the Faerie burn, Mist suddenly walked out of the night. Moshee was startled. He had not heard the Wolf's approach over the tumult of the wind. The grey-mane passed the Caribou silently. The wind whipped the Wolf's long Winter coat. His ears stood up straight. Bou looked on as Mist walked to the edge of the pillar of fire that swirled about Ainafare. *What are you doing? This is madness.* Then the mighty Wolf strode forward into the flames. Untouched and unburned, he moved to the very center of the firestorm to stand beneath the Faerie. Ainafare's tears fell upon the Wolf, but everywhere they struck him their fire was extinguished and his fur was made wet. Moshee watched, spellbound.

What craft is this?

The grey-mane looked up at the Faerie for a moment and then threw back his head and howled. The sorrowful sound rose over the wind and the flames and rolled down the mountainside.

Soon Polaris came to stand beside Moshee, and eventually Bree. The three animals stood together in silence. They watched the Wolf and the Faerie as the late morning sun broke over the eastern lowlands.

Where is Taiga? The young bull wondered.

At last Ainafare's fire began to diminish, and with it, the winds that blew up the mountain. Mist ceased his howling and looked up at her. Slowly, the flames fell away, until only the Faerie's body flickered. But these flames also gradually died until at last only her eyes smoldered. It was then that her exhausted arms fell to her sides. Her head hung forward and her wings began to slow. A final, fiery tear gathered in one of her eyes. It fell, and she with it, both landing softly in the long scruff-fur of the grey-mane's shoulders.

High up in the sky came the cry of an Eagle.

chapter 22

Windshim & Aquila

OCTOBER

Aquila's transparent second eyelids slid closed across his eyes and opened again as he and Windshim soared over the southern mountain ranges. From their great altitude they watched the sky blush orange with morning. Each day the darkness widened, and the sun came later and later. The Eagles flew near to each other.

"It is three moons since we left the Caribou," Windshim said. "We have done as Blinn asked. We have circled the Old Crow Basin and the Eagle Plains. We have carried word to Polaris at Lone Mountain. We have been to the shadow-walker's den at Tombstone Mountain, and west and north again, searching. There is not a whisper of him anywhere."

"Then only one task remains for us." Aquila peered at her. "We must find Moshee. By now he must have what he seeks. Let us find him and the Wolves and keep watch over them."

"Yes, let us search them out," she replied. "It is strange, though. We have taken countless Hares and not one among them bore a message from the Gnome. None among them brought word to us of the Breschuvine."

Aquila considered this. "It is too dangerous. The Gnome is wise and has much craft. He knows the shadow-walker is not bound, as we are. Grotto would have captured a Hare and wrung the message from it. Or he might have bade his Crows to watch where we perched and circled in the sky, giving clues to where the Breschuvine lay. We ourselves might have led him to his prize."

"That is true. Still, it is hard to fly and see as we do, to have an eye upon all the northlands, and still be of no service. I am curious to know what Blinn has learned of Grotto." She looked toward the dawn. "Too much time has been wasted searching for this shadow-walker, who somehow evades us, even though we can spy a Hare upon the plain from the top of a mountain. Now the season is grown late, and we do not know where to look for Moshee. Still, we are bound to watch over him and guide him to the Gnome at Hart River."

Aquila stared straight ahead as he spoke. "Then look there, Windshim, beyond the edge of the southern range. I cannot be certain at this distance, but if pressed, I would say that is Bear Cave Mountain. And look, upon its summit, a fire burns out of season and reaches up into the sky."

Windshim's transparent eyelids blinked and her yellow eyes focused. "That is not a fire by lightning out of season, Aquila. Look how it rises in a spire of flame. Do you see the white light that blazes near its base? It is the Faerie, Ainafare. Blinn warned of such a thing, but he could not have guessed at this darkness. Beset by grief she has cast aside her covenant. She burns with rage for the shadow-walker." The Eagle flapped her great wings. "Fly, Heart-feather. With Ainafare we will find Moshee and, by the look of her fire, Grotto too."

As Aquila and Windshim approached the mountain, the flames that rose from the summit faded and died in the early sun. The Eagles soared above the peak and upon the mountain they spied the Wolves, Polaris and Mist. With them were Moshee, and his sibling, Bree. They could not see the Faerie at first, though they were certain she was there. Nor had there been any sign of the old cow, Taiga. Farther down the slopes they had seen the Bear, Arktikos, with her cubs, all together in a clearing, at work upon the remains of some animal that was obscured by their brown bodies.

The Grizzly does not sleep yet. It is late in the season to keep her cubs from their den, Aquila observed.

When they arrived, Windshim flew down to the little band of animals, seeking news and counsel with Ainafare. Aquila circled Bear Cave Mountain alone, keeping watch, as the sun climbed higher. Little time passed before his mate returned to him in the blue, morning sky.

"It was Ainafare that burned," Windshim said. "The hard stone of the mountain has been scorched. Arktikos will find the entrance to her den blackened when at last she rests." The Raptors circled on warm thermals that blew in from the eastern lowlands and rose up from the mountain. "It is as Blinn warned. The Faerie's covenant is broken. She has confronted the shadow-walker. He is a Wolverine grown beyond all reckoning, they say. The Faerie has wounded him with her fire. But he has escaped through the Bear's den, and the caves that lie beyond. Polaris cannot scent or track him."

Aquila considered this news quietly. "And what does the Faerie say?"

"She says nothing. She is spent, exhausted by wrath and sorrow. Look closely, she sleeps, collapsed upon the back of the mighty grey-mane, nestled in his thick scruff. It is a strange sight to behold."

"Very strange," Aquila replied. "Her grief runs deep. It is different, the way of the Faeries." Aquila looked down at Mist. "In our many Springs together, how many fledglings have we watched slay their siblings to rule the nest and lay claim to the food we bring? We accept these sacrifices. It is the way of our brood. Always there is another Spring, another clutch. But the Faerie is driven almost to madness by the loss of just one."

Windshim gazed down at the grey-mane. "It is not the same with them." Her eyes focused, and she saw the Faerie's little figure, nestled in Mist's scruff-fur. Ainafare rocked gently as the Wolf moved carefully over the land. "They are mysterious, these Tuatha De Danann, and long-lived. The Gnome says that some among them are lucky to produce a single fledgling in an age."

Windshim blinked, and her voice was soft. "Think on it, Aquila, Heart-feather. It is as though our every nest, our every clutch, our every surviving fledgling had been swallowed at once by the shadow-walker and taken from us. I too, would burn, if I had the craft."

Aquila looked at her. "And what of the cow, Taiga?" he asked.

"The cow is no more. She is fallen, put down by Arktikos the Bear when she sought to protect her yearling, Bree. Moshee will not speak of it. He did not learn of his mother's death until after the spectacle of the Faerie. Now he is confused, filled at once with sorrow and bitter anger."

"That is sad news."

"The news grows darker still." Windshim looked at her mate as she spoke. "It was the shadow-walker that led Moshee to the Breschuvine. The Caribou has only half the flower within him. The Wolverine consumed the other half before the Faerie drove him off."

"What does this mean?"

"I do not know. We must watch over the Caribou as they cross the dark path of the Cargoth. Blinn has bade us to lead them back to the meeting place of the Hart and Peel Rivers. It is there he will await them. If any may know what it means for Grotto to have the Breschuvine within him, it will be the Gnome."

The Wolves and the Caribou moved southeast at Windshim's bidding. Ainafare still lay sleeping between the grey-mane's wide shoulders. The Wolf strode with great care and grace over the frozen ground, and the Faerie was carried along with him, like a little leaf upon a gentle river. As they moved out onto the vast lowlands that lay between the Western and Eastern Mountains, the

Golden Eagles flew together in wide circles, searching for signs of Grotto amid the Spruce trees.

"It is hopeless," Aquila said. "For three moons we have searched for him and found nothing. Now he ranges darkly and carries within him the Breschuvine. He will not be found if he does not wish it. Let us hunt. Let us perch and eat for strength, so that we may watch over the Caribou. If the shadow-walker comes, he comes. But he has been wounded, and I do not think he will risk the Faerie's fire again, nor the teeth of the grey-mane, if he has been weakened. None among those we watch over, not even Ainafare, knows where the Gnome will await us. There is nothing the shadow-walker can gain from them. He has already found what he wanted. They are as safe now as they can be."

Windshim nodded in agreement, and the Raptors turned east together and soared high above the Caribou, the Wolves, and the sleeping Faerie.

Windshim and Aquila hunted Ermine, Pika, and Hare across the plains near Branch River. There were no messages sent among the Hares. *It is well,* thought Aquila. *No word has come to us. The Gnome ranges south without hindrance.* They perched upon high rocky precipices that overlooked the river. There they rested and fed, as Moshee travelled with Bree and their company of Wolves.

Windshim went down to the land-walkers often. There was no

sign of Grotto, she told them, or the Crow, Hugin. On one occasion Aquila spotted a Red Fox that seemed to follow the strange little band. But when the wind swung from the north to blow due west, the scent of the big Wolves came to the Fox, and it turned and fled.

Snow fell among the Black Spruce and dusted the land. Now more than half the day fell away into darkness. The Eagles watched from above, as the Caribou crossed the Whitestone River with the Wolves. On the east side of the river, and to the north, there was a group of Caribou that had already come down from the coast. The little herd was made up of cows mostly, and yearlings that had survived the Autumn. They moved east, and the wind kept the scent of the Wolves from them. Aquila watched Moshee as he stopped on sparse rises to look north. *He sees the herd. Perhaps he even scents them. His eyes were keen already, and now the Breschuvine is at work within him.* As the Raptors watched from above, Moshee and the others suddenly stopped.

The young bull turned to face Bree. The two Caribou stood for a time, nose to nose, and then Bou seemed to butt Bree gently with his head, until she turned and walked a few paces away. The yearling bellowed at him and moved to stand at his side. But Moshee moved quickly toward her, once again, and butted her — this time more aggressively. Surprised, she cantered away a little and then stopped and turned to stare after him. Moshee looked at her for a moment and then turned to join the Wolves. The yearling stood and stared after them as they walked away. They did not look back. The Eagles could hear her bleating faintly.

"He begins to understand," Aquila said simply.

"Yes," replied Windshim. "He has already lost the she-Wolf and the cow. He has learned how dear a loss the Faerie suffered when I summoned her to the Peel River. There is no place upon his path for a yearling Caribou. Much has been sacrificed. Much will be sacrificed. There is no need to imperil her."

For a time the yearling followed her brother and the Wolves, stepping in their broad hoof and paw tracks and keeping a careful distance. But at last, the big grey-mane turned and stood in her way, as Moshee and Polaris continued on toward the dark path of the Cargoth. Bree stood her ground and looked at the enormous Wolf. But he would not waver. The yearling paced and turned, filled with confusion.

Aquila watched them carefully. "She is heart-sore and full of questions," he said. "I wonder what the grey-mane says to her?"

"I cannot guess," Windshim replied.

"I do not think there is any tenderness left in him," said Aquila.

"Perhaps. Though Polaris says he stood with Ainafare in her fire. That he was unscathed by the flames. That he howled for her as she burned, until she fell, exhausted, where she now lies."

"That is strange craft for a Wolf," Aquila said. "Can it be the Root Troll's blood that courses in him?"

"Who can say?" Windshim thought for a moment. "A Caribou has been chosen of Rahtrum. A Wolverine ranges darkly. A Faerie burns and scorches the earth. And now, a Wolf unlike any we have seen before, rises in the north. Who can say what the Cargoth and the Binder have set in motion? Who can say what lies before any of us now?"

They watched as the yearling hung her head and turned slowly away from Mist. The grey-mane stared after her for a little while before he followed the others.

At Windshim's bidding, Aquila remained behind to watch over Bree and ensure she was able to find the other herd of Caribou. "She will not survive long on her own," his mate had said. Aquila agreed.

Now, as he looked on, the yearling seemed to wander aimlessly, stopping here and there to dig at Sedges. She lifted her head often to scan the surrounding land. *She is stricken with fear. And why not? She has been guarded by Wolves and a Faerie. Saved by a Root Troll. And now she is alone, abandoned by her kin. She must search her instincts, for she knows little of being Caribou.*

He circled high in the air above her, keeping watch. When at last she crossed the Whitestone River it was clear that she would continue on this path, away from the small Caribou herd, until she stumbled into the range of the Nahoni Wolf Pack. Aquila went down to her. She was startled at first and reluctant to listen to him, but at last he convinced her to turn and follow him. They travelled this way, with him above, calling to her occasionally as he guided her to where the other Caribou grazed.

When Bree stood at the edge of the little herd, the cows

raised their heads one by one and eyed her. Some of the yearlings bleated. But all of the Caribou eventually ignored her, pushing their muzzles into the snow to graze. Bree wandered ever closer, and soon she was among them.

She will feel safe now. It is the way of Caribou to be among one another. The Raptor wheeled and flew in search of his mate. He scanned the ground with his keen eyes and searched for the tracks of Moshee and the Wolves.

Aquila's feathers shone golden brown in the afternoon sun. Below him, rivers coiled and slithered around rolling hummocks and through Spruce and Birch forests. It was not long before the Eagle spotted the wide tracks that the grey-mane and his companions made through the snow. Ahead he saw the dark path of the Cargoth where it snaked across the Eagle Plains.

It is like a scar upon the land. What creature can make such a path? What animal may cleave the north in two?

As though in answer to his question, a dull roar sounded in the sky above. The Raptor peered up and saw one of the Cargoth's giant silver Eagles glinting in the sun high above. It left a thin trail of cloud behind it. Aquila called out and looked east. The dark path drew near. His clear eyelids blinked as his eyes drew focus and followed the tracks of Moshee and the Wolves into the distance.

First he saw Polaris, who kept watch at the rear, as the little group approached the path. Moshee was ahead of him, trotting quickly through the Spruce trees. Well out in front was Mist, and it was he who came first to the edge of the dark path. The grey-mane climbed carefully up the steep embankment of stone and scree that rose above the frozen ground. When Mist came to the top, he stood upon the wide path and looked up and down its length, scenting the air. Satisfied that all was well, he crossed and descended the embankment on the other side. Well behind the Wolf, Moshee broke into a canter and was fast approaching the steep edge of the path. It was then that Aquila heard Windshim call out. He looked for her and found her circling in the sky, high above the path. She called again and looked down at Moshee.

She is distressed. Something is not well. His eyes watched behind the Caribou. *Is he pursued? Has the shadow-walker followed us?* But the Eagle could find no sign of any animal tracking Moshee; only the black Wolf who now ran easily through the shallow snow, ten strides behind the Caribou.

Windshim called again, and at last Aquila saw what troubled her. There, upon the dark path, a beast of the Cargoth, coloured blue like the sky, galloped toward the Caribou at great speed. It passed through a valley just south of the grey-mane's crossing and was hidden from the Caribou's view as it raced up a slope to meet him. Powdery snow and dust rose behind the beast's round, black hooves. Aquila judged Moshee's speed as the Caribou mounted the bank of the path. He looked again at the blue beast, as its frightful growl drew nearer.

It will fall upon him. He does not know his danger.

The Eagle looked up to find his mate. Windshim was already in motion. She folded her wings in, clutched her talons behind her tail, pointed her beak to the ground and fell, sharp as a golden fang, out of the sky.

Windshim! No!

Aquila quickly folded his own wings and fell into a predatory dive. But he was too far from the path. The wind whistled over his feathers as he cut across the sky. Moshee, who did not know his danger, had mounted the bank and burst onto the dark path. The Caribou froze as the blue creature came growling over a rise and bore down upon him. The beast made a terrible bellowing noise, again and again. Windshim broke her dive between the Caribou and the creature. Her mighty wings opened wide and she pumped them furiously. Her sharp talons made ready to try the strange blue hide. But at the last moment, the beast skidded and swerved.

It was too late. Windshim was struck. She spun in the air and collapsed onto the path. Several of her feathers drifted in a cloud of snow and dust. Polaris, who was just behind Moshee, scrambled desperately out of the way of the creature as it slid sideways over the edge of the path and tumbled down the embankment. There it crashed against the trees and lay still upon its back. Moshee stood motionless as the snow began to settle. The black Wolf descended cautiously to where the beast lay. The creature's belly was caked in mud and snow and its black hooves still turned slowly.

Aquila landed beside his mate. He hopped close and leaned in to her. "Speak to me, Windshim." She moved and he backed away to give her room.

Windshim flapped her left wing and soon stood upon her talons. "I am here." Her right wing was stretched out at full length beside her. It was bowed and bent where it should not be. She dragged it in the snow, and it made streaks of red. "Where is Moshee?"

The Caribou approached. He looked down at her wing. "You have saved me," he said quietly.

Mist, who had been drawn back by the sound of the blue beast, stood at the far edge of the path. "Moshee, come," he called to the Caribou. "You cannot stay here. It is not safe."

Bou answered without turning. "But what of Windshim? I cannot leave her."

Aquila turned to the bull. "Go, Caribou. Your precious life is purchased once again. Leave now, before another of the Cargoth comes upon us. Do not make a mockery of this sacrifice."

"Be gentle, Aquila," Windshim said softly. "Moshee, my mate speaks truthfully. I will be well, but you must go now. It is not safe."

"I did not ask for this." The Caribou looked at each of the Eagles. "Not for any of it."

"It is all right," Windshim said quietly. "Go."

Moshee turned, he paused at the edge of the path to look back at the Raptors, and then he followed Mist.

Polaris climbed up again onto the path and approached the Eagles.

"I fear my prey was too large for me," Windshim said to him.

"And yet it is fallen." The Wolf looked at her wing.

"I do not think the blue beast truly wished to fall upon us," she said. "At the last it veered to pass us and lost its balance."

"That may be so, but it is fallen. I have looked through the strange ice-skin upon the head of the creature. Two Cargoth lie within, both red with blood. One is a mature female. She is also fallen, for no breath comes to her. But the other is male. He is no fledgling, but I do not think he is come fully into his seasons. To him breath still comes, though he appears to sleep."

"What of them?" Aquila snapped at the Wolf. "Do not speak to us of Cargoth. Time is short. Windshim cannot stay here upon the path. She must be moved."

Polaris stared at the Raptor.

"Do you not hear me, Land Crow? Let us help her to the eastern bank of the path."

Polaris did not answer.

Aquila flapped his wings in frustration.

"Heart-feather," Windshim said gently, "you speak wisely. It is not safe here upon the dark path. Who can say when another of the Cargoth's beasts will come? Or where the shadow-walker lurks? That is why you must go."

Aquila stared at her.

"Think on it. Only you can lead Moshee to Blinn, now. For only we know where the Gnome awaits him."

"Then we will tell the Wolf."

"No." Her voice was weary. "Blinn has entrusted this to us because we are Eagles. Because we, alone, remain beyond the reach of Grotto. Any among the land-walkers may fall to him and give up their secrets."

"But he has been burned. We do not even know if he lives. He is gone," Aquila protested. "There is no sign of him. It is safe."

"It is not," she replied. "We could not find him before, and yet there he was upon Bear Cave Mountain. Think Aquila. You must go."

"Let the Wolf leave first then," the Raptor said with quiet resignation. "I would stay with you."

"No," Windshim answered. "I, too, know where the Gnome awaits Moshee." She glanced at her wing. "I am no longer beyond the Wolverine's reach. You know already what must be done. The Wolf must stay a little while with me."

Aquila looked at her twisted wing. He could find no words.

"Fly, brave Aquila," she said calmly. "Go. Watch over the Caribou. See to it that he reaches the Gnome, for he will yet do wondrous things."

Aquila stared silently into her sharp, yellow eyes, then lowered his head and spread his broad wings out along the ground. His voice faltered as he spoke. "I will do as you ask because it is you who asks it, mighty Windshim, Sky-mate, and Heart-feather. Always you will be upon my wing." He then lifted up his head and turned to look at the Wolf. "Be merciful and quick, Land Crow, or I shall come and circle Lone Mountain each Spring to pluck your pups from the mountainside and teach them to fly."

"I will be like lightning," the Wolf replied.

As the Raptor strode up into the sky upon his wide wings, he peered down once more. The black Wolf moved in a blur to take up Windshim in his jaws and shake her violently. Aquila looked east and called out into the wind.

A red beast wound its way along the dark path. It crossed the valley and galloped up over the rise. It slowed and stopped where the path was stained with the life of the Raptor and scarred by the felling of the blue beast. Large, strange-looking ears swung forward on either side of the red creature's broad head, and from out of each one stepped a Cargoth.

chapter 23

Moshee, Chosen of Rahtrum

NOVEMBER

The Gnome called Blinn, Eye of the North, lay curled in the snow atop a large stone. The rock sat upon a stony promontory that looked over the place where the Hart River flowed into the Peel. Though he rested, Blinn's keen, black eyes kept a constant watch. He waited on the tip of a small island that had been carved out of the landscape by the waters of the Peel River. For two days he had lingered, waiting for signs of Moshee. As the sun sank behind the horizon and stained the dark clouds red, Blinn considered all that had happened.

Only the day before, the Eagle, Aquila had circled above and cried out. The Gnome had made himself visible to the Raptor, who came down to him. Blinn listened carefully to the Eagle's news. He heard how the cow, Taiga, was fallen and how the Wolverine had consumed half the Breschuvine. He heard how Moshee, burdened with loss, had chased Bree away that she might be safe, and how Windshim had fallen upon the dark path of the Cargoth. He heard, too, how the Faerie, Ainafare, had lit up the night with her fire and burned the shadow-walker. How Mist had stood with her, until she had collapsed upon him in exhaustion.

"There the Faerie lay," Aquila said to him, "and did not awaken from her slumber until we were across the dark path. It was only after Windshim was struck down, and before we all parted ways, that she first stirred. Ainafere she calls herself now, First of Fire. Flame still smolders in her eyes. It is strange to see."

Blinn considered the Eagle's words in thoughtful silence.

"It was the Caribou that called us together and bade each of us to leave him," the Raptor continued. 'Go,' he said to us. 'Each of you in your own direction, whatever your destination.' At first the Wolves would not hear of it, but the bull is grown strong of will and body, and he would not put another hoof forward until they yielded. 'If Grotto still follows us, then this sudden disbanding will confuse him. It is clever,' he said. 'If he does not follow us, then what difference can it make?' So, at his bidding, I took the Faerie aside and told her where you would await them. It was then the grey-mane left us to run north. Polaris turned back toward Lone Mountain, and I continued on to bring you word. The Caribou comes to meet you. He is accompanied by the Faerie, Ainafere, for she will not leave his side. She is certain that through Moshee she will again find Grotto."

"Thank you for this news," Blinn answered. "I am sorry for your loss, brave Aquila. Far-sighted Windshim was bound to Rahtrum, and she was his chosen. Twice over she has protected the life of the Caribou. May she ever be upon your wing."

"Will Moshee truly wake the Cargoth?" the Eagle asked, as he prepared for his departure.

"None can say for certain," the Gnome replied. "But there is one more thing you might do Aquila, to aid us, and to honour Windshim."

"Ask it."

"Fly to Skull Ridge. There is a Troven there, a high counsel of the Tuatha De Danann. Bring news to them in my name and the name of Ainafere, and they will hear you. Tell them all that you know and all that you have seen. Say to them that Moshee has the Breschuvine within, and bid them send word to the Earthshaker. Will you do this for me?"

"I am bound. It will be done." The Eagle leapt into the air and ascended into the sky.

Blinn watched him go.

A day had passed since the Eagle flew for Skull Ridge, and now, in the gloaming of early Winter, the Gnome lay upon his large stone with his tail curled over his muzzle and all of the Eagle's news turning in his mind. As the last light failed, he saw a motion upriver. A shape moved on the stone wash where the two rivers met. It was accompanied by a small, white light. Blinn's black eyes widened and focused, and what was distant drew near. He watched the young bull step carefully upon the snow-covered rocks until he stood at the river's edge. Moshee stopped there, and stared downstream toward the Gnome. The Faerie hovered beside him.

He looks this way. Surely he cannot see me at this distance. The Gnome stretched his back before standing up on his two hind paws. Snow twirled from out of the clouds. Blinn watched as the Caribou strode forward into the river. *He does see me. Perhaps half the Breschuvine will be enough. Yes. It must be enough.*

The bull swam easily with the current, and when he reached the little island he clambered out of the dark water to stand eye to eye with Blinn, atop his tall stone. Ainafere glowed white in the air beside Moshee, and her eyes flickered orange with fire. Her light illuminated the bull Caribou. Vapour rose from his body, newly warmed by his labour.

He is strong. The Breschuvine is at work within him. He is ready.

"We are here, Blinn," Moshee said coolly, as he looked over his shoulder at Ainafere. "What is left of our company."

"It is good to lay eyes upon you again, Moshee. Aquila came to me yesterday. I have heard much of your journey." The Gnome considered the Faerie for a moment. He turned again to the Caribou. "The seasons are not ours to waste. We must strike west and cross the mountains before Winter is upon us."

"That is all?" The Caribou's voice was bitter. "After all of this, I am to follow wherever you lead?"

"Yes. After all of it, you are to follow wherever I lead. What else is there, Moshee?" The Gnome was impatient. "Do you want me to tell you that I am sorry?"

"Yes. Tell me that you are sorry. Tell me something. I have found your precious Breschuvine. What now? Where have you been, Blinn? Where were you when Arktikos felled my mother? When the shadow-walker was upon us? Where was the Eye of the North when mighty Windshim fell to earth?"

The Gnome stared into the Caribou's eyes. "I am sorry, Moshee. I am sorry for all of them. I am sorry most of all for Ainafere." He glanced at her. "You want to know where I have been? Where have I *not* been! I have held counsel with Rahtrum. I have ranged far in the north, seeking news of the Wolverine called Grotto. His scent is faint, but there is a trail. We must learn all we can of the shadow-walker, for he is a mystery to us. He is," the Gnome searched for the right word, "*unexpected*. As for our precious Breschuvine, you have consumed but half of it." He looked accusingly at the Faerie. "If it were not enough to contend with Grotto as he was, now he has the Breschuvine at work within him, and none of us knows his purpose. So you see, Moshee, I have been kept busy."

The Caribou huffed. "And why must *I* go with you?"

"Where else will you go?"

"You misunderstand me, Blinn. Why must I go with you? You say that I am chosen of Rahtrum. But why? Why not the Eagle, Aquila, or the Wolf, Polaris? Why must it be me?"

The Gnome stared at him. "You are chosen of Rahtrum, Moshee, but you are not the first. The Breschuvine grows but every fifth Autumn. By my count, six have gone before you, Eagles and Wolves among them. All of them fallen. Each of them lost before the first bite of Winter. The northlands are unforgiving." Blinn's eyes grew wide. "Do you not see? You are the first to find the Breschuvine. You are the first to carry it within."

The bull was surprised. "There have been others?"

"Yes. It is as I have said," the Gnome replied. "You are the seventh."

The Caribou fell silent for a moment, but at last he gathered his wits. "Then why me on this occasion? Why not a Lynx or a Bear?"

"I do not know why the Binder does all that he does. It was the turn of the Caribou this year," the Gnome replied, "and so here you are."

"I still do not understand." The bull cocked his head slightly. "Why *me*? Why not choose another? We Caribou are like a sea when our herd comes together on the Coastal Plains. We are teeming in the north. Why choose, Bou, calf of Taiga?"

Impatient, the Faerie drifted in front of Blinn. "Meddling Gnome. Do you think that he carries the burden of action but cannot shoulder the truth of it? Do you think it will bow and break him? Look at the loss he carries already. A moon has not passed since his own mother fell, and yet, he stands before you. He is strong. Stronger than the others."

The Gnome's eyes narrowed.

Ainafere ignored him and turned to Moshee. "Even as a yearling you could see what others could not. You remembered what others of your kin had forgotten. Have you not felt different from the very beginning? Have you never felt a strange strength inside of you? Even before the Breschuvine?"

Moshee stared at her. His head nodded slowly.

Her voice softened. "Sometimes, when a great tree stands directly before us we see only the wide trunk in our way. We do not always see its broad foliage, reaching into the sky above, protecting us from the chill of a cold rain. You see only the great challenge that is set before you, Moshee. You see only Bou, yearling of Taiga. But who among the Porcupine Caribou has sired a far-sighted Caribou with long memory? Who is your father? Who gives you your name?"

The young bull's eyes began to widen.

"Think on it, Moshee, and you will begin to see," said the Faerie.

"Do not press him, Ainafere," the Gnome said softly. "For everything a season."

"Do not coddle him, Blinn," she replied evenly.

The Caribou seemed not to hear them. "It cannot be."

The Faerie hovered before his muzzle. "And yet it must be."

"Then it was him." The Caribou's eyes moved from Faerie to Gnome, desperate for an answer.

"You are Caribou, Moshee," said Blinn, "but you are so much more."

"Yes," said Ainafere, "It was him. The same that came to you in Winter. The same whose antlers wove high into the air. The same that was ringed by Faeries and Root Trolls. The same that was attended by Gnomes," she pointed at Blinn, "the Eye of the North among them. The same that set you upon this path. Do you now see the broad foliage that is above you? You are not only Bou, yearling of Taiga. You are Moshee, calf of the Earthshaker, chosen of Rahtrum."

The young bull stepped back until his rear hooves were again in the river. He huffed and shook his head as he considered her words. He stood in silence for a moment. "What does this mean?"

Blinn held a paw up to hush the Faerie. "It means that you are more than Caribou. It is why Rahtrum has sent you to find the wildflower. With the Breschuvine within, you can do what no other animal can." He sighed. "But this you will discover for yourself. Now we must go, Moshee. The seasons will not wait and the shadow of the Cargoth is growing."

"Where are we going?" the Caribou asked.

Blinn pointed. "For now, we go west."

Moshee stood motionless. "I do not know how to wake the Cargoth. I did not wish for any of this."

Blinn spoke with deliberate patience. "The Cargoth grow as a long shadow with the setting of the sun. They must be awakened before it is too late. The one called Grotto ranges darkly, and now he carries half of the Breschuvine within. Still, we do not know his purpose. You may be set upon a path not of your choosing, Moshee, but you are what you are, and this you must do. There is no other way before you. All other paths are gone, but this one."

"Much has been sacrificed for you, Moshee. Do not waver," Ainafere said.

"But what hope have I? Have you not gazed upon the shadow-walker? He is a nightmare come to life. And the Cargoth are a plague. What chance have I of waking them? What hope can there be for any of us?"

"What do you know of hope?" The Gnome's voice was cold, and

his black eyes flashed. "Do not speak to me of hope, Moshee, unless you can show it to me – unless you can tell me what it is. Can you hunt it? Will it feed you? Can you drink it when you are thirsty? Go then. Search for hope. Graze upon it and see where it will lead you." The Gnome spat his words. "Always it will lie beyond you, like a shadow in the fog, like a trick of sunlight in the distance; a whisper on the wind."

Blinn grunted and looked Moshee in the eye. "Hope is for your kin," he said, waving his paw through the air, "for all in the north who follow in the tracks of a thousand generations. Let them nurse their minds upon it, while they busy themselves with survival. Hope is for the Cargoth. It is how they sleep, lost in their long dream of hunger, hopeful that they will not fall into the darkness of their own shadow." He pointed at the Caribou. "Hope is not for you and me. It is not for Ainafere or Polaris; not for Mist. Hope is most assuredly not for the shadow-walker. Do you think you will find him curled in the warmth of his den, wishing for things?"

Blinn shook his head sadly. "No. Hope is not for us. For we are all of us bound to action. When the time for counsel is ended, though we are burdened with fear and sadness, we must press forward. Always you must press forward. For you are Moshee, and you carry the Breschuvine within. And now, the time for counsel is ended."

The young bull stared at the Gnome and the Faerie in turn. Then he swung around to face the mountains in the west. He stepped out into the river and took a deep breath. "If that is who I am, so be it." His body grew taller and wider as Ainafere and Blinn looked on. "I will go with you." He looked over his shoulder. "I will go for Tundra, and for Mother, and for Windshim. And I will go for you, Ainafere — for your fledgling. For all that has been sacrificed."

As he spoke, new antlers sprang up from where he had dropped the last season's. They grew quickly and wove high into the air above him, until he wore a mighty rack that suited his new stature. He seemed not to notice.

"Let us go if this is the only path left to us. I am what I am. If the Cargoth can be awakened, then I will wake them. I *will* find a way."

Fire flashed in the Faerie's eyes as she glanced at Blinn. A look of relief washed over the Gnome's face. The three unlikely companions struck out together toward the mountains.

chapter 24

Hugin
DECEMBER

Hugin sat alone atop a tall stone in the darkness. He fluffed his sable feathers to keep warm and shivered against the deep, sharp bite of Winter. He covered his legs and feet with his body. The Yukon sky was a canvass of eternal night, sequined with stars and constellations. There was no moon. Ghostly rivers of green and blue and violet drifted silently above.

Hugin did not notice the Wolf until it already stood beside the stone. He gave a little squawk of surprise and began to spread his wings. His talons scratched and clicked on the cold rock as his weight shifted. The Wolf dropped a lifeless Hare upon the ground. Hugin eyed it. The Hare was still warm by the look of it. Its blood leaked like a black shadow onto the snow. The Crow's empty belly churned. The Wolf was dimly lit by the Aurora Borealis. Its muzzle was stained with the life of the Hare, or perhaps another. It was immense.

The great Wolf breathed the frigid air and exhaled a cloud of vapour. "It is cruel, this World, is it not, Crow?"

The predator turned to Hugin, and for the first time the Crow saw the night sky glimmer in the Wolf's golden eyes.

"I am called Mist, Grey-mane. Cub of Root Troll and Wolf of Lone Mountain. I hunt the Wolverine, the shadow-walker called Grotto. Tell me all that you know, and you may yet see the Spring."